W9-AAS-838

LAWLESS LAND

OTHER FIVE STAR WESTERN TITLES BY LES SAVAGE, JR.:

LAWLESS LAND

A WESTERN DUO

LES SAVAGE, JR.

FIVE STAR
A part of Gale, Cengage Learning

Detroit • New York • San Francisco • New Haven, Conn • Waterville, Maine • London

GALE
CENGAGE Learning‑

LIBRARY OF CONGRESS CATALOGING-IN-PUBLICATION DATA

Savage, Les.
    Lawless land : a Western duo / by Les Savage, Jr. — 1st ed.
      p. cm.
    ISBN-13: 978-1-59414-837-8 (hardcover : alk. paper)
    ISBN-10: 1-59414-837-6 (hardcover : alk. paper)
    1. Western stories. I. Savage, Les. Trouble in Texas. II. Title.
PS3569.A826L435 2010
813'.54—dc22   2009037792

First Edition. First Printing: January 2010.
Published in 2010 in conjunction with Golden West Literary Agency.

Printed in the United States of America
1 2 3 4 5 6 7 14 13 12 11 10

CONTENTS

★ ★ ★ ★ ★

Trouble in Texas

★ ★ ★ ★ ★

I

After Knightland threw the steer and hog-tied it, he dragged the wild, thrashing beast over to a coma tree and snubbed it up tight with a pigging string. His movements had held a wild reckless grace, but as the violence of it ceased and he straightened up to step back, his tall gaunt body took on a strange indefinable awkwardness. The great bony barrel of his chest was still heaving with the breath passing through it when the brush popped behind him. A man on a big blue-tick roan came into the open.

"You can just take them piggin' strings back off that cow and let her up, Bob," he told Knightland.

Turning, Knightland saw that it was Cannibal Moore. "You got the wrong dogie, Cannibal. This is one of Bayard's steers."

"And these are my thickets and you're working for the Blackjack now from what I hear," said Cannibal Moore. "If Bayard wants his beef, he can come in here after them. But not one of you damn' syndicate riders is putting a foot in my brush, Knightland, and that goes double for you."

Knightland stared up at Cannibal Moore for a moment without speaking. Cannibal was well over fifty, his baldhead scabrous with brush scars. He had little eyes, bloodshot and unwinking as a bull's, and heavy bulldog jowls that only gave accent to the stubborn line of his thick neck. His body belied his age, bulging with muscle built from the beef and beans and man-killing work of the brush since he was a baby.

"Cannibal," Knightland said to him, "you ain't going to win out with this attitude. The syndicate's here to stay and it ain't no use trying to fight it. I've known you since I was a button and you never made enough off your cattle to do anything but eat. This way you get a price that means something. I'll even put you on one of my crews. Time you're through you'll have enough to live rich the rest of your life."

"Where?" said Cannibal. "If I ain't got no land, where'll I live?"

"Corpus Christi's a good town."

"I don't like towns. I like my brush and I'm keeping it." Cannibal's ancient, rawhide-laced rig creaked as be leaned forward, planting one hand on the rope-scarred horn. "There's a lot of others in this stretch that feel the same way, Bob. They feel you turned your back on the brush folks when you hired on to the syndicate. I understand your pa's one who thinks that."

The dark look shadowing Knightland's face seemed to give his tall, awkward length ominous accent. The hungry hollows of his cheeks deepened, filled with a week's growth of matted, ruddy beard, showing how long he had been chousing these cattle in the brush. His shaggy mane of hair had that same ruddy cast, almost black in the shade, glinting with red lights under a strong sun, matched by the heavy, expressive brows that rose to peaks filled with the devil, above his somber, smoky eyes. He was clothed in the traditional rawhide of the brush, the leggings clinging tight as a second skin to his long legs. The grease and filth ingrained into the hide was criss-crossed with a white lacing of scars from constant contact with the brush.

"Dad's a stubborn old, fool," he said at last. "The bunch of you are fools. You've been working this brush on the same shoestring scale for fifty years, each man tending to his own little pasture and never getting beyond a dog-run shack and a six-cow thicket. That's why this brush is just as full of wild ones that have never been branded as it was when the Spanish had it a hundred years ago. There's a cattle boom building up north, Cannibal, but you'll never be able to profit by it unless you learn a new way of working this brush."

"Did it ever occur to you," said Cannibal, "that maybe some of us don't care about getting beyond a dog-run shack?"

"Bayard did," said Knightland. "He got more money in one chunk than he ever knew existed."

"You did, too, didn't you, Bob?" Cannibal smeared a hand thoughtfully across his jowls, studying Knightland. "Seems to me you always had ideas a little too big for your britches. They never really showed up like this till you came back from the war. It really made you restless, didn't it? And that woman."

"She doesn't have anything to do with it."

"I think she has a lot to do with it. You've been casting calf eyes at Madelaine Wade ever since you was a kid. A man has to be somebody to have a woman like that, don't he? Is that why you're so het up over Victor Cordon's syndicate, Bob?"

"If your brains are too clabbered to see what it can do for this brush, Cannibal, I'm not going to waste my time talking. I'm going to leave this steer tied up and come back for it in a couple of days. And I want to see it when I do come back."

Cannibal spurred his roan up against Knightland, bending toward him. "You're unhitching that steer right now."

A bleak, savage expression rent Knightland's face as he spoke. "Don't cross me. Even an old friend like you. Don't do it."

Cannibal leaned a little farther forward in a confiding way. "The odds ain't even, Bob."

Cannibal had not actually been looking behind Knightland, but some vagrant flicker of the man's attention caused Knightland to turn his body far enough so he could see. The other horseman had come into the clearing without a sound. He was a tall, lean figure with an enigmatic face the color of oiled

11

mahogany. He was Cannibal Moore's man, who claimed to be a Karankawa Indian. The Karankawas had been an early tribe of Texas Indians known to have been eaters of human flesh. Knightland had rarely heard him speak, and he sat the animal in statuesque silence now, his eyes forming sharp, glittering flashes in the shadow of his hat brim.

"I didn't think it would ever come to this, Cannibal," said Knightland.

Cannibal took a heavy breath, straightening up in his saddle. "I guess two men ought to recognize when they're looking at each other across the fence, Bob. Will you get off my land now?"

"With my steer," said Knightland, and moved to get around Cannibal's horse. He knew it was only a gesture, and was ready to jump back when the man put spurs to that big blue tick and drove the animal into Knightland. The heavy, speckled chest surged by Knightland as he threw himself away. Cannibal's leg was before him and he caught it.

Cannibal tried to rein the horse up but not soon enough. Knightland's grip pulled him off balance before the animal would stop. He came from the saddle heavily. Knightland had to release his hold and keep on jumping backward to stay out from beneath Cannibal's falling body. At the same time he heard the Karankawa's horse coming in from behind him, and whirled back that way to see the man hurtling bodily off the animal right on top of him.

Knightland could not get out from under this time. He went down with that twisted, savage face looming into his and the flashing sight of a knife off to one side. He was stunned by hitting earth, with the Indian coming down on top of him, but he still had enough sense left to make a grab for that knife wrist. He felt it strike between his thumb and index finger, bearing his own hand back with the force of the blow, but his block managed to deflect the knife enough so it only ripped at his shirt.

Then he stretched one leg out for purchase and rolled the man over while the Indian was still off balance from the impetus of that thrust.

He heard Cannibal grunt behind them with the effort of rising from that stunning fall off the horse, and knew this had to be quick. He caught the Indian's long black hair in his hands, ignoring the knife, and beat his head into the ground. The man gasped, bringing the knife in from the side. It was a feeble jab that raked across Knightland's ribs.

At the same time, Knightland heard Cannibal grunt again, this time right above him. He threw himself aside. There was a savage blow on his shoulder. He rolled out from under it, leaving the Indian, and saw that Cannibal had struck at his head with a gun. The man was recovering himself and whirling, raising the clubbed revolver to strike again. Knightland came up off the ground at him, driving his numb shoulder into the man's belly. This carried Cannibal backward across the Indian. He halted there, with the Karankawa beneath their struggling feet. Grappling into Cannibal, Knightland felt the Indian pawing at his legs, trying to rise with the knife.

Knightland caught Cannibal's gun hand in both fists, pinioning it for that moment, and then half turned to find the Indian's face, freeing his right boot from the man's pawing hands, and kicking him in the head as hard as he could. The Indian sank back with a deep groan.

"Damn you, Bob!" snarled Cannibal, trying to wrench his gun hand free. Knightland came back into him, still gripping that wrist, and then twisted his whole body the other way, putting the pressure of all his weight into his hold. Cannibal gasped with the pain, and the gun slipped out of his spasmodically opened fingers. Knightland released the wrist, kicking the gun away from them. Then came back into Cannibal.

The man set himself, blocking Knightland's first blow. He

13

counterpunched heavily, awkwardly like a great bear. Knightland ducked aside, sweeping the fist off his shoulder, and got inside. Then he started punching Cannibal viciously, brutally, as hard and fast as he could hit, driving the man backward, giving him no quarter, not allowing him to push away, until Cannibal went over backward. Knightland stood swaying above him, chest heaving with the breath passing through it. Cannibal started to rise.

"Don't do it, Cannibal," said Knightland. "Say you're through, because you aren't getting up if you're not through."

Cannibal lay there a long time, staring at him. "All right," he said at last. "Take your steer. But don't let me catch you in Karankawa Thickets again, Knightland. I won't use the butt of my gun next time."

II

Corpus Christi in 1870 was a town still humming with a boom started by General Taylor in the Mexican War, when he camped his army here and brought a flood of federal money. A strange, exotic, contradictory town, where the buzzing Yankee commerce of newer brick buildings was flanked by the sleepy indifference of one-story adobes a hundred years old. Where one of Concord's new road buggies pulled by a team of prancing blacks had to wait half an hour while a stream of ancient, creaking Chihuahua carts rolled past, hauled by oxen as lazy as their Indian drivers, piled precariously high with goods from El Paso and farther south into Mexico.

Bob Knightland had to thread his way through one of these caravans on his way to the Blackjack offices in one of the older adobe buildings overlooking the sullen waters of the bay. Despite the weariness of a long ride, he held all the casual, slouching grace of a centaur, bringing his buttermilk horse in to the tie rack. But when he swung down off Clabber, hitching the reins, and stepped up onto the walk, that sense of great, tall awkwardness was in the jerky, loose-jointed movements of his body. There was an arcade, supported by adobe arches, before the building, to cast the sidewalk in shade, and he was beneath this before he saw who the woman was standing near the door.

He stopped to stare at Madelaine Wade. Her rich, braided hair held a shimmering hint of newly minted gold. There was something haunting about her face, perhaps the oblique shadow shifting vagrantly beneath her cheek bone, or the strange disturbing depths of her blue eyes. Her lips made Knightland think of ripe fruit that had yet to be tasted. Some movement, with the sight of him, drew the tightly cut Garibaldi blouse away from the proud maturity of her breast.

"Bob," she said, catching his wrist to pull him in a doorway. "I hear you and your dad had a fight."

He shrugged, acutely conscious of the light touch of her hand on his wrist. "It's been coming a long time, I guess, Madelaine. He always got up on his hind legs when I tried to do anything like this."

"But . . . they say . . . they say . . ."

"He disowned me?" he finished almost defiantly.

"Surely, Bob, he can't mean it. He'll be all right when you see him again."

A dark, brooding look entered his face. "Not Pa. He told me if I signed on to the syndicate I needn't ever come back to his house, and he meant it. He said I was turning my back on my folks and everybody in the brush when I took a job here. He said a man can't get big fast without hurting somebody, and the ones I hurt will be my friends." Knightland brought his eyes to hers. "You don't think that's true, do you, Madelaine?"

She was watching him closely. "What do you think, in your heart?"

"I think a man who won't accept change is a fool," he said,

hotly. "This brush is changing, Madelaine. The ways of working cattle are changing. Victor said the first herd up the Chisholm had a thousand head in it. The most my dad and I ever got in one roundup was a hundred and seven. It's obvious we can't make any money out of the cattle boom by those methods. The days of working a few hundred acres of your own pasture are through and nobody'll get hurt if they accept that. A lot of them have already sold out."

"That wasn't exactly an answer to my question, was it, Bob?"

A stormy light filled his eyes as he stared down at her; his mind was still filled with Cannibal. "You aren't siding with the brushpoppers?" he said.

"Is it a matter of sides?" she asked.

"Madelaine . . . ," he said, filled with a poignant need in this moment to explain himself to her, to tell her all the things he had wanted to so many times—how symbolic she was of the things a man born to poverty and hardship could yearn after. Yet, as it had happened before, she seemed to sense his thoughts, and a strange indefinable withdrawal filled her eyes, a cold, speculative light, studying him that blocked the words in his throat, filling him with the bitter frustration of a man with nothing to offer, wanting a woman who had everything in the world.

"Yes, Bob?" she asked softly.

"Nothing," he said. "I'd better go in and see Victor."

"Before you do"—her voice stopped his motion—"Dad's throwing a little party to celebrate the forming of the syndicate. A lot of the stockholders will be there. Since you're one of us now, Bob, I wish you'd come, too." He could not help the starting negative shake of his head, and, although he tried to halt it in time, a small frown puckered her brow. "You aren't worried about your clothes, Bob?"

His eyes flashed. "I assure you I won't embarrass you, Madelaine," he said stiffly.

"Bob, don't be like that. You haven't been paid your first month's salary, have you? Is that it? If you want a little advance . . ."

He felt pride thicken his throat and tried to stifle it, knowing how foolish that was. Yet he could not. "I said I'd make out, Madelaine. What time will it be?"

"Saturday at eight."

He tilted his head in acceptance and turned to go into the building. Mixed with the angry pride, however, was a growing sense of elation. It was the first step, wasn't it? Since he'd been a kid, he could remember passing that vast, brick Wade mansion out on the Brownsville road whenever he came into town, watching it till the building was out of sight, plied with the awe and the wonder of the riches it signified. And since he'd been a kid, he'd wanted to get inside, not just to gape at it but to move through every room as Madelaine's equal.

He reached Victor Cordon's office to find the door open. The only one inside was a thin, dark man with a neat spade beard shot with gray, his black serge clothes rumpled and travel-stained.

"Mister Cordon?" the bearded man asked, and went on without waiting for a reply. "I'm Alvaraz Orvado. I handle the properties of the Gomez family and have offices in San Antonio. I was down here collecting rents out on the Gomez Strip and heard your men are running the cattle regardless of the brand. I want your assurance that this will be stopped immediately. I want every Gomez cow returned by next Saturday to the corrals at Angelita. I'll have a man waiting there to receive them."

"Wait a minute," said Knightland. "You've got the wrong man. I only rod the crews for the Blackjack. I'm not Cordon . . ."

He halted, with the feel of someone's hand on his shoulder,

and the vibrant, cultivated voice of Victor Cordon in his ear. "Something wrong, Bob?"

Cordon moved by as Knightland stepped in to give him room, a square, vigorous man in his impeccably tailored suit with a vividly handsome face, curly black hair, eyes that sparkled.

"I'm Cordon." He smiled, holding out his hand to Orvado. "What's this about the Gomez property? Our legal staff made a very patient and thorough tracing of all title. Our findings showed the Gomez people didn't have any legal claim. Not so, Harper?"

Harper Miller had come in behind Cordon. He pulled shrewdly at his long Yankee nose with a thumb and forefinger, fixing Orvado with a chill blue eye.

"Yes, Vic. They lost title after the Revolution. Their claim was so obscure Texas took over the land and threw it open to the veterans with land scrip. I've got some of that scrip we bought up right here in the office."

"I don't know at what Land Office you got information like that," said Orvado. "I have clear title right here in my briefcase going back to the original grant the King of Spain gave *Don* Cervalle Gomez. The Republic of Texas honored those grants as well as the state."

Harper Miller's lean body made its swift, incisive motion past Knightland, as he said: "Mind if we see them?"

Cordon moved over to the desk, also, as Orvado opened his case and pulled out a sheaf of papers. Both men leafed through the sheets. Knightland watched them narrowly, a vague disturbance stirring in him. Finally Cordon pointed a finger at something on the paper.

"What's this seal drawn on the original royal grant?"

"Naturally the papers had to be countersigned in the New World," said Orvado. "It is the seal of Governor-General Alvaraz."

"I never saw it printed before, did you, Harper?" said Cordon.

The lawyer raised his chilly eyes to Cordon's for a brief moment. Then something altered subtly in his face. "No," he said. "No, I never saw it printed."

Orvado frowned. "What are you getting at?"

"I've seen the Alvaraz seal on other grants," said Cordon, dismissing the whole case of papers with a wave of his hand. "It's always been made by the seal stamped into hot wax right on the paper. There are other discrepancies. You'd better get out, Orvado, before I call the law."

Orvado was so angry now he began to tremble. "*Señor,* I still don't understand. Are you saying . . . ?"

"That these are counterfeit," said Cordon. "Get out before I throw you out!"

Orvado gathered up his papers in a stiff silence, stuffing them into the case with shaking hands. At the door he turned to speak.

"I give you my last word. If the Gomez property is not returned and your men don't stop working those thickets by Saturday, I will institute legal proceedings that will ruin your syndicate."

Cordon turned his back on the man and walked to the window. When Orvado had disappeared, he wheeled around, staring at the door.

"You didn't tell me there was some doubt about the Gomez Strip, Vic," said Knightland. "I've had two crews in there."

"There wasn't any doubt," said Cordon angrily.

"You sure those were counterfeits?"

"Sure, sure. I've seen enough of those old grants. We've had to trace a dozen of them buying up these thickets." He faced Knightland squarely, a hearty laugh obliterating his anger. "Forget it, Bob. How we doing in the brush?"

"You just about got your first trail herd," said Knightland. "Last count was seven hundred and ten for all six crews. There's a hundred in the Angelita corrals, a hundred and twenty-three in the Kingstown . . ."

"OK, OK." Cordon grinned, slapping him on the back. "How about that?" he asked, cocking his head at Miller. "Didn't I tell you Bob was worth it? He isn't any ordinary ramrod you can pick up for fifty a month. He asks for two percent of the gross and makes you like it."

Miller smiled, pulling at his nose. "I still think it's a crazy way to pay your foreman."

"He's not our foreman," said Cordon. "He's a partner, Harper. We used to run the brush together. We went through the war together. I promised him something good if he'd string along with me. Come along, now, Bob. We're cashing in on your name. More of those brushpoppers have heard you're with us. They've come from a hundred miles away to sign on."

There were a couple of dozen men gathered in the adobe corrals at the rear of the building. Knightland lined them up along one wall, then went to the head of the line.

"Still the best all-around hand in Nueces County, Dale?"

The scarred face of the short, bowlegged little brushpopper at the head of the line spread into a wrinkled smile. "Ain't been topped yet, Bob. You really think this is a good thing? I wouldn't've come if I hadn't heard you was rodding things. There's a lot of talk ag'in' it in the brush."

"There'll always be talk against something new," said Knightland. "If you want to sign on, you'll see cattle making real money for the first time. And I'll be with you all the way."

"Sign me on, then." Dale grinned.

The humor was still in Knightland's face as he passed on to the next man. It fled, then, and he did not stop, moving to the third in line. The man he had passed straightened a little against the wall.

"Ain't letting personal feelings mar your judgment of a good hand, are you, Bob?" he asked.

"My personal feelings are surprised that you'd even come here today, Sinton," said Knightland.

Cordon was at Knightland's shoulder. "What's the matter with this man, Bob?"

Knightland turned to him. "You asking me that?"

Cordon's brows raised. "Only thing I ever heard of him was he could rope rings around most hands."

"You ought to wash your ears out then," said Knightland. "I don't want him, Cordon."

"You can at least give me a reason," said Cordon.

"Why embarrass the man?" said Knightland.

"You ain't embarrassing nobody, Bob," said Sinton Dexter. "Give us that reason."

His body had inclined itself away from the wall a little, as casual and lazy as his voice, a long, lean man, epitomizing a country of much dust and little water, with grime etching his face and filth and age obliterating the original color of his patched striped pants. Knightland's eyes, filled with the murk of rising storm, dropped briefly to the Remington that Dexter carried in his belt.

"You've spent so much time fixing your mind on that iron, Sinton, that I don't think you've had any left to practice with the branding iron. Is that plain enough?"

"You ain't calling me names, are you?"

"I don't want to talk about it any more," said Knightland.

"Give the man a fair hearing, at least," interposed Cordon.

Knightland turned on him. "Maybe you'd rather pick the crews out."

For a moment Cordon's fare darkened. Then, with an effort,

he brought back that smile. "Take it easy, ramrod. This is your show. I'm sorry I interrupted."

Knightland stared at him a moment longer, puzzled by something. Then he turned back to Dexter, inclining his head to the gate. "You can go."

Dexter straightened up, hooking his thumbs in his belt. "Maybe I don't feel like it."

Knightland was only a pace away from the man. He brought his right arm up in a vicious, jabbing blow as he took the step. Dexter had no time for reaction. The fist caught him deep in the belly, and he was carried heavily back against the wall, doubling over. Knightland withdrew his arm to strike again, hitting him at the side of the neck. Dexter fell to the ground with a sodden sound.

"Dale, you and Karnes pick him up and put him on his horse," Knightland said. "I think he'll go now."

III

It was late afternoon before the work of picking his crews was over, and Knightland came from the door out onto Water Street tired and dusty and ready for a meal. He still had a bad taste in his mouth from Sinton Dexter. He knew it had been brutal but the man had been bound on making an issue of the incident, and it was no use leaving anything undecided in the minds of men as rough and elemental as the crews were. He was unhitching his horse when he saw the wagon coming down Water Street. It was an old linchpin, standing out among the Chihuahua carts like a sore thumb.

The man driving was tall and spare with the same inexplicable look of awkwardness Knightland held at times. He was dressed in the inevitable greasy rawhides of the brush, his gaunt head topped by white hair, as shaggy and coarse as a broomtail's mane. Even at this distance, the scarred, gnarled size of his great, bony hands was evident. Knightland left his horse and moved past a Chihuahua cart to intercept the linchpin. He was almost to its line of direction as it passed. He held out a hand, calling: "Pa?"

Micah Knightland did not turn his head. Those great hands seemed to tighten somewhat on the reins of his team. He sat, stiff and motionless, eyes straight ahead, and the wagon rattled past. Bob Knightland dropped his hand, staring after the man. A strange, sick feeling gripped the pit of his stomach.

"Don't take it so hard, Bob," said someone behind him. "Your father's a stubborn man, but he'll come around when he sees what a good thing the syndicate is."

Knightland turned to see Sam Burman standing beneath the portal of the Blackjack building, a small, wizened, baldheaded man with squinted, twinkling eyes. Knightland moved back to his horse.

"I'm glad to meet somebody who sees a little good in the syndicate," he said somberly.

"The first thing a tailor has to learn is how to change with the styles." Burman smiled. "I think you can apply that to almost everything in life. It's changing all the time. I used to own a Kentucky pistol that only shot once. Now I have a Colt that shoots six times. This growing demand for cattle is going to force men to band together and work them instead of each one running a few in his own pasture."

"You're a philosopher, Sam," said Knightland. "Do you believe in the Blackjack enough to give its ramrod some credit on a suit of clothes."

Sam Burman smiled softly. "I believe in its ramrod enough to do that, Bob."

Knightland went down with him that day for the first fitting. Then he rode out into the brush for the remainder of the week to finish the first roundup with his crews. When he came back

Friday afternoon, he got the second fitting. The suit was ready the next day along with a new white Stetson and a pair of bench-made boots.

Harrison Wade had been one of the original founders of Corpus Christi, coming in with Kinney when he established his trading post before the Mexican War. He was one of the major backers of Victor Cordon's syndicate, and his house was out of town on a bluff overlooking Nueces Bay, a two-story mansion of red brick and tall pillars. There were already a number of horses and rigs in the yard, and a Negro servant came to take Clabber from Knightland.

He was then ushered into an entrance hall, dazzled by the light from a hundred candles reflected in a row of ornate, Adamesque mirrors. Madelaine met him, the wine of her moiré gown in startling contrast to the cream of her flesh. Cordon was right behind her, chuckling as he came up to Knightland and clapping a hand to his arm.

"Well, well, so this is what the well-dressed young ramrod is wearing these days."

Then it was Madelaine: "Come on, Bob, you'll have to meet Dad." And the two of them dragged him over to the distinguished white-haired man talking to Madelaine's brother and another man in a black swallow-tail.

"Ah, yes," said Harrison Wade. "The Knightland boy. You've grown up, Bob, you've grown up." His head tilted back a little. "Ah, yes."

Something fluttered across Madelaine's face, and her breast rose with a quick breath as if she meant to speak, but Cordon broke in swiftly. "Bob's been doing a great job with the cattle, Harry. We'll have seven hundred on the trail next week. Does that convince you he's worth the extra money?"

"Well . . ."—Harrison Wade tilted his head back again—"yes. Shall we have supper?"

There were about a dozen at the long, glittering table. Madelaine and her mother were the only women. The talk seemed mostly politics. Knightland felt lost in it.

"I hear Governor Davis is going to be reëlected."

"It'll mean the end of Texas."

"Oh, I don't know, Harry, just because he disbanded the Rangers . . ."

"How about you, Knightland? Think he'll get the vote?"

"I don't know much about the man."

"Bob's been working pretty close to the brush, Harry. Only election you get out there is who stuffed the ballot box on the last calf count."

Genteel laughter billowed around the table at Cordon's sally. Knightland stared around at the pink scrubbed faces swimming in the reek of expensive cigar smoke. His hands, against the pale, soft hands holding glasses and moving across glittering silver, stood out like great, scarred paws. He found his hands moving with the impulse to hide beneath the cloth, and then, in an angry defiance, shoved them out again, reaching for his wine glass. He saw he was using the wrong fork for his salad and put it down hastily, staining the cloth with the dressing. His guilty upward glance met Madelaine's. She tried to erase the frown from her brow. Her smile held definite effort.

He started to feel embarrassment but that faded before another feeling. He stared around the table again, and the laughter and the soft, cultured talk took on a dim, unreal sound, as if he were not here, as if he were above, somewhere, or beyond, observing in a detached, untouched way. It seemed to be resolving something within him. But before he could identify that, a Negro servant came softly to Harrison Wade's side and whispered in his ear. Wade inclined his head, caught Cordon's eye. He and Cordon excused themselves and Madelaine took over. In another moment the Negro came and whispered in

Knightland's ear that he was wanted in the parlor. He passed through the heavy jade hangings dividing the two spacious rooms. Sheriff Barton Clane was waiting.

"Hate to interrupt the party, Bob," he said. "But I understand you and Cordon were among the last persons to see Alvaraz Orvado alive."

Knightland stared at him a moment. "I don't know. He was in the office last Wednesday."

"He was found murdered near the old Brownsville road yesterday," said the sheriff. "An attempt had been made to hide the body, but some half-breed hog-toler driving his razorbacks through the thickets came acrost him."

Knightland's eyes squinted. "Any papers on him?"

Clane shook his head. "Why do you ask?"

Knightland found it an effort not to look at Cordon. "He had a briefcase full of them when he was with us."

Clane shook his head. "That was gone as well as his money belt. He came down monthly to collect the rent from these cotton farmers on the old Gomez Strip, it seems. I guess there's enough men around these parts who'd kill a man for that amount. I just wondered if you had any additional light to shed on the thing."

"Yes, Victor," said Knightland. "What could we tell the sheriff?"

Cordon's brows raised and he shrugged. "I can't think of anything, Bob," he said, watching Knightland intently. "Can you?"

"I'll have to think it over," said Knightland.

"If there's anything I can do," said Harrison Wade, "let me know, won't you, Clane? I know you'll excuse me now if I go back to my guests."

Clane nodded, turned to Cordon and Knightland. "If you do

recollect something that might help, I'd appreciate your letting me know."

"We will, Bart, we will." Cordon smiled, clapping the man on his arm. "And don't forget to drop around for that beer tomorrow. We're always stocked, you know."

Clane nodded, grinning, and turned to go.

"You ought to be in politics," Knightland told Cordon, after the man was out of earshot.

"You ought to play more poker." Cordon grinned, coming in close. "That was keeping the cards in close, Bob. But you can see what any connection with Orvado now would do to our business. It would be a shame to endanger any of the credit or goodwill we've established, and, as long as that briefcase is gone, nobody'll know Orvado was trying to pull a phony title deal on us. Not that we have anything to hide, but there's no use linking our names to anything like that unless it's necessary."

"Have we got anything to hide, Vic?" said Knightland, meeting his eyes.

Cordon chucked him in the ribs. "Bob, you aren't still mad about Sinton Dexter?"

"You know I'm not thinking of that, Vic. It's Orvado."

"All right, so it's Orvado. A two-bit shyster trying to cut in on our good fortune with counterfeit titles. It's been done before, Bob. He'd probably done it before himself. Once a crook always a crook. Maybe one of his old enemies was just paying a debt."

"Or one of his new enemies?"

Cordon's eyes flashed, and little muscles twitched about the corners of his mouth, as if with the effort of retaining his smile. "Bob, you're making it hard for me. Just what's on your mind?"

"I think you know."

"What possible reason would I have for wanting to do that to Orvado?"

"That's what I'm wondering," said Knightland. "What possible reason."

"Bob, let's not quarrel again. We never used to. What's happening? Come on back in and enjoy the party."

"I can't, Vic. Make my excuses, will you?"

Cordon stared at him. "You're going out to think things over, maybe?"

"A lot of things."

"Include this, then," said Cordon. "Remember what you've wanted so bad as long as I've known you. You're on the way to that now, Bob. This syndicate is going to be big, and the men in it are going to be big. You may never get another chance like it. Only a fool would spoil that chance now."

Knightland spent the next four days out in the brush with his crews, gathering into one big herd the cattle they had caught and driving them in to Corpus Christi. He tried all the time to get Orvado off his mind. He tried to tell himself it was foolish to think of it in those terms. But every time he did, Victor Cordon would come to his mind, and he would find himself studying the man, analyzing him, wondering.

They had known each other as kids. Cordon had been born in the brush but an uncle in town had taken him out of it young. He had disappeared for a while. There was talk of Chicago and New York, school and business. When he had come back a couple of years before the war, the change was apparent. The simplicity, the crudity of the brush was gone from him; he was an impeccably tailored, cultivated, ambitious young man who had talked himself into the partnership of a business. With the war the business failed and Cordon had joined the Army with most of the other young men in the vicinity. He and Knightland had been thrown together, renewing an old friendship. Even then Cordon had been talking of the syndicate.

Knightland searched those years for some hint that Cordon could be capable of what had happened to Orvado. The man had killed. Knightland had seen him more than once. But they had all done that in the war. Then why should this insidious suspicion keep coming? Knightland was unable to answer it.

When the herd was just outside of town, Knightland left it and came into Corpus Christi with Kenny Dale to make his report.

There were half a dozen men in the Blackjack offices when Knightland arrived—including Victor Cordon, Harper Miller, and Arnold Wade, Madelaine's brother. Arnold was a slim, weak-chinned fop Knightland had never cared for, standing over against the window in obvious subservience to Cordon. Then, as Knightland moved on in, he saw Sinton Dexter lounging in the corner behind the door. He could not help draw up at sight of the man. He moved on in with Kenny Dale coming behind. Cordon rose with his usual heartiness.

"You look dusty as a wagon track in July, Bob. How about a beer?"

"I could use one," said Knightland. "Wasn't that Cannibal Moore's Karankawa I saw leaving here?"

Cordon had gotten a bottle from the cooler and was opening it. His eyes seemed to seek Harper Miller's in a fleeting look before they came to Knightland's again. "Sure thing." He smiled. "Good news, too. Not so, Harper?"

"That's right," said Miller. "Good news."

Cordon waved to a sheet of paper on his desk. "Cannibal sent us a note he's ready to sell out and you can start working Karankawa Thickets right away." Arnold Wade made a move-ment in the window seat that caught Knightland's attention. But when he looked Wade would not meet his eyes. "I hate to send anyone right back out, Bob, but I'd like that stuff in this herd. Cannibal has some prime beef, you know."

"Most of the men are pretty well played out, Vic," said Knightland. "They've been with the brush nearly three weeks without a day's rest. I'll be willing to work but I'll need some fresh hands."

"That's why I thought of Sinton," said Cordon. As Knightland started to protest, Cordon came around the desk, speaking swiftly. "Bob, you can't condemn a man for a few mistakes. There are a lot of men handy with a gun in your crews. Sinton needs a job pretty bad. His wife's sick out there in the thickets, and he hasn't worked in months. I think you're being too hard on the man. Don't you, Kenny?"

There was a pause. Cordon had been looking at Knightland. He changed the direction of his gaze, brows raising quizzically.

"Yeah," said Kenny Dale finally. "Yeah, Bob. You been riding with a pretty tight cinch lately. Why don't you ease up?"

Knightland turned to stare at Dale, but the man was watching Cordon.

"Give him a chance, anyway," said Cordon. "He'll be fresh, and he's a good man."

Knightland turned to Dexter. "You carrying any grudges?"

Sinton eased himself away from the wall. "I reckon not, Bob. I was baiting you the other day, all right. I got what was coming to me."

Knightland nodded. "Let's have a meal before we step on again, Kenny. Meet you here in an hour, Sinton. Have your war bag filled for a week."

Kenny Dale and Knightland ate at a little greasy sack outfit around the corner and picked up Dexter in front of the office.

The Karankawa Thickets were on the other side of Nueces Bay, near San Patricio, and they did not reach them till near evening. Planning to use Cannibal Moore's corrals, Knightland started right out flushing the cattle.

They had a half a dozen pigging-stringed by dusk and were separated, running a big patch of black chaparral, when Cannibal came. Knightland had flushed a big mouse-colored dun from some cactus and was crashing through the chaparral after the steer, surrounded by the wild, abandoned sounds of his charge, when the brush began popping off to his left and a horseman broke a hole right through the white brush there, charging down on Knightland.

IV

"Damn you, Knightland, I told you what would happen if you busted my thickets again!" shouted the man. He had pulled his gun.

"Cannibal!" shouted Knightland. That was all he got out before the man shot.

Clabber lurched beneath Knightland. Knightland kicked free of the stirrups and took a dive, doubling over to smash into mesquite and chaparral. A branch caught him across the back, taking all the breath from him, and then he was rolling over the ground, fighting for air, and coming to a stop heavily against a stump of chaparral. He heard Cannibal thrashing around in the brush behind him.

"Cannibal!" he called again, in a gasping way. "Hold off, will you, Cordon told me . . . !"

The gunshot cut him off. Cannibal had wheeled his big blue tick roan and was pushing her through brush this way. He loomed up above Knightland with that gun back of his ear to throw down. Knightland, with his own gun halfway out now, knowing it was his only chance, could do nothing else. His Navy bucked in his hand.

Cannibal's gun came on down from his ear as if he were going to throw down and shoot anyway. But the weapon fell from his hand at the bottom of its arc and he started pitching over onto Knightland. Knightland tried to roll away. The big roan whinnied wildly and spun off on her heel, crashing back through the brush. Cannibal's foot caught in the stirrup and he was dragged with her.

Knightland came to his feet, starting after them, but he could not keep up. They were out of sight by the time he came into the trail where he had been chasing the steer. Clabber had gotten back onto his feet and was standing there, wheezing, the blood coming out of his chest in great gouts. Then Knightland heard someone calling him from the thickets. In a few moments Kenny Dale and Sinton Dexter came into view.

"Cannibal jumped me," he told them. "He threw down on me and I had to shoot him. He's out there in the thickets somewhere. I saw him drop off but haven't been able to find him."

"He must be still alive, then," said Dexter. "Man must be crazy. Let's get out of here."

"I want to find him," said Knightland. "He may be unconscious out there somewhere."

"You can't find him tonight," said Dale. "Those clouds won't let any moonlight through. If he's staked out for you, he'll finish you for good the second time. Cool off, Bob. The best thing for you to do is get out of here."

"Kenny's right," agreed Sinton. "Climb up behind my saddle and we'll lead your animal."

"Clabber's through," said Knightland.

"Maybe he ain't," said Sinton. "I had a horse shot like that once, that lived to a ripe old age. Climb on and we'll see if we can't lead him back to camp."

Reluctant to leave the horse, Knightland stepped aboard Sinton's fiddling mare, and they took up Clabber's trailing reins. The buttermilk horse balked for a moment but finally started moving after them. They went at a walk for a couple of miles. The bleeding stopped. For a while Knightland thought they would make it. Then, abruptly, the horse went down. Knowing it was dead before he got off, Knightland stood staring down at the animal.

"That's one you owe Cannibal," said Dexter.

"Are you sure it's Cannibal I owe?" asked Knightland.

This brought Dexter's narrow head around sharply. "What do you mean, Bob?"

They got back to Corpus Christi two days later, three grimy, saddle-weary men heading their sweat-streaked animals down Water Street. Before they reached the Blackjack offices, however, Sheriff Clane appeared on his stockinged bay, quartering across the street toward them.

"You looking for your boss, Bob?" he asked. "I just saw Vic and Harper heading out toward the Wade place. Ain't that a new favorite?"

"I left Clabber in camp a few days," said Knightland, glancing at the bald-faced animal he rode. "All this cow work used her up pretty much."

"What thickets you been working, Bob?"

"Westward."

"How far westward, Bob?"

Knightland met his eyes squarely. "What's the matter, Clane?"

"I just got word from the San Patricio sheriff that Cannibal Moore was found dead in Karankawa Thickets yesterday. It looked like cold-blooded murder. His gun was in his holster and not a shot had been fired from it."

"In his hols . . . ?" Knightland halted, mouth open. Then be clamped it shut.

"Shock to you, Bob?"

"Cannibal and I were old friends," said Knightland.

"I reckon you were, Bob." Clane peered at him narrowly, then turned away, saying the last almost absently: "All right, Bob. All right."

Knightland watched him go, then viciously wheeled his horse around and headed toward the Brownsville road. The others followed. They found Cordon's horse, along with Harper Miller's, hitched to the tie ring before the Wade house, and a Negro boy watching the animals said the gentlemen were out in the summer house. Arnold Wade and Victor Cordon and the lawyer were the only ones there, seated comfortably in cane chairs, with a cut-glass decanter of expensive whiskey on the table in the center.

"I'd like to see that note Cannibal Moore sent you," Knightland said, before Cordon could speak.

"Why, Bob?" said Cordon, surprised.

Dexter started: "Cannibal was . . ."

"Shut up, Dexter," Knightland told the man before he could finish. "I'd just like to see it, that's all. Come on, Vic."

"What's the matter, Bob? I don't think I have it. I don't keep things like that long, got so much paper work as it is."

Knightland paced forward. "What did it say, Vic? Just what did it say?"

"I don't understand you, Bob. Has something happened? I told you what it said."

"Cannibal didn't even give me a chance to talk. The minute he saw me he threw down. Those weren't the actions of a man who had just written you he was ready to sell out and I could start running his cattle anytime."

Cordon's lips parted. "You had a fight?"

"I had to shoot him," said Knightland. "I thought his horse dragged him off but it must have dropped him somewhere. The brush was so thick around there we couldn't find a thing. We even went to his house but he wasn't there. Now Clane tells me

34

Cannibal was found out in Karankawa Thickets, murdered. His gun was still in his holster, unfired."

"Sounds like you were mistaken about his throwing down on you," said Cordon. "We'll do everything we can to keep this quiet, Bob. Who else was there? Just Kenny and Sinton? If they're the only witnesses, you'll be safe, you know that . . ."

"Safe from what?" said Knightland angrily. "I didn't murder Cannibal. It was self-defense and you know it!"

Cordon raised quizzical brows. "I do?"

"You sent me out there deliberately," said Knightland hotly. "Maybe you hoped it would be the other way around. Is that it, Vic? Cannibal was pretty good with his gun. Maybe you were getting spooked about Orvado."

"Well . . ." Cordon let it out on a soft breath. He pursed his lips, began to toy with a glass on the table. "You're talking pretty wild for a man in such a tight spot. Why should I know it was self-defense when the law is calling it cold-blooded murder? You don't want to antagonize any of the people upon whom your life depends."

Knightland stared blankly. "My life?"

"How many men were in the office when I sent Bob out to Cannibal's, Harper?" asked Cordon.

"Let's see"—Harper Miller squinted one eye—"there was Arnold Wade, Kenny and Sinton, you, and myself."

"That would carry a lot of weight if they all got up on the witness stand and told how Bob went to Karankawa Thickets the night before Cannibal was murdered, wouldn't you say, Harper?"

"I would say."

"And then if Kenny and Sinton were to tell how they were chousing cattle in the thickets and heard the shots and all. Just about clinch the rest of the evidence, wouldn't you say, as a lawyer?"

"As a lawyer, I would."

Cordon lifted his eyes from the glass, staring quizzically at Knightland. "Now what was that you were saying about Orvado?" Knightland glared at him, savage expression filling his face. He tried to speak but only made a guttural sound. There was nothing to say. Cordon drew a swift, smiling little breath. "On the other hand, Bob, it might be as you say. It is strange about the gun being in Cannibal's holster but something funny might have happened, and you really might have shot him in self-defense. If that's true, we wouldn't want to send an innocent man to death, would we? And if you're innocent, there's no use involving ourselves in such an unsavory mess. It would be very bad for such a struggling young business. Do you think, Harper, if Bob kept in line and worked very hard at getting more cattle for us and followed our every order explicitly, do you think we might keep this little secret between us?"

Harper Miller pursed his lips and inclined his head forward. "We might, Victor. We just might."

"I wonder"—Cordon was suddenly interested in something on the ceiling—"I just wonder if Cannibal had any heirs."

The scent of oleander had a sickening oppression to Knightland as he walked back through the trellises of the summer garden and down the brick walk flanking the main house. His body was drawn so tight the slightest shift of pressures would cause a violent explosion. He tried to find logical thought through the veil of frustration that gripped him. Then, abruptly, Madelaine was before him.

She must have come out of the house. There was something infinitely cool to the coif of her golden hair, swept upward off her face, and the dimity of her summer dress. But her face reflected none of this; it was pale and strained, an expectant, waiting look to her eyes.

"We heard Cannibal was found murdered," she said.

"Did you?" His voice was grating.

"What happened out in the summer house between you and Victor?"

"Nothing."

"Don't be silly. It's in your face. You've got that look again. I'm always afraid you're going to kill someone with your bare hands. What is it, Bob?" She paused as if searching his face, and then her voice came again. "Did you kill Cannibal?"

It was hard for him to breathe looking at her. "Why do you say that?"

"My brother Arnold is a weak man, Bob. Victor has him under his thumb. He'd do anything for Victor. But he drinks sometimes, and he's been confiding in his sister so long it's natural to talk. Arnold was there when Cordon sent you out to Karankawa Thickets. Cannibal wouldn't sell out, would he? It's a logical conclusion to reach."

"No, Madelaine"—Knightland found his hands gripping her shoulders and was surprised that she did not pull away—"you've got to believe me. One person in this world has got to believe me. I didn't murder Cannibal Moore. He had his gun out and he shot twice before I did. Cordon told me Cannibal had written a note, telling us he was ready to sell out, and I could start chousing his cattle anytime. I saw the note on Cordon's desk and I saw the Karankawa leaving the office."

"You didn't actually read the note?"

He shook his head. "No. That's why I can't put it together. Cannibal wasn't the kind to deliberately set a trap for me."

"That would put it right back in Cordon's lap," she murmured, frowning. "Why should he send you out if he knew Cannibal still didn't mean to sell?"

"Maybe he was getting afraid of what I knew," Knightland told her. "You heard about the Orvado killing? Orvado was in the office, just before he died, with titles to the Gomez Strip.

Cordon claimed they were counterfeit. But they were gone when Orvado's body was found. If they weren't counterfeit, Orvado could have well destroyed the syndicate by court action. We had been running those Gomez cattle, all right. Something like that would make the investors lose faith in Blackjack, and the court costs alone would eat up the margin we'd been running on."

"Would Cordon take the chance of practically rustling cattle if he knew there was no chance of getting title to them?"

"I think he made an offer to the Gomez family in Mexico City, not knowing they had a representative up here," said Knightland. "When they refused, he went ahead working the cattle anyway. You know how lax the absentee ownership of some of those Mexican families is. There was rustling going on in the old Portrero for two years before any action was taken. Cordon is the kind to work on the edge that way, planning on having the Blackjack so big by the time the Gomez family did anything that he could squelch it."

"So Victor was afraid of you," she said. "You were the only one beside himself who knew what had gone on between him and Orvado."

"Harper Miller was there."

"Victor's right arm," she said. "And they either had to get rid of you or put you in a spot that you couldn't tell. Cannibal offered a perfect solution, didn't he? If he killed you, that was all right. If you killed him, you'd be in just such a spot as you are now. Who do you think put the gun back in his holster?"

"It couldn't have been his gun. He dropped that. It must have been another. Dale and Dexter were both out in the brush. They didn't come up for a few minutes."

"Time to find Cannibal's body and hide it where you wouldn't find it. Time to put a fully loaded gun in his holster."

"You do believe me."

"Oddly enough," she said, as he dropped his hands from her

shoulders, "it never particularly mattered to me whether your killing of Cannibal was murder or self-defense. I'd like to know what you are going to do about it."

"What can I do about it?" he said.

She studied him a moment. "Bob, whenever we've been brought together in the past, I always felt the conversation you made was a surface thing, that underneath you were thinking something else, wanting to say something else. You never tried to make love to me. Didn't you want to?"

"Madelaine . . ."

"Forget your pride for a minute," she said, coming closer. "It's reached a point where I've come to know what you feel, and I'm not going to play the coy, waiting woman any longer. Was it the difference in our stations that kept you quiet?"

He could not help that lowering of his eyes toward the grimy, brush-scarred clothes, the great, calloused, scarred hands. "I guess you're right," he said in a low voice. "The time has come to speak out. It's funny. A man can fight other men and not be afraid, or go through a whole war and never turn tail and run, or take a run through brush that a lot of men would never chance. And yet when it comes up to saying just a few words to a woman, it's like he was the biggest coward in the world. You can never know how it feels to want a woman and have absolutely nothing to offer her. What good would it have done me in the past to talk of love, to even hint at it? I guess I wanted to every time we met. It wasn't only that gulf between us, Madelaine. Every time we seemed to hit a mood, and I'd start, I sensed something in you drawing away and getting cold."

"It didn't have to do with the patches on your pants, Bob," she said. "It had to do with exactly what is happening tonight. If I seemed to pull away when you were about to say what you really wanted, it was because you had something in you I could never quite pin down. It felt shaky and dangerous beneath my feet. I want a man who's sure just where he stands, Bob, right or wrong. You weren't sure then. You went back on your friends when you joined the syndicate, Bob . . . your friends and everything you stood for. And now that you see what a rotten thing it is, you still haven't got the courage to quit."

"How can I quit," he said desperately. "When a word from Cordon will . . ."

"I suppose you're right," she said in a subdued, withdrawn disgust. "I guess I couldn't expect it, could I, in a man like you?"

V

Knightland rode out into the brush to try and clear it up within himself. But nothing would come. He saw now Madelaine was right in a way. There had been a sacrifice of principle, so subtle, so finely shaded, that even now it was hard to see, yet it had been there all down the line—with his parents, Orvado, not speaking up to the sheriff that first time, with Cannibal. Yet, at the time, it had seemed logical. He had wanted to climb so badly.

He returned to town near evening. He had meant to eat, but sight of Clane at one of the stools in the café Knightland frequented made him turn back to the Blackjack office. The trail crews were working late getting the cattle out of the corrals, and there were lights within the building. Kenny Dale was the only one in Cordon's office, seated casually at one of the chairs, feet crossed on the desk. He uncrossed them with Knightland's entrance, and lowered them to the floor. Bob Knightland stood looking at him bleakly.

"I always prized your friendship highly, Kenny," he said.

"Likewise, Bob," said Dale, watching his face.

"How much did they pay you?" asked Knightland.

"Now, Bob . . ."

"Who was it put that gun in Cannibal's holster? You, or Sinton . . . ?"

Dale stood, wiping his hand across his mouth. "Bob, there's no use talking, the thing's over, your fight isn't mine . . ."

"You're the last man I would expect to sell out."

"Look who's talking," said Dale.

Knightland stared at him as it came home. Then all the sand leaked out of him. All he felt was a bitter defeat. He heard the shuffling of boots behind him and turned to see Cordon coming in.

"Well . . . Bob." Cordon smiled. "Knew you'd get over your sulks sooner or later." He went to the desk and shuffled through some papers. "We're going to work on east from Refugio to the Guadalupe now, Bob. There's a big patch between Refugio and Greta owned by some Eastern money. We haven't been able to contact them yet, but you can go ahead and clean out the brush, and we'll probably have the proper clearance by the time you get back. Run the Sliced Moon or some crazy brand like that."

"I suppose they have someone occupying the place."

"Naturally, naturally. A Mexican crew or something, I don't know exactly. You won't have any trouble."

"Suppose I do?"

Cordon raised his head. His teeth showed in a smile. "Do I have to tell you, Bob?"

"Listen, Cordon, I'm not going to use those methods to . . ."

The entrance of Sinton Dexter halted Knightland.

"Vic," he said, "I'd like to see you alone . . ."

"In a minute, Sinton," Cordon said. "Bob was thinking he might have some trouble in those patches running the Sliced Moon. Mexican crew over there, isn't it? Bob was a little reluctant to go. Tell him about Clabber, Sinton."

The man looked at Knightland and dropped his eyes.

"What about Clabber?" Knightland asked.

41

"Why, Sinton," said Cordon, "just the way you told me. How you knew just where Clabber was. Not out in the open where any of Sheriff Clane's routine investigations would come across him. Hidden off in some thicket where you could find him. What do you suppose Clane would do if you told him where the horse was?"

Sinton wiped his mouth. "Ask a lot of questions, I guess, I don't know. Listen, Vic . . ."

"I think he'd do more than that, don't you?" said Cordon. "If he found Knightland's horse out there, quite near to Karankawa Thickets, shot to death, I think it would just about clinch the case for Clane along with all the other evidence, don't you, Bob?"

Knightland licked his lips, staring at Gordon, remembering Sinton Dexter's insistence that they try and lead the horse away, knowing it would die, yet wanting it where it would put Knightland in just this sort of a spot. Seeing how far ahead Cordon had planned this thing made Knightland sick at his stomach. He stared at the man in a bleak, helpless rage, unable to speak. His hands twitched with the desire to get them on Cordon. It caused him actual pain to restrain himself.

Cordon's eyes were drawn to that twitching, momentarily, then he raised them again to Knightland. "Take all your men, Bob. And you'll do me a good job, won't you?"

Knightland turned stiffly to walk out the door. He stood by his animal for a long time, faced in against the steaming, fetid heat of its body, under a hot sun, trying to find one clear thought in his mind. Nothing was there but rage, and the dim, desperate realization that he had to do Cordon's bidding or go on the run for good, and he had seen too many men out there in the brush with too many years of running behind them.

With a sullen curse he stepped aboard his bay and swung it out into Water Street. He was a block from the Blackjack building when he saw the wagon. It was an old linchpin, drawn up in front of an open Mexican market with a stirring, nervous crowd around it. Doc Mayer was crouched in the bed, tending Micah Knightland, and Bob's mother sat up on the seat, twisted back over her husband.

Knightland galloped his horse heedlessly into the crowd, swinging off when he could not get in any farther, fighting his way through the last press to grasp at the side of the wagon.

"What is it, Doc, what's happened?"

"Gut-shot, Bob," said the doctor. "He'll go if I try to move him. There isn't much I can do . . ."

"Dad," cried Knightland, grabbing a front wheel to climb in, "Dad, what happened?"

"Don't get in my wagon," said Micah in a groaning voice. "And don't call me Dad."

Knightland's face went white. His mother was sitting up on the seat, turned around to face the rear, over Micah's head. She looked at Knightland with a hollow lack of expression that knotted up his stomach.

"Ma," he pled. "Ma, he doesn't mean that . . ."

"I think he does, Son," she said emptily. "He told you what happens when a man tries to get big too fast."

"You mean . . . they . . . ?"

"What do you mean, *they?*" she said. "You, boy. Your syndicate. I'm surprised you weren't with them. He told that man a dozen times he wouldn't sell out. Even had me write it in a letter. He heard our cattle was being run today, and got his gun and went out to stop the man . . ."

"What man?" said Knightland, and even as he said it found his head snapping back toward the Blackjack office. Doc Mayer made some small grunting sound, and it brought Knightland's head around.

"I'm afraid he's gone," Mayer murmured.

43

Knightland's hands slid off the wagon and he dropped back onto the road. He knew what that lack of expression on his mother's face was now. It was too big for feeling, too soon. At least for grief. But there could be anger. A different kind of anger than he had felt with Cordon earlier. A steadily mounting, implacable anger that turned him around and started him walking toward the Blackjack office.

"Bob," called someone, "what are you going to do?"

Without stopping he turned his face to see Madelaine Wade, coming out from beneath the arcade. She caught his arm, walking swiftly beside him, looking up at him, trying to see behind the mask of his face.

"Cordon?" she said, breathlessly. He did not answer, walking on, in long, vicious strides that she could hardly match. "Bob, they'll have someone to send after Clane. You know that. They'll know you're coming, now, and they'll know why, and send somebody to him with the word. It'll mean the end of it . . ."

"Isn't this what you wanted me to do?"

"But not this way"—tears suddenly filled her eyes—"they'll kill you."

Sinton Dexter appeared at the door of the Blackjack. He was faced this way as he came out, but he took a couple of steps toward his horse at the tie rack before his eyes accustomed themselves to the blinding sun. He saw Knightland. His lean, slouching body continued the movement toward the horse indecisively, then stopped. Knightland kept on coming, and Dexter broke and dodged back into the building.

"Now they know, Bob," pleaded Madelaine. "Stop, please, I can't keep up with you. They know and they'll be waiting. Please. If Clane finds out about what happened that day . . ."

"I thought you wanted a man to know where he was going," he said.

"Bob!" she cried, and stumbled, and fell, and then had to

release his arm, unable to keep up with him any longer, because his walk had been gaining speed steadily, until he was moving in on the Blackjack in what was almost a run.

He stopped at the door, pulling his gun. There was movement far down the hall. He ducked around the edge of the opening and threw himself against the wall to avoid being skylighted. The hallway was empty.

He started stalking down the corridor unable to muffle the tap of his boot heels. Again that sound. Then movement coming from a shadowed room. He was between two doors, and threw himself against the one on his left, catching at the knob with his free hand. It opened with him and he was already halfway inside when the shot crashed.

He saw that it came from a room beyond Cordon's office. He did not try to answer it. The door he had jumped into opened on Harper Miller's empty office. These windows were shuttered against the sun. They opened out toward the corrals behind the building.

"Bob!" It was Cordon's voice coming from down the hall. "Unless you put that gun away and come out, I'm sending Harper after Sheriff Clane. He'll tell Clane everything. It won't matter if you get us or not, then, Bob. You'll hang for Cannibal. If we don't get you, the law will."

"The law can have me after I'm through with you, Victor," said Knightland. "Did Sinton kill Orvado as well as my father?"

"Don't be a fool, Bob. I'll give you one minute. If you're not out here without your gun by then, Harper will be on his way to Clane."

"You'd better not even wait that long, Victor. I'm coming right now and my gun's in my hand."

In a gesture of vicious anger, Knightland caught up a chair and flung it crashing through the door. Again the deafening smash of shots rocked the hallway out there. Knightland was already tearing open one of the shutters and slipping his leg across a broad windowsill. He ran down this outside wall, passing the shuttered windows of a storeroom. There was the flash of movement from the end of this wing of the building, about fifty yards on down, and Harper Miller dashed across the open space between corrals and building.

Still running, Knightland raised his gun but the lawyer was behind the protective network of corral bars. From there he must have seen Knightland. His voice came sharp.

"Hold up, Sinton! He's outside! He's outside!"

It was too late. Sinton Dexter had already appeared in the open space, running hard. Miller's words, however, caused him to try and halt himself as if wanting to turn back. At the same time he had seen Knightland and began to shoot. Knightland held out his own gun at shoulder level and fired once.

Dexter crumpled to the ground.

Knightland could hear the hasty, diminishing pound of Harper Miller's boots, too far down the line of corrals to reach now. Knightland himself was by the windows of Cordon's office. He lifted one leg over the low sill and gave the shutters a smashing kick. They gave, with a splintering of wood. He kicked again, with his gun held in on the opening. The shutters smashed open this time, clattering back against the wall.

The office was empty.

He knew the sight of Sinton Dexter going down out there would have stopped Cordon if Cordon had been following him out. If Cordon had turned back, he was still out in the hall somewhere, either between this door and the rear one, or on up toward the front. Knightland paced across Cordon's office to the hall door, standing ajar.

Then up the hall toward the front there was a shuffling noise. Knightland shifted till he could see down the corridor without moving the door. He must have made some sound, however, for it was Kenny Dale coming out of Harper Miller's doorway, and turning his way as if drawn by Knightland's sound.

"Look out, Bob!" shouted Dale. "Vic's in the room across . . . !"

A great, deafening crash drowned him out, the sound of gunfire in the corridor. Dale was carried back against the door frame, bent in the middle. Knightland whirled the other way down the hall. The door to the last room before the end of the corridor was ajar enough to leave a wide crack. Knightland had to shoot from the hip, emptying his gun into that door belly high, one shot right after another, his whole body jerking with the gun.

In the ear-splitting noise of his own fire he was vaguely aware that a shot came from that dark crack, or two shots, he did not know how many. He saw the flame and felt adobe chip off against his face. Then the hammer of his Navy made a dull metallic clank on a fired shell, and all the thunderous, racketing sound ceased abruptly.

He lay on the floor feeling pain in his thigh for the first time. One of Cordon's shots had caught him and he had not even felt it in the excitement of these few moments. He dragged himself to a sitting position against the wall. His blood was seeping out onto the floor now. He saw that the door had opened into that other room.

Cordon must have had his hand on the knob, and dragged the portal back with him as he fell. His legs were visible in the dim light, up to the knees. He lay on his back with the toes of his polished boots toward the ceiling. Knightland turned his head down the hall where Kenny Dale lay hugging his stomach.

"Why'd you do it, Kenny?" he asked. "You could have had me."

"I guess I just couldn't take it any more," groaned Kenny. "It came on me while we was waiting for you here. Their money had looked pretty good at first. But it kept getting redder and redder, and I saw it was blood, and I couldn't put your blood on it, too, Bob, I just couldn't . . ."

He trailed off, breathing feebly. Then it was Madelaine, appearing at the door, calling to Knightland. He could not rise. She came running down the corridor, dropping to her knees.

"Bob, Bob, you've got to get up. Clane is coming. Harper told him everything."

"My leg won't take my weight," he said. She stared at him, and then sobbed his name, dropping to her knees beside him. "Why do you care . . . so much?" he asked.

"Because I see finally what you really are," she told him. "It really started at the party, didn't it, Bob? And ended with your father's death today. Something inside you resolved itself during that period."

"I guess it did," he said. "It's funny. I told you how I wanted to meet you on your own level for most of my life, how your money was a symbol of everything I had to attain to meet you on that level. Being invited to that party should have been one of the biggest milestones in my life. But it wasn't. It wasn't anything. I realized I didn't belong and never could . . ."

"A man can develop taste in clothes, Bob, or learn which fork to use at the table . . ."

"And what if he learned and still didn't belong? And didn't want to? That's what went through me, Madelaine. It should have humiliated me deeply to see what a bad fit I made. It should have made me mad, made me willing to do anything, learn anything to belong. But I wasn't embarrassed. I just realized that I didn't belong. And I didn't care. I knew then that I couldn't have you even if I did have money because I could never be happy living like that."

"I told you, Bob," she said, "that when you sensed a withdrawal on my part, it didn't have anything to do with the patches on your pants. I wanted a man who was sure where he stood. I'd live in a cave with that man, if I loved him."

He stared at the tearful, glowing light in her eyes, realizing what she was saying, yet unable to believe it. Then Sheriff Clane was pushing his way through the crowd that had gathered in the door and was gradually filling the hall. He glanced at Dale, and Cordon, and stopped above Knightland.

"Doc Mayer'll be here in a minute," he said. "Right now, I'd like to have a word with you, Bob. I guess you know what Miller told me."

"Sheriff . . . ," began Madelaine in a swift pleading way.

"Never mind" Clane grinned. "Ever know a sheriff who could speak Karankawa?"

"I never knew anybody who could," she said puzzled.

"I grew up out on Dagger Island," Clane told them. "That was the last home of the tribe. I speak their lingo good as they do. I found Cannibal Moore's Karankawa out in the bush the other day. He saw the fight between Cannibal and Bob. Said Cannibal shot twice before Bob did. Then he saw Sinton Dexter find Cannibal when that roan dropped him, and put his own six-gun into Cannibal's holster. Cannibal really sent a note to Cordon but it didn't say he was selling out. It said the next time Cannibal found a Blackjack man in his thickets, he'd shoot."

Knightland stared, open-mouthed, at the sheriff. None of them spoke. Finally Clane looked at Cordon's boots. "Victor wanted to get big fast, didn't he, Bob? I think he was using you more than you realized. Your name meant a lot in the thickets. Half the men working for Blackjack are in it because you thought it was a good thing. Your killing Cannibal was obvious self-defense. How'm I going to fix this up?"

"Sinton Dexter started shooting before Bob did on the outside," groaned Kenny Dale from where he lay. "And Vic Gordon was set to shoot Bob in the back on the inside . . ."

"That's it." Clane grinned. "You're free on three counts of self-defense, Bob. If they want to make a jury trial of it, they'll have to corral you out in the thickets themselves. How about your father, Miss Wade? Did he know what Cordon was doing?"

"No," said Madelaine hotly. "He was only one of the stockholders in the syndicate. Cordon was running the works."

Before Clane could answer, Doc Mayer had shoved through the press and was kneeling beside Kenny Dale. And then Knightland's mother. She stopped above him. Then she was on her knees beside him, sobbing softly.

"You've come back, Son. You've come back."

"I guess so, Ma," he said. "If the ways of working cattle are changing, they'll have to get somebody else to do it. I found out just how good a dog-run house and a six-cow thicket are."

"Maybe somebody else has, too," said Madelaine quietly.

He looked at her but spoke to his mother. "Think our house would hold three, Ma, till I get another one built?"

His mother raised a tearful smile to Madelaine. "It'd seem empty with any less after all these years."

★ ★ ★ ★ ★

LAWLESS LAND

★ ★ ★ ★ ★

I

In the cell, in the heat, in the stripes of blinding sunlight that slanted through the barred windows, the droning of a fly was the only sound. The old Navajo sat on the rusty cot, staring fixedly at the adobe wall, his eyes as blank as glazed beads.

"Jahzini," Lee Banner said. *"Sixoyan bica dahndinza?"*

The Indian's slack lips worked soddenly at the words. *"Do ya ah-shon dah . . ."*

"No good?" Banner's voice sounded exasperated. "Of course it's no good if you won't tell us anything." He turned helplessly to Cristina. "Explain to him that we can't help him unless we know everything that happened."

The girl began speaking to her father, intensely, swiftly. Banner could only catch a word here or there and gave up trying to follow. He leaned tiredly against the barred door, tall, blond, broad-shouldered, in a blue serge filmed at the cuffs and coat-tails with Arizona dust. He had a high forehead, sharply squared off at the temples. His deeply recessed eyes gave his lean face a brooding quality that made it appear older than his twenty-five years.

Cristina broke off finally, waiting for her father to speak. Sunlight made a shimmering circle on her black hair as she turned to Banner. "He will not even answer me."

Banner shook his head defeatedly. "I guess there's nothing more we can do, then."

Her eyes widened, dark with plea. She had spent six years at

Carlisle, and spoke English with the peculiar precision of one who had learned a foreign language well. "Lee, do you believe my father killed Wallace Wright?"

Banner stared into her delicate face, knowing it would haunt him now. This was really the first time he had seen Cristina since her return from Indian school a few weeks before. She had left a child; she had come back a woman. Yet there would always be a child-like quality to her, no matter how she matured. The fruit-like curve of her cheek glowed like sun-tinted copper, the reed-like slimness of her body, in the boarding-school dress of flowered calico. The hair, parted in the center like a little girl's, was so black it drank in all the light and left only the faintest sheen over the top of her head.

He reached out to grasp her arm. "You know I can't believe Jahzini did it. The man I remember couldn't kill anyone. I may be in the prosecutor's office, Cristina, but I'll do everything in my power to help your father." He watched that draw a shining hope into her eyes, and then turned to call: "We're through now, Charlie!"

There was the raucous squeak of a swivel chair. Charlie Drake appeared at the end of the cell-block, rattling through the keys on his ring. He unlocked the door and pulled it open. "I don't see what you hoped to gain outta that Indian. They got enough to hang him a dozen times over."

Banner walked through with stooped shoulders. "What would you do for a friend, Charlie?"

The sheriff pulled the door shut after them with a clang. "Don't get sucked into anything, Lee."

Banner's boots beat a hollow tattoo against the cement floor. The outer door creaked dismally on unoiled hinges. He followed the girl into the furnace of Mexican Hat in June. Banner's eye automatically registered the picture—the buildings across from the courthouse, the curlicued façade of Blackstrap

Kelly's saloon jammed up against the row of enigmatic adobes, the false fronts of Sam Price's Mercantile and the harness shop. For six blocks it ran, the old and the new, fronted by the inevitable sagging hitch racks, the rusty ring posts.

He felt Cristina's hand on his arm, and realized they had reached Jahzini's old Studebaker wagon, its split front axle bound with rawhide. He halted awkwardly here, not knowing what to say. Cristina's lower lip trembled.

"Judge Prentice has a pretty full docket," he said. "They haven't set any date for the trial yet, but I imagine it won't be till late summer. Maybe something will turn up by then."

The shadow of a man came into Banner's vision. It touched the wagon, stopped.

"Checking up on the case, Lee?"

"Doing what I can, Arles."

Arles took a deep drag on his cigarette, smiling loosely. He was tall, dour, slack as a piece of old hemp. Beneath the battered brim of a ten-gallon hat, his face was burned almost black by the sun. In the shadow of the brim, the movement of his eyes from Cristina to Banner made a shuttling gleam. "I thought Henry Dodge had already questioned Jahzini."

"He has, Arles."

"Doing some leg work, maybe."

"Not exactly."

"Oh. Not exactly." Arles took a last drag on his smoke. Then he pinched it out between his thumb and forefinger. He saw their eyes on it, and smiled. "Most folks won't believe them rope calluses are that thick. I can pinch a match out the same way. Don't feel a thing."

"Don't you?"

Arles flicked the cigarette butt away. He turned to Cristina. "Rainbow Girl," he said. It brought a flush to her face. "Maybe you asked Banner to defend your father," he said.

"You know it's as good as an insult to use their Indian names," Banner told him. "Why do you keep on doing it?"

Arles looked at Banner. "You going to defend Jahzini?"

"Why don't you let it go, Arles? It's been hard enough on Cristina."

"Dodge wouldn't like you defending Jahzini. Not when he's prosecuting the case. Be like his own son turning against him. Dodge always said you was like his own son."

Banner's voice was thin: "How about Hackett?"

"Hackett wouldn't like it, either. Nobody would. There's a lot of feelings against the Indians about this. You know how much trouble they've caused us over that railroad land. The case is open and shut, anyway."

"That sounds like something Hackett told you to memorize."

Arles's eyes flickered. The loose grin formed slowly, with palpable effort. "Don't make me mad, Lee."

"This isn't any of your business, Arles."

"I just wanted to put you right, Lee. You've got too big a future in that prosecutor's office. You don't want to ruin it over some old drunk Indian that never did any good for . . ."

"He's not an old drunk!" Banner was surprised at how loud his voice was. "He's my friend and he was my father's friend before me."

"Take it easy, Lee. You'll bust a gut."

"Then leave us alone, Arles. Cristina's in no shape for this kind of thing."

Arles chuckled softly. His eyes passed over the girl slyly. "I hadn't thought of that," he said. "See you so much with Julia Wright, I hadn't thought of that at all. You'd be a fool to mess your whole career up over some little desert slut . . ."

Banner's violent lunge cut Arles off, driving him back so hard he crashed into the wagon. As he went, Arles slapped at his gun. But Banner grabbed the wrist in his left hand, pinning it against

Arles's side. With his other hand he bunched the man's shirt up across his chest and threw the whole weight of his body into holding Arles against the wagon. His voice shook when he spoke. "I told you to leave her alone, Arles. Now get out of here, and don't ever let me hear you talk that way about her again."

He held Arles a moment longer. The man's frame was rigid against Banner, and there was a vicious rage stamped into his face. Banner stepped back, releasing him.

Arles's whole body came forward involuntarily, his hand gripping the gun.

"They'd lynch you for that," Banner said. "Not even Hackett could save you."

Arles hung there a moment longer. At last he brought his rage under control. His voice had a rusty sound. "Mighty safe without your cutter, ain't you?"

"You can have it any way you want it. All you have to do is unbuckle your belt, if you aren't through."

The man's narrow head lowered a little. He did not speak. He did not move. The breath passing through him had a husky, animal sound. Finally his boots scraped softly against the sun-baked earth. "You're a damn' fool, Lee," he said. He glared at Banner a moment longer. Then he wheeled around. His shadow slid off the wagon.

Banner felt Cristina's hand on his arm. "It is always like an explosion, when you get mad."

He tried to relax, tried to smile, couldn't. "He built me up to it."

"He has always hated me," she said. "Ever since he tried to make love with me at the trading post that time and I scratched his face."

Banner was frowning now, still watching Arles cross the street. "Why should he have done that? Any of that?"

"He was probably speaking for Hackett. Why wouldn't Hackett want you to defend my father?"

"I'd like to know," Banner said.

After Cristina said good bye, after she got into the wagon, and turned it down Reservation Street, Banner remained in front of the jail, watching her go. She would be returning to her mother, out there in the lonely hogan beyond Yellow Gap. Banner had spent a year in that hogan, after his father's death. He had been twelve years old, and Jahzini had been his father's only friend in this barren country. The old Indian had taken the boy in, had treated him as his own son, till Banner's uncle had come West to care for him. All the memories of that year welled up in him now. Jahzini, sitting cross-legged in the hogan, kindness and warmth in every seam of his nut-brown face, holding Banner and Cristina, round-eyed and spellbound, as he recounted the ancient myths of his people. Jahzini, half drunk on *toghlepai,* a chuckling little gnome lying on his back and thumping his belly like a drum and singing the "Clown Song" till the children and even his sober wife were doubled over with laughter. Jahzini, forcing his portion of mutton on a hungry boy when a bitter winter had left them without enough to go around.

In this mood, he crossed the street toward Henry Dodge's law office. Before he reached the bank, the outside stairway coming down from above began to tremble, and finally Banner's uncle stepped out onto the plank sidewalk. Fifty, white-haired, ruddy-faced, Dodge was inclined to paunch and seat. He saw Banner and halted on the walk, grinning at him. "Looking for you, son. The sheriff got permission from Fort Defiance to impound all of Wright's official papers till the trial. Might be some evidence among them that would help the People. I'd like you to pick the stuff up."

"Isn't that Sheriff Drake's job?"

"He and I both thought it would be easier on Julia if you did it," Dodge said. "Better take the wagon. Might be a load."

Banner's mind was hardly on what Dodge was saying. "Henry, I can't believe Jahzini did this. There's something funny about it. He's so changed, so dazed. All he does is sit there and tell us it's no good . . ."

"And claim he didn't do it," Dodge finished. "Of course he's dazed. I'd be dazed, too, with the evidence piling up against me like that." Dodge put a fatherly hand on Banner's shoulder. "I know how far back your attachment for Jahzini goes, Lee. But he was drunk when they found him. A man ain't in his right mind when he's drunk. And you know the trouble Jahzini had with Wright. The Indian was on one of those alternate sections the government gave to the railroad. Wright got the order to move him to land just as good. Jahzini wouldn't go. He was drunk that time, too, and he threatened to kill Wright if the man came again. And now we got a statement from Jess Burgess saying that he had arranged to buy wool from Jahzini in town on the day of the murder. That'd mean Jahzini was coming through Yellow Gap about the time Wright was killed there. Cristina herself said Jahzini started out with the wool. He never reached town. To top it all, they found Wright's burned saddlebags in Jahzini's hogan."

"That's it," Banner said. "Why would he want the saddle-bags?"

"Those Indians are natural-born thieves . . ."

"Now you're talking like Hackett."

"What's Hackett got to do with it?"

"That's what I'd like to know. Why should Hackett be afraid I might defend Jahzini?"

Dodge's twinkling eyes went blank. "You, defend Jahzini?"

"Hadn't you considered the possibility, Henry?"

A little muscle twitched in Dodge's cheek. His voice came from deep in his throat. "Son, you might as well stand out here on the street with everybody watching and slap me in the face."

Banner grasped his arm, suddenly contrite. "It won't come to that, Henry. You've always said a prosecutor owes as big a duty to the accused as he does to the People. I know you'd do everything you could to get Jahzini free if you thought he was innocent. Now, why is Hackett so interested?"

"How would I know, Lee?"

"He's one of your principal constituents, isn't he? Without his support you wouldn't be district attorney today. And now he's pushing you toward that superior bench . . ."

"Now you're goin' off half-cocked like you always do, jumpin' in with both feet before you even know what's there."

"Or maybe you don't want to know what's in Hackett's mind," Banner said. "Maybe you're afraid to dig any deeper than this."

"Son, stop it! We never talked like this before."

"Maybe it's time we did."

Dodge's voice sounded guttural with restraint. "Don't make me mad, Lee."

Banner frowned at him. "It's funny," he said. "That's the same thing Arles told me."

II

It was 1:00 P.M. when Banner came back to Reservation Street with the cut-under spring wagon. He was still depressed and confused from his talk with his uncle. Had his usual impulsiveness led him to jump to the wrong conclusions? He tried to tell himself Dodge would not compromise on this case. His faith in the man's integrity went back too far. Moodily he pulled up before Blackstrap Kelly's. Under the curlicued façade, the saloonkeeper sat on an upended barrel, lovingly blowing the head off a beer.

"I swear," Banner said, "you get more kick blowing that foam off than you do drinking the stuff."

Kelly thumped the barrel with his wooden leg. "Head's the best part. Look at this now. Frothy. Lacy. Like something a woman would wear."

"Tilfego inside?"

"As usual. Out back, proposing to my cook." Kelly sent him an oblique look. "You going in?"

Banner frowned down at the man. "What's the matter?"

Kelly brushed a bulbous thumb across his nose. "You ain't really takin' that Injun killer's case, are you, Lee?"

Banner's voice grew low. "You, too, Blackstrap?"

The man tapped his wooden leg uncomfortably against the barrel. "I'm sick of this Injun trouble. Some of my best friends got holdings north of the railroad. Only last week some Injuns run off a hundred of Elder's cattle."

"Which they claimed he originally cheated them out of."

"That ain't true. He bought 'em from Hackett. He's got a legal bill of sale."

"Then maybe it was Hackett that cheated them."

"They're always claiming something like that. What they makin' such a fuss over losin' a few acres for, anyway? They've still got half of Arizona. They signed a dozen treaties . . ."

"All of which we broke."

"Damn it, Lee . . ."—the man twisted angrily on his barrel, looking up at Banner with a flushed face—"that's exactly what I mean. You keep on talkin' this way and you'll lose every friend you have in this town. These Navajos have pushed us too far. This murder is the last straw. There wasn't a better man in the world than Wright. He didn't have an enemy in this town. If he couldn't settle this trouble with the Injuns, nobody could. He never raised a hand to 'em. He did more for 'em than their own people would. And what do they do? Kill him. Shoot him from

61

ambush like the dirty coyotes they are."

"Is that the feeling in town?" Banner asked quietly.

Blackstrap looked morosely at the plank walk. "I've heard talk of lynchin'."

"So you wouldn't want me to come into your saloon any more, if I was going to defend Jahzini."

"Dammit, Lee, I didn't say that . . ."

"I'll tell Jigger to bring you out another beer," Banner said.

Somberness left Banner's eyes half-lidded, made his face older, as he went into the saloon. He hadn't fully realized until now what the feeling of the town was about this killing. Absently he caught Jigger's attention, jerking his thumb toward the front door, and the bartender began drawing another beer for Blackstrap. Banner passed the trio of townsmen at the bar, the bored faro dealer smoking over an empty layout. He pushed open the kitchen door. At the big table sat Tilfego, broad, squat, sloppy. He had the cook on his lap, poking at her amplitude with a hairy finger.

"So much ripeness I have never see. If someone they do not come along and pluck you, Celestina, you will fall off the bough."

"Will you really marry me, Tilfego?" she asked.

"You and six hundred others," Banner said.

They both turned in surprise. Then Tilfego grinned.

"You are just in time the best man to be, Lee. Celestina, this is my very good friend, my best friend, my only friend. He and I we grow up together, both of us."

"How about a little hunting?" Banner asked.

Tilfego's eyes glowed eagerly. "Hunting?"

"You'd better," Banner said. "A married man doesn't get out much."

"If you will allow me to rise, my dove, my pigeon, my little *chile pimiento,*" Tilfego said, "married we can get upon my return."

"I don't think you mean to marry me at all," she said.

"On the honor of my grandfather."

"The horse thief?" Banner asked.

Banner finally got him out into the wagon. As they were rattling down Reservation Street toward the desert, Tilfego slid off his ancient sombrero and ran thick fingers through hair like the roached mane of a horse.

"*Qué barbaridad,*" he sighed. "I never see so much heat. Hunting you do not want to go in this furnace?"

"Not really. You been tracking for the Army lately?"

"No. And something I got to make soon. My money he is all spend."

"How about reading some sign at Yellow Gap? I'll buy you a beer afterward."

Tilfego slapped him on the back. "Who cares for beer? I have not see you enough lately. And now is this business of Jahzini. And you do not think he kill Wright."

Banner glanced at him, grinning ruefully. "I hope you find sign that easy at Yellow Gap."

"Is not hard for to see how you feel, Lee. Perhaps the land she will tell us what we want to know."

They had left the town. They were in the land of illusion, the Painted Desert, where the colors were constantly changing with the caprice of heat and light and desert dust, where vast distances staggered the eye. They crossed a meadow of sacaton grass that rose to meet them like the restless swell of a tawny sea. They dipped into a gorge cut by eons of wind and water. They finally reached its eastern end and rolled into an endless greasewood plain, studded with castellated mesas. The cut-off to Yellow Gap was ten miles east of Mexican Hat, the gap itself three miles north along the cut-off. It was fissured and shelved by erosion, its walls sculptured into weird mosques and minarets. The road followed the rim for half a mile, then shelved down the west wall. It was a sandy, slippery descent, with the brake shoes shrieking most of the way. The horses hit the bottom, blowing with relief.

Far ahead they saw the towering column of rock near which the Indian agent's body had been found. Tilfego made Banner stop the wagon a hundred yards from the spot and they went the rest of the way on foot. Finally Tilfego halted, staring at the yellow earth.

"*Qué barbaridad*," he said. "Look at the mess they make."

"I guess that's why nobody else could read much sign," Banner said. "The bunch that came down to get Wright's body wiped it all out."

All Banner could see were the imprints of shod hoofs and boots and the wheel tracks of wagons criss-crossing the sand. But Tilfego finally began picking his way carefully through the marks until he reached a spot a few yards distant. He squatted down there and traced the outline of a man's figure with his hairy forefinger. It was like dawning light. Banner could see clearly the depression the body had left, with all the other prints superimposed upon it.

Squatting there, the seat of Tilfego's greasy buckskin *chivarras* shone wetly across his broad rump. The Mexican was studying the surrounding terrain now, his brown eyes squinted almost shut with concentration. Finally Tilfego pointed at a patch of creosote, twenty feet away.

"Somebody he stand there. Twig he is break."

"Could it be the bunch that got the body?"

"Many men they would have break more brush."

Tilfego rose and moved over to the creosote, studying the earth for a long time.

"He come down here from the east rim, then he go back up,"

the Mexican said at last. "While he stand here, something she make him jump. You can see where his boots they have change the position. If it was behind him, he would have turn. But he did not turn." Tilfego looked across the cañon. "I think she was something up on that west rim."

They got into the wagon again, drove back up the road to the rim. They left the wagon in some greasewood and worked their way northward along the rim. It was a long, maddening search. It took the Mexican over an hour to find it. At last, in a thick growth of prickly pear, he squatted down.

"One man. On a shod horse. Coming from the north. About three days past."

Excitement lent Banner's face a boyish eagerness. "The day of the murder."

Tilfego rose, following the tracks toward the rim of the gap, halting again in a stand of wind-twisted junipers that overlooked the cañon. He studied the surrounding trees for a long time, finally fingered a wisp of something from the rough bark.

"Horse he is a bay. Scrape his hair off here."

"It couldn't have been the killer?"

"No. This man he did not even go down into the gap. He wait here a while, then he turn and go back north."

"Then that's what startled the killer, down in the cañon. He saw this man up here."

"Maybe not the man. Trees hide him. Maybe just his movement."

"What's the difference? There's every possibility that this man saw the murder. Do you realize what an eyewitness could mean, Tilfego? If Jahzini didn't do it, this would save his life."

"Not so quick, not so quick." Tilfego chuckled, holding up his coffee-colored palm. "Let us read some more."

He spent a long time studying the sign, recounting little details about the horse and rider that would have amazed anyone who had not known Tilfego's uncanny ability. But added up, they did not give Banner much more to go on.

They returned to the bottom of the gap at last, and Tilfego began to work again. Going to where the unknown man had stood in the creosote, near the body, the Mexican began backtracking along the man's trail, up to the east rim. He was silhouetted at the top among the ocotillo, then he disappeared back of the drop-off.

Banner paced restlessly around the wagon, making sure not to spoil any sign. It must have been half an hour before Tilfego reappeared. He came down from the rim and stopped in the creosote ten feet from Banner.

"This man he hitch his horse 'way back in the piñon where the rim she starts to drop off."

"Not the bay again?"

"No. This is different man. The horse I know. She got three nail is missing in the left hind hoof."

"Whose horse?"

"In them rocks a long time he hide. A lot of cigarette he smoke. Then he shoot Wright."

"Why did he come down here?"

"To see if Wright was dead for sure, I guess. And while he stand here, the movement of that man on the bay catch his eyes."

"What have you got in your hand?"

"I tell you he smoke cigarette. He try to grind all the butts out with his heel. But one get shoved under a rock."

He brought it over to Banner. The butt was about half an inch long.

"An ordinary man, he crush it out against the ground," Tilfego said. "This one is pinched out, like between the fingers."

Banner raised his eyes to Tilfego's sweating face. His voice had a hollow sound. "Arles?"

III

After that they went to the agency. It took them an hour, through the castellated mesas and the tortured gorges and the mesquite-choked washes. Then the horizon flattened out and the buildings appeared as if rising from the ground. Timber was precious in this land, and they were all of adobe, beaten by the wind, the sun, the rain, till they had taken on the hues of the earth itself.

Calico Adams's trading post was first, a tawny cube of a building. The other buildings were behind the trading post, the schoolhouse, the agency living quarters, the shaggy ocotillo corrals. There was a pair of Navajo ponies racked before the post, heads bowed, tails frayed by the wind.

"You won't mention what we found," Banner said.

"My mouth she is sealed," Tilfego said, his eyes on those ponies. His nostrils began to flutter. "Chile peppers!"

"Chile peppers," Banner snorted disgustedly. "How can you tell there are any women around?"

Tilfego's grin tilted his eyes into an Oriental slant. "I don't know. When there are chile peppers around something inside me just start for to buzz like the bee. I look around, I sniff the air, I turn the corner. ¡Hola! Chile peppers."

Banner pulled up by the door of the trading post. "Be careful of those Navajo girls. You know what they think of Mexicans."

Tilfego climbed off the seat, chuckling. "Before I am Mexican"—he thumped his chest—"I am man."

Banner shook the reins out and drove the wagon around the trading post toward the agency quarters. He saw that there was a sweat-caked roan standing ground-hitched before the long building, and a man at the doorway.

He turned sharply as Banner approached, and Banner recognized him as Victor Kitteridge. He made a tall and narrow shape in the doorway, his faded denim shirt and jeans so worn they were paper-thin at the elbows and knees. The suspicious calculation in his eyes seemed to have sucked all the warmth from his face.

Julia Wright stood behind him, just within the doorway, and Banner tipped his hat to her before speaking to the man. "Didn't realize you knew the Wrights, Kitteridge."

The fine weather graining looked like tiny scars at the edges of the man's lips. "Man should stop to pay his respects," he said. "*Ipso facto,* Counselor."

Banner's grin was wry. "No law against it. How's the roundup coming? They tell me your increase has been so good you had to hire a Mexican hand."

"Did they?"

Banner's grin faded. "Get any more beef and you'll have to lease some of that railroad land like the rest of the outfits."

"Will I?"

The hammerheaded roan grunted tiredly as Kitteridge stepped over and pulled the latigo tight. He took up the reins, toed a stirrup, and swung aboard. Glancing obliquely at Julia, touching the brim of his battered hat, he turned the horse down the road. Banner watched him go, frowning.

"Lived out here three years and I don't think he's been to town a dozen times. Do you suppose he's on the dodge?"

Something passed through Julia's face as she turned sharply toward him. "I don't know. Dad did him a favor once. He stopped to express his regrets."

Banner swung from the wagon, wrapping the lines around the whipstock. She waited for him silently. The strain, the grief of the last days had left her face pale and drawn. She was a tall woman, almost as tall as Banner. The swell of her breasts was deep and round against the bodice of her watered silk dress, the nearest thing to mourning she could approach in this outpost.

He had heard her called a "handsome" woman. It was a good

word. Her brows were heavy saffron sickles above eyes so blue they were almost black. There was a honeyed abundance to her high-piled mass of golden hair.

He stepped into the door and caught her hands. He saw the tension die a little at the corners of her lips.

"I'm so glad you came," she said, her voice low, husky with strain. "You helped so much the other day."

He took her hand. "I'm sorry I couldn't make it sooner. I'm on an unfortunate errand. Dodge got permission from Fort Defiance to impound all your father's official papers till the new sub-agent came out. It was really Sheriff Drake's job, but both he and Dodge thought you'd been through enough already."

Her hand slid from his; she gave a little shake of her head. "It does make it easier, having you do it. But why impound anything? Isn't that a little irregular?"

"Dodge thinks there might be something among the papers that would help the prosecution."

She nodded, turned to lead him across the room. It was cool in here, the coolness of thick adobe walls and heavy earthen roof. Julia led him into her father's office. It still smelled faintly of his pipe tobacco.

She threw open a small trunk. "Most of his official stuff's in here. The more recent letters are in the desk. He had one ready to mail to the commissioner when he . . . left." She sat down at the old roll-top desk, began pulling documents from the pigeonholes. Then she spoke again, without looking up at him.

"Did Cristina ask you to defend her father?"

He knew a vague surprise. "Were you in town today?"

"Hackett was by. Arles had told him about it." Tension dug a little crease in the soft flesh beneath her chin. "How could Cristina ask such a thing? Dodge is like your own father. To take the case against him . . ."

"She didn't ask me to do that," Banner said. "But don't blame her. After all, Jahzini is one of my oldest friends in this country . . ."

He broke off as she flung up her head, her eyes filled with a naked anger. He stepped forward, grasping her shoulder.

"Julia, I know how you feel, but . . ."

"Do you?" she said. It was as if the words brought her to her feet. "That you could even talk to that woman!" Her voice was vitriolic. "Or with Jahzini . . ."

"Julia, I had to . . ."

"Why? What could you possibly gain?"

"I didn't mean to discuss it with you today, Julia. I wanted to spare you. But if you insist, I doubt very much whether Jahzini murdered your father."

The blood drained from her face. He saw a little vein surface in her temple, beating frantically.

"How can you say that? Every shred of evidence points to Jahzini. I saw him fight twice with Dad over moving from that land. They found Dad's saddlebags right in Jahzini's hogan! All she had to do was come up and ask you. The way she swings her hips . . ."

"Julia."

"You're defending them now. That filthy dirty swine murdered my father and you're . . ."

"Julia!"

He almost shouted it, catching her by the arms and shaking her. When he realized what he was doing, when he saw the pain his grip brought to her face, he stopped. She stared up at him, eyes flashing, and he thought she was going to lash out again. Then, abruptly, all the sand went out of her. Her head dipped against his chest, all the weight of her body sagged against him, and she was crying. He held her tightly against him, speaking in a husky voice.

"That's better. You should have done it the first time I came out. You can't keep it all inside."

She didn't answer. She continued to cry, the sobs racking her body. When at last it was over, she leaned against him, wet cheek pressed to his lapel.

"I'm sorry, Lee . . ."

"I guess you had to let it off somehow. Why don't you come back into town with me? The sooner you get away from here the better."

She shook her head. "I've thought it over. I don't have anywhere to go. No relatives in the East. This has been my life the last five years. I'd miss teaching those Indian kids. Missus Adams said she'd put me up at the post when the new agent came."

"Maybe you're right. I don't think they'd ever get anybody as wonderful with kids as you."

She put a hand on his wrist. "Now, what was it you said about doubting whether Jahzini . . . Jahzini . . . ?"

"I don't want to upset you again."

"Tell me," she said. "I can't be like that again."

He frowned. "Julia, what about that trouble your dad had last year with Hackett over Broken Bit cattle grazing on Indian land?"

"They settled that."

"To the Indian Bureau's satisfaction, maybe. But was your dad satisfied?"

"You know he wasn't," she said. "That's one of the few things I thought he was wrong about. Hackett acted in good faith."

"Did he?"

"Lee, what are you driving at?"

He glanced at the papers in the trunk. "If your dad had been working on anything out of the ordinary, concerning the Indians, it might be in those papers."

"Would we have the right to go through them, Lee?"

"If it meant a man's life . . ."

"How do you know it means a man's life? What are you going on, anyway?"

He had the impulse to tell her what they'd found at Yellow Gap. Yet he knew it was not completely conclusive, and would only upset her again.

"Maybe I'm wrong, Julia. I shouldn't have imposed this on you in the first place. Forget it."

"I will," she said. She touched his arm with sudden contrition. "If you'll forget what I said about Jahzini and . . . the girl."

"Of course I will," he said. And knew, somehow, that he wouldn't.

With all the letters, the documents, the forms in the small trunk, he left Julia and drove back up to the trading post. He halted the cut-under wagon beside the ratty Navajo ponies, swung down, went inside.

There was a richness to the cool gloom of the room. A richness of barbaric colors blazing from hand-woven blankets, of dully gleaming silver heavy to the hand, of *yei* masks topped with the exotic splendor of *guacamaya* plumes from Yucatán. The counter ran down one side of the dim room, with the shelves behind it carrying the beads, the coffee, the tinned fruit, the bolts of gay cloth, the rack of Winchesters. Calico Adams stood there, trying to trade with a pair of Navajos. They were hardly listening. Their attention, sullen, watchful, was on Tilfego.

The Mexican sat on the *bayeta* blankets piled against one of the peeled cedar posts that supported the roof. The girl on his knee was buxom for an Indian. When Tilfego saw Banner, he grinned and pinched her cheek. "Like the peach, no, *amigo?* She is going to marry me."

"*Do tah,*" the girl said. She giggled and pushed his hand away. "*Do tah.*"

Calico's snowy head glowed like a nimbus in the gloom of the room. "Can't you get that Mexican out of here?" he asked Banner. "He's ruining my business."

"I've got the papers," Banner told Tilfego.

"How you like the tickle, chile pepper?" Tilfego said, probing at her with a sly finger.

"Tilfego," Banner said.

"Let us stay a little longer, Lee. The best man you can be."

"You'll have to walk back."

"What a barbarity," Tilfego said. Then he gave an immense grunt, getting up. The girl stumbled backward, sputtering angrily. Tilfego shrugged helplessly. "Tomorrow, chile pepper, Tilfego will come back and marry you then."

In the wagon, rattling down the road, Banner said: "I don't see how you do it. The ugliest man in the world."

Tilfego grinned blandly. "Have you ever see a bird charm' by a snake?"

"You should be more careful with those Navajo girls. Those Indians were mad enough to do a scalp dance."

Tilfego shook his head sadly. "Always you preach. Like the voice of my conscious."

"Conscience."

"*Sí,* conscious." Tilfego raised his head. "Somebody coming."

Banner could see nothing at first. Four riders finally appeared on the horizon.

"One is Arles," Tilfego said, before Banner could differentiate between horse and man. "Clay Hackett. Big Red." The Mexican squinted. "The fourth a stranger is."

The quartet was coming down the road at a ground-eating canter, and Banner could make out Clay Hackett now. One of the biggest ranchers in the county, his six-foot body had a slouched ease in the saddle, broad-shouldered, lean-shanked. His grin was broad and confident, but his black eyes could take a bite out of a man. He pulled his horse down, black as sin, without as much as one white stocking on it, and let the animal stir up the yellow dust with its nervous little dance.

"Glad to find you, Lee," he said. "Henry told us you'd come out to impound those papers. We can take them off your hands now. This is the new agent. Claude Miller."

"Claude R. Miller," Arles said.

Banner nodded at the agent. He was slim, dark, in well-cut blue serge. He had a little mustache and a string tie and, in a country where the sun made even the white men dark, his face looked pasty. Big Red sat a roan just behind him. Red was three inches taller than Hackett and weighed two hundred and fifty pounds, no fat. His face had a ruddy glow.

"You got a court order for the papers?" Banner asked.

"Dodge said we didn't need that. The sheriff would have to be along to make this official."

"I'm acting for the sheriff," Banner said. "They're officially impounded as of the time I got them."

"Miller just wants to go through them and see if there's anything that might be necessary for his administration," Hackett said.

"He'll have to see Dodge about that," Banner said.

Tilfego grinned blandly at Arles. "You better get the new left hind shoe for that horse. Three nail she is already gone."

Arles was rolling a cigarette. "I'm thinking of running her barefoot," he said.

Hackett stopped his black from fiddling. "What the hell," he said. "Henry told us to pick up the papers."

"That's the gospel," Arles said. He licked his folded cigarette paper, sealed it, looking at Banner all the time.

"I'll be getting along," Banner said.

Hackett leaned forward in his saddle, fixing Banner with his eyes. "Not till you give us the papers."

"I can't give them to you."

"Get them, Red," Hackett said.

Big Red reined his short-coupled roan around the slim dark agent, around Arles, around Hackett. He checked it beside the wagon.

Banner's eyes glittered. "Don't do it, Red."

"Arles," Hackett said.

Arles took a long drag on his cigarette, sidled his horse around to help the redhead. Big Red's saddle creaked as he put all his weight onto his left stirrup, swinging off into the bed of the wagon. He bent over to lift the trunk onto the rump of his roan. Arles reined his horse against the outside of the roan to hold the trunk once it was on the horse. Banner jerked the whip from its holder and lashed it across his nigh animal.

The horse screamed, rearing.

Banner hit the other horse. They both bolted. He heard Big Red shout behind him, pitched off his feet. The whole wagon shuddered as the man's great body struck its bed. Hackett had to dance his black aside to keep from being struck by the rig as it shot by him.

Dust spewed from beneath spinning wheels, iron rims clanged against the rocks of the road. Banner heard a running horse off to his left and saw Arles spurring his mount to catch the wagon. His animal caught up with the rear wheel, drew toward the front. Banner snapped the whip over the team again, trying to get more speed. He heard Big Red scrambling to hands and knees in the bed behind.

Then Arles drew abreast of the front wheel and jumped off his horse at Banner. His body smashed into Banner, knocking him over against Tilfego. Arles braced one leg against the dashboard, hit Banner in the face.

It knocked Banner into Tilfego again. Blinded by the pain, he felt the reins torn from his hands. He lunged back up into Arles.

The only thing that kept Arles from pitching out was his hold on the reins. It pulled the team hard to the left. Banner felt the wagon slew beneath him as the animals turned sharply.

"Jump!" Tilfego shouted. "She is going . . . !"

The horses plunged into the ditch siding the road and went down. The wagon overturned.

Tilfego's form flashed by Banner, like a jumping cat. He pushed off after it. He had a dim sense of Big Red pitched from the bed, as the wagon went on over. And of Arles, jumping too late, caught by the edge of the seat as it came down on him.

Then Banner hit, balled up, and rolled, coming to a flopping halt in a spiny patch of creosote. He turned over and saw that the horses were down, kicking in their traces. Arles was pinned beneath the overturned wagon, apparently unconscious. Big Red was on his hands and knees in the road, shaking his head. Then Hackett came up on a running horse and pulled it to a vicious halt above the trunk, where it had been thrown from the wagon into the road. He leaned out of the saddle, scooping at the handle. Banner got to his feet and scrambled out of the ditch and ran for the man.

Hackett straightened with the small trunk and tried to wheel away. Banner caught up with him, grabbed his arm. Hackett fought. Banner pulled him out of the saddle.

When he realized he was going, Hackett let go of the trunk and tried to come down on Banner. The lawyer jumped away.

Hackett hit on hands and knees and came up like a rubber ball. Banner blocked aside one of his flailing arms and hit him in the face. But Hackett's rush carried him on into the lawyer and he kept driving and it knocked Banner off balance and finally spilled him.

Banner rolled over to see Hackett still coming in, jumping to spike him with high heels. He flopped out from under and came to hands and knees before Hackett had wheeled back. Banner got to his feet as Hackett rushed. One of Hackett's fists rocked his head and he staggered backward. He caught himself, blocking the next blow, coming inside it. He hit the man in the belly twice, short, vicious blows. They stopped Hackett.

Banner shifted his feet and hit him in the belly again. He put all the weight of his body behind it. Then he hit him in the face.

It straightened Hackett to his full height and spun him around on his heels and pitched him full length to the ground. He lay on his belly, making sobbing sounds into the dirt. Banner stood above him, panting, waiting. Then he heard something behind him, and turned to see Big Red coming toward him, still shaking his head.

"No," Tilfego said. "You better not."

Big Red stopped. Tilfego sat in the ditch, grinning blandly. He had his gun out.

Hackett had trouble getting to his hands and knees. Blood dripped off his face into the dirt.

"You still want that trunk?" Banner asked.

The breath sounded squeezed out of the man. "I'll get it." He spat a tooth. "Damn you. I'll get it."

He tried to get up and almost fell. When he finally gained his feet, he spread them wide, swaying dizzily, wiping blood from one edge of his mouth. The new agent sat his fiddling horse a dozen feet back of the overturned rig, face filled with a foolish expression.

"Look here," he said. "Look here."

"Those horses don't look like they've broken any bones," Banner said. "You can help us get this wagon turned back over. If you want to look at the papers, they'll still be in Dodge's office."

Tilfego chuckled. "What a barbarity."

IV

Henry Dodge was in his office when Banner got back. The door was open. He was sitting tilted back in his chair with his white-stockinged feet propped up on a pulled-out drawer. The awesome reek of his cigar filled the room and ashes littered the calf-bound copy of Coke's *Commentaries* in his lap. As Banner walked in, carrying the small trunk, the old man's leonine head lifted. Then he put the book hurriedly on the desk, swinging his feet off the drawer at the same time.

"You got it. Good!" He leaned forward, rummaging through the litter of papers on the floor. "Just lemme get my shoes on now and we'll go through it. They . . ."

He stopped, holding to the tongue of a shoe he had uncovered. He looked up again, at the bruise mottling Banner's cheek, the jagged tear in his coat sleeve.

"What in the Johnny hell happened to you?"

Banner heaved the little leather-bound trunk onto the desk. "Hackett tried to take it away from me."

Dodge set the shoe on the pulled-out drawer, frowning at Banner. "Didn't he tell you? I said it was all right, son, if he met you on the way back. I didn't expect that new agent so soon. He'll probably need some of the stuff himself. He told me he'd hold it all for whenever I wanted it."

"His name is Claude Miller," Banner said. "Isn't that Hackett's cousin? The man who's been clerking for three years at Fort Defiance, waiting for Hackett to pull some strings and get him an agency?"

"I suppose so. I don't see why you wouldn't hand the papers over. They're his by right, now."

"And since he's Hackett's cousin, I don't doubt Hackett will get a look at anything he wants. Why should Hackett be so eager for those papers? It made me suspicious right there. So suspicious I went through the trunk on the way in here."

Dodge's eyes widened. "You? A lawyer . . ."

"Don't cite the book at me now, Henry. I'd break a hundred laws if it would save an innocent man's life." Banner got the envelope he had opened from his pocket, pulled the letter from it. "Wright had written this to the commissioner the very day he went out to be killed. Want to read it?"

Dodge snorted. "I won't compound a felony."

"I'll tell you what's in it, then," Banner said. "Wright told the commissioner that for the last six months he had been gathering proof against Clay Hackett. Wright claimed that now he could prove in court, beyond a doubt, that Hackett was mixed up in one of the dirtiest swindles that had ever been perpetrated against the Indians."

"You're talking about that grazing trouble again. It was all settled last January."

"In this letter, Wright said that the January arbitration was just a farce. Hackett hasn't observed a single article of his agreement. Wright claims he has statements from two sub-agents that Hackett used his influence with the Indian Bureau to have at least six different families forced off their rightful lands, some of the best graze in the Corn River bottoms. He has depositions from two white ranchers that Hackett used force in a dozen instances to drive other Indians off their graze. He has a hundred statements from Indians and traders of beatings and burnings and mass slaughter of their sheep."

Dodge leaned back in his chair, a deep frown ridging his forehead. "I can't believe it. I just can't believe it." He looked up. "Those depositions, statements . . . ?"

"I couldn't find them. They weren't in the trunk. We even ripped out the lining. I think Wright must have been carrying all that proof with him. Remember the burned saddlebags they found at Jahzini's?"

Dodge spread his hands. "But without them . . ."

"We've still got a case." Banner pulled the stub of the cigarette from his pocket, put it on the desk. "We found this at Yellow Gap. Pinched out. Who else around here but Arles puts his cigarette out that way?"

Dodge stared at it. "Arles might have stopped for a smoke on that rim anytime during a week before or after the killing."

"There was other sign. Tilfego recognized the tracks of Arles's horse, the back left shoe with the nails missing. Arles's own tracks led down from the rim to a spot near where Wright's body was found."

"Would you swear they were Arles's tracks?"

Banner hesitated, frowning at him. "I . . ."

"You know you're not that good. And how much would Tilfego's word mean to a jury? He's already been in jail on a perjury charge."

"That stupid case about the horse. He was proved innocent."

"Stupid or not, he lied under oath. A prosecutor would bring that out. You know what it would do to the jury."

"You're quibbling," Banner said. "You're overlooking the whole point entirely. I know just about how significant this proof would be in court. I've seen you tear a lot stronger evidence than this to shreds. But we're not just talking about the legal technicalities of evidence. We're talking about a man's life."

"Lee . . ."

"What's happened to you, Henry? I've seen you actually hand items like this over to the defense. You always bent over backward to see that a man you were prosecuting got a fair trial." Banner drew a soft little breath. "But those cases didn't involve Hackett, did they?"

The old man's eyes flashed up to his in an instant of anger. Then as they dropped to the cigarette butt again, he settled into his chair. The lines seemed to deepen in his face. "You shouldn't have said that, Lee."

Banner wheeled to the window, unable to bear the hurt he had caused in this man who had been a father to him, staring out at the twilit town through slitted eyes. Tilfego was still sitting where Banner had left him in the cut-under wagon at the hitch rack before the office stairs.

Dodge's chair creaked softly with his turning motion. "Lee, I know what kind of a man Hackett is. I watched him grow up in this town. You know how no-good his folks were. It didn't leave Hackett much. All he's gotten in this world he's gotten the hard way. It's left him a hard man, I guess. But not the kind of a man who would murder."

Banner saw Tilfego's head raise. The man seemed to be sniffing the air. Suddenly he climbed out of the wagon and disappeared around the corner.

"I disagree," Banner said. "Everybody knows Hackett's land south of the railroad is drying up. If he doesn't keep what he's grabbed north of the railroad, he's through. If Wright's proof was ever brought to light, the Indian Bureau would push Hackett back to his old pastures if it took the U.S. Army to do it. Everything that he's fought for ten years to build here would be wiped out. He's up against the wall, Henry."

Dodge did not answer. Tilfego reappeared on the street below, hanging onto the arm of a girl. He pulled her halfway across the street before she stopped, trying to tug free. He whispered something in her ear. She giggled. She went on across the street with him. They disappeared into Blackstrap Kelly's.

"Did you ever wonder why I wanted to be a lawyer so badly?" Banner asked.

It took Dodge a long time to answer. Finally he sighed heavily. "Natural, I suppose. Growing up in the house of one."

"Not just any lawyer's house, Henry. You used to wonder why I played hooky from school so often? It was to watch you try a case. I wanted to be a lawyer like the other boys wanted to be Billy the Kid or an engineer on the railroad. It's something to watch you in court, Henry. A man couldn't see you in action without wanting to be a lawyer."

"Lee . . ."

"I guess that's the same way you've wanted to sit on the superior bench, isn't it? I guess I didn't really know how much it meant to you till just now. You've been talking about it ever since I can remember. I didn't really take it in, how much it meant to you. If you want that judgeship as bad as I wanted to be a lawyer, I guess I should understand . . ."

"Lee, don't . . ."

"And you won't get the bench without Hackett's support, will you?"

"Dammit, Lee, here you are goin' off half-cocked again!"

Dodge's husky shout lifted him up out of the chair. He stood in his stocking feet, hands opening and closing at his sides. Through the window, Banner heard a shrill feminine squeal from Blackstrap Kelly's. Then a sharp slapping sound. The batwing doors flapped open as the girl pushed through them and ran down the street. Tilfego came running out behind her. He stopped on the sidewalk, staring after her figure.

"*Qué barbaridad*," he said.

Banner put his hat back on, taking a deep breath. "You'll turn Wright's letter and that cigarette butt over to the court as items for the defense?"

Dodge spoke in a low voice. "Of course."

"And that's all."

Dodge held out his hand. "Son, we can't swear out a warrant on this evidence. What else can I do?"

That somber look settled vague shadows beneath Banner's prominent cheek bones. He shook his head tiredly.

"Nothing you don't have the courage to do, Henry," he said.

V

Dusk was a stain on the town when Banner reached the street. Tilfego was not in sight, and Banner supposed he had gone home. The young lawyer climbed into the wagon and lifted the reins and turned down Aztec to the house he and Dodge shared. Vaguely he tried to find an excuse for Dodge. Had he been too harsh in his judgment?

As he passed the jail on Aztec Street, he found himself staring at the barred windows. It took his mind off Dodge. It brought him the picture of Jahzini again. Not as he had been this morning, dazed, incoherent, shrunken, but a man so much more human than anyone in Mexican Hat would ever realize, a man whose intense affinity with the earth and the sky had molded into him a strange mixture of childish naïveté and aged wisdom, making him one moment a clown, the next a mystic.

Banner could remember a potbellied little gnome whose black eyes twinkled with mischief, teaching a blond boy to play *nan-zosh* and running with him after the hoop and shouting as gleefully as another child. Or he could remember sitting out on a lonely mesa with the dawn-tinted statue of a man, so steeped in his closeness with the earth that they could unspeakingly know things together that no white man with all his words and all his sophistries would ever know.

These memories still filled Banner's mind as he reached Dodge's house. It was a long adobe, shoulder to shoulder with a row of other long adobes that fronted right on the street. Banner passed through the wide gate in the patio wall and drove across the flag-stoned garden to the stables. Unharnessing the team, watering them, putting two quarts of grain in the trough, he went inside and washed up.

Dodge's bustling Mexican cook fixed him something to eat, but he had no appetite. Finally he took a pot of coffee to the study, tried to settle down to work. He had some conveyancing to do, a codicil to add to a will. But Banner found himself unable to fill out the codicil; the proper phrasing would not come. His mind was still too filled with memories of Jahzini, and with what had happened this evening. And with a bay horse. Finally that was his uppermost thought. A man on a bay horse who had seen a murder.

He put the deed away, staring blankly at the wall. It seemed hopeless, at first. There were thousands of Indians north of the tracks. A dozen white ranchers and squatters. Hackett himself ran a crew of thirty men. Or it might have been a stranger, wandering in from nowhere.

But Banner's mind clung stubbornly to it. It wasn't logical that Hackett would allow another of his men to wander down that way, knowing Arles would be waiting to kill Wright.

And how about the stranger? The tracks had come out of the north. If it was a stranger, that meant he would have passed through a lot of Indian land. He couldn't do that without being seen, or at least his tracks being seen.

Could it have been one of the Indians themselves? This was shearing time, when they all stayed close to their hogans, joining in the work. That cut it down considerably. Banner had seen only a few in town these past weeks. The route through Yellow Gap led to only Calico Adams's trading post or to town. It would not be hard to find out what Indians had been at those two places the week of the murder.

He went to his bedroom, making a blanket roll. He buckled on his gun. He put enough grub for a couple of days into his saddlebags. He left a note for Dodge saying he had gone hunting. Then he saddled up and rode.

He rode till the moon began to fade, and then stopped to sleep in the shelter of a ridge. He awoke with false dawn flushing the sky and started again without breakfast, for he knew that would be waiting ahead. He was deep in the reservation now. He came upon the hogan at dawn.

It was what the Navajos called a logs-stacked-up house, made of piñon logs, boughs, cedar bark. It looked indescribably lonely, huddling there with the desert stretching out as far as a man could see on every side. Banner hailed the house.

In a moment the door of woven yucca stalks was pushed aside and Cristina stooped through, straightening to stare at him. She recognized him and came swiftly forward.

"Lee, what are you doing this far north?"

His center-fire rig creaked softly as he stepped off the horse. "I have reason to believe your father isn't guilty of the murder, Cristina. I'm traveling north to try and find out. I could use your help."

He saw her lips part. In the milky dawn light the piquant oval of her face held a waxen hue. When she finally spoke, her voice trembled with suppressed emotion.

"There is great hurry?"

"Time to tell you about it."

"Come in, then. You surely have not eaten breakfast."

She turned and led him through the low door. Banner stooped through, straightened within the mingled smells so characteristic of these dwellings. The greasy reek of mutton seemed to pervade everything, and with it the penetrating odor of the sumac and piñon gum with which they made their black dyes. Sitting over by the fire was the bent old woman, shawled in her worn *bayeta* blanket, Jahzini's wife, who had been mother to Banner during that year. She came to him with her hands held out.

"Ahalani, shiyaazh." Greetings, my son.

"Altalani, shima." Greetings, my mother.

She stood a long time gripping his fingers in her sinewy brown hands and staring at him with eyes almost blind from bending over a lifetime of smoky cook fires. Then she waved at the pallets along the wall. He turned right as was the custom of Navajo men upon entering and seated himself upon one of the rolled sheepskins. Cristina ladled mutton stew from the copper kettle into a pottery plate traded from the Pueblos. As she bent to put ash cakes beside the stew, it drew her heavy skirt tightly across one hip, revealing surprising fullness. He began to realize how deceptive her apparent slimness might be.

As she took up his meal, he told them about Wright's letter, recounting as much as he could in Navajo so the old woman would understand, then what he and Tilfego had found at Yellow Gap.

Cristina had just poured a cup of coffee, and she turned toward him, still holding it. "Arles," she said. There was a thin bitterness to her voice.

"I think he's our killer," Banner said. "He must have done it for Hackett. He probably came down to the body to get those saddlebags. All the proof Wright had been collecting against Hackett must have been in them. Arles burned it, but the bags weren't completely destroyed, so he planted them here in your hogan while you were out with the sheep to make it even worse for your father."

"There is a chance, then, if we find this man who saw the murder, this eyewitness on the bay horse?"

"*Haut iish baa yanilti?*" the old woman asked.

Banner realized that he and Cristina had reverted to English, and the old woman had asked what they were talking about. Cristina turned and explained the last part of it. When Cristina finished, the old woman turned to Banner, her smoke-squinted eyes luminous with grateful tears.

"*Ah-sheh heh, shiyaazh.*"

Banner turned to Cristina, frowning. "I don't remember the first word."

"Perhaps you never heard it," she said, smiling softly. "It is a word we hardly ever say, even to each other. She said . . . 'Thank you, my son.' "

They went outside after breakfast and walked to the corral and Banner helped Cristina rope out a shaggy little pinto, lifting the saddle for her. She worked in silence, tugging the latigo tight. Her profile was like a glowing copper cameo. She must have felt his attention on her; she looked up self-consciously, cheeks flushed.

"We will start with the Indians first?"

"They'll be the biggest job," he said. "But we'll do two things at once. They'll know if any strangers passed through the reservation going toward Yellow Gap. We can find out at the same time what Indians went south last week."

They rode out a narrow arroyo, topped a ridge, and looked out over a desert turned to a green ocean by the early morning light.

"This is the trail north," Cristina told him. "It will take us by many hogans."

They dropped down off the ridge into the vastness of the desert. Before noon they reached the encampment of Cristina's cousins at Red Forks. Three logs-stacked-up houses and a big corral, the flock of sheep held in a brush corral by the boys, the sacks of unwashed wool piled against the houses. The sweating faces and the shy smiles and the greetings. And the questions.

"Any strangers?"

"No strangers."

"How was Mexican Hat?"

"I have not been to Mexican Hat since the Mountain Chant."

Wasn't that one of this clan down by Yellow Gap last week? None of us has been down that way in a long time. Perhaps a cousin. Yes, a cousin, from up by Chin Lee. When did he go? In the Month-Of-The-Big-Crust. That's January.

They rode again. Banner lost count of the hogans they had stopped at, the grinning faces, the disappointments. But at none of them had they heard word of a stranger. There had been a new trader up by Ganado. But he had come in by wagon, and had gone on to the north. Nobody had even seen the tracks of a stranger heading south.

In the afternoon they began to run into big bunches of Hackett's Broken Bit cattle. Banner saw the angry flush it brought to Cristina's face. This was far north of the checkerboard sections the railroad leased to Hackett. This was deep into the Indians' land.

They finally reached a country of gorges and cañons and were soon lost in the aimless meanderings of a chasm cut a hundred feet deep into the surrounding tablelands. The horses started to spook and shy. Then Banner felt the trembling of the earth. The girl pulled her pinto in, turning to stare at him anxiously.

"What is it?" Her voice sounded small.

Before he could answer, the first whitefaces plunged around the turn ahead, spilling from the narrow notch into the broad cañon floor on which they stood. Banner spurred his chestnut up beside Cristina and then neck-reined left, forcing her dancing pinto over to the cañon wall, where a narrow cleft turned the cattle away from the wall in a little eddy. For a moment the cañon was filled with a sea of plunging backs and tossing horns, and then they were past, and the dust was whispering back into the earth.

A quartet of riders appeared in the notch behind the cattle. Banner saw Hackett's black horse. As he passed the cleft, Hackett caught sight of Banner and the girl. He waved two of his riders on after the cattle, and turned his black toward the wall, pulling it down to a walk. Arles wheeled to follow, a cigarette in one corner of his mouth.

"Looks like we almost wiped you off the walls," Hackett said. He wasn't smiling.

"Couldn't have done better if you'd tried," Banner said.

"We could have done lots better," Arles said, "if we'd tried."

Hackett touched his hat brim. " 'Afternoon, Cristina."

She dipped her head soberly.

Arles shifted in the saddle. "My back's still sore."

"I was hoping maybe that wagon broke it," Banner said.

Hackett ran a finger inside his lip. "I'll have to get me a new tooth. Dentist said it'd cost twenty dollars."

"An expensive fight," Banner said.

Hackett chuckled suddenly. "Just like when we was kids, Lee. Remember how we used to fight all the time?"

"It wasn't serious then."

The humor was wiped off Hackett's face. "No," he said. "It wasn't serious." He leaned forward in his saddle. "Nosing around, Lee?"

"I guess so."

"Finding out a lot of things?"

"Enough things."

Hackett slapped a hand across his saddle horn. "Damn it, Lee, why in hell did you want that trunk so bad yesterday?"

"Why did you want it?"

"You raised my back hairs. It was Miller's by rights. You know damn' well you didn't have any official hold on it."

"The sheriff has it now, if you want it."

"Charlie Drake?" A crooked smile crossed Hackett's face. "Well," he said, "maybe so." He wiped sweat-caked dust from his angular brow. "Got to be getting on after my beef."

"Isn't it a little north of your leases?"

"Few strays get over the line. You know."

"More than a few."

"Don't take too big a bite, Lee. A man can only chew so

much." He sent Cristina a sharp glance. "Did it ever occur to you, Lee, that you might be getting sucked into something?"

"It's pretty evident what I'm getting into, Clay."

"Is it, now?" Hackett gathered his reins, emitting a rueful little snort. "You're a damned fool, Lee."

"Am I?"

Staring at Banner, Arles took a last drag on his smoke. Then he pinched it out between his thumb and forefinger and dropped it. "Yes," he said. "You are."

Hackett laughed. Arles glanced at him. Hackett spat. They lifted their reins and necked their horses around and spurred them into a gallop. Banner and the girl sat silently till the men were out of sight.

"Did you see how Arles was watching you?" she asked. "He never took his eyes off."

"I saw."

"Do you think he knows, Lee?"

"That I know he killed Wright?" Banner asked. "Maybe."

VI

They rode on down the cañon. The sunlight waned from the narrow strip of sky above and the shadows darkened and Banner found himself looking over his shoulder more and more often. And finally he pulled up, angry with himself, while he searched the cañon walls until he saw a bench. He rode toward it and scrambled his horse up the ledge that led to the top and Cristina followed him. They sat their blowing animals behind a screen of junipers for a while, watching the cañon below.

"Is there any other way he could follow us?" Banner asked.

"No. If he is following us, he will have to come by horseback down this cañon."

They waited. The horses fiddled beneath them.

"Let's go. If he was coming, he'd have showed up by now."

They rode steadily northward, with the rocky walls rising against the sky above them. Finally Banner pulled up again.

"Am I just jumpy?"

"We could climb a mesa. We could see some distance from there."

"We'd better."

He started to wheel his horse. The shot made a deafening smash. His horse reared and he pitched off the rump.

Hitting hard, with the breath knocked from him, rolling over, he heard Cristina's animal grunt, heard the sudden clatter of its hoofs as it broke into a wild run down the cañon. He kept rolling over, dazed, knowing only that he had to gain some sort of cover. There was another shot. Sand kicked up three feet to his right. He kept rolling till a scrubby juniper stopped him. He flattened beneath its thick branches.

He could hear the sound of the horses down the cañon. It faded, died. He was no longer dazed. The pain was coming. His head was beginning to ache; his whole back throbbed. He got out his six-shooter.

He shifted over to one side, trying to see the rim. But dusk was thickening, rapidly becoming night. He hunted for a way up to the top that would not leave him open. He found it, finally, a fissure, choked with brush. He began to crawl toward it. He thought he saw motion above, and stopped. He was sweating.

When nothing happened, he moved on. He reached the fissure and began the climb. It seemed to grow lighter as he rose. He reached the top to find that twilight still turned the sky pearly up there, while the cañon bottoms were black as ink.

The mesa spread out to the east, yellow with flowering greasewood. Erosion had turned it to a labyrinth of shallow gullies. Beginning to work his way down one of these, he heard a horse snort.

It stopped him sharply. It had seemed to come from his right.

He took a chance, worked his way to the top of the gully. The greasewood was knee-high here, so thick he could not see through it. He bellied down and began a snake-like passage across the sandy flat. The horse snorted again, closer, but still to his right. He started to veer that way when the other sound came. It was a soft click. It sounded like a cocked gun.

He stopped, trying to cover his breathing. The click had come from his left, and ahead. Was he taking a direction that would put him between the man and the horse?

Carefully he eared back the hammer on his own gun. Then he began to crawl again, more slowly, more painstakingly. Finally he reached the edge of another shallow gully, which ran out to the wall of the main chasm.

At the mouth of the gully, behind the rocks, looking down into the cañon, crouched the man. His figure made a vague silhouette. The silver bow guard on his wrist, the silver *conchas* on his belt gave off a dull glitter in the last of the twilight. But the weapon in his hands was no bow. It was a Winchester, with its lever pulled out to half cock. Banner finally made out the edges of his hair, against the coppery sheen of his flesh. It was long hair, uncut, and Banner knew he could not use English.

"*Taddoo nahi nani,*" he said. Stand still.

The Indian stiffened. Then, slowly, he turned his head, till he could see Banner, holding the gun on him. After a long moment, he let his Winchester slide to the ground.

Cautiously Banner made his way down into the gully, moved toward the Indian. The man was young, maybe twenty. He was naked to the waist, wearing only buckskin leggings, a pair of Apache war moccasins, curling up at the toes. He turned to Banner, the whites of his eyes gleaming like marble in the growing night. Banner tried some more Navajo on him. The Indian would not answer. Then Banner heard the rustling in the lower cañon, and he moved forward, keeping his gun on the Indian, till he could make out the shadowy movement below. Two horses, only one ridden.

"Cristina?"

"Lee? My horse ran away. Are you all right?"

"I've got our bushwhacker. Stay down there."

He jerked his gun back into the gully; the Navajo started walking, and he followed, till they reached the horses. There were three of them, one with a pack slung over its back. Banner got their lead ropes, then went back to the edge of the gully with the Indian. It became a fissure, crawling down the cañon wall, slanting enough to take the horses. Banner slapped them on the rumps and they began scrambling down, squealing angrily. Then he picked up the Winchester, followed the Indian down after them. Cristina rounded the animals up as they hit the bottom. She dismounted when they were quieted, coming forward to meet Banner as he slid into the sandy flats after the Indian.

"*Ahalani, tineh.*" Greetings, young man.

The Indian did not answer.

Cristina tried again, asking his name. "*Haash yinilege?*"

For a while, Banner thought he would not answer this either. Then, sullenly: "Nishtli Adakhai."

"He says he is Adakhai," she told Banner. "It means The Gambler. I know him now. He comes from Chin Lee. He is the most famous gambler on the reservation. He is also known for his hatred of whites."

"No wonder he won't talk to me. Ask him why he shot at us."

She spoke to the Indian again. He answered, a long speech, with angry gestures. Finally she said: "He says he did not shoot at us. He has been south, hunting, and was riding home. He heard the shots and came to find out what they meant."

"Do you believe him?"

"I don't know. He is one of the wild ones, who will not adopt the ways of the white man. Most of them at Chin Lee are that kind."

"Would they know about a stranger?"

"No stranger could pass through this country without their knowledge."

"Then let's go on up there with him."

"It might be dangerous, Lee. If they all feel against the white men as this one does . . ."

"And yet they might be the very ones who could help save your father. We've got to go, Cristina."

Banner was reluctant to give Adakhai his rifle back, but Cristina asked him if he would use it if they returned it, and he said no. He did not want to take them to his clan, but Cristina told him they would go anyway; she knew where it was. Sullenly the Indian mounted one of his animals, picked up the lead rope, started down the cañon. They left it in a short while, breaking onto a desert bounded on the south by a great rock-ribbed escarpment that seemed to run endlessly to the east. They followed the base of this wall, riding behind Adakhai. Cristina dropped back.

"Did you notice his horses?"

"Hard to see anything in this light."

"One of them is a bay."

Banner looked at her sharply. Then he heeled his horse into a trot, trying to catch up with Adakhai's spares, trying to see if they were shod. But it was too dark. He heard the ring of shoes against rocks, didn't know which horse had made it.

Then the darkness was spattered with light.

It came from ahead, winking, dying at a half dozen points. It finally became the wavering plumes of cook fires. The Indian shouted something. The fires were blotted out by the fluttering passage of running figures, swiftly gathering around Adakhai

94

and Cristina and Banner. There were a few women in velvet tunics, voluminous skirts. The men were all thin and stringy, the copper of their bodies grayed with caked dust. Few of them wore shirts; their pants were buckskin; some only wore G-strings.

With a soft rustle of moccasins in the sand, a slight tinkle of heavy hand-hammered silver, they were gathering. None of them spoke. None of them smiled. Cristina sat straight in her saddle, eyes moving slowly through their ranks.

Adakhai had slid off his pony and was unlashing the carcass of a deer. A pair of boys helped him, and he spoke to them in short, thumping gutturals.

An old man was shouldering through the other people now. He was short and squat and bowlegged, with stringy gray hair and a scarred face. He halted before Cristina, speaking in a guttural voice.

"Ahalani, cikeh."

"Xozo naxasi, natani. Sa ah hayai bikehozoni."

She called him chief. Called him *natani,* and wished him long life and happiness. His eyes glittered, staring at Banner. He waved at the cook pots, inviting them to eat.

Cristina stepped off her horse, and Banner put his weight into the left stirrup, hesitating just a moment, and then swung down. They stepped back for him, a stirring of moccasins, a tinkling of silver. It was like stepping into a den of wild beasts. The smell of wildness was so strong, so rancid, he almost gagged on it.

He looked at Cristina, and she nodded at the saddles. He stripped the sweat-sodden gear from both animals, carried it to the fire. Then he led the two jaded beasts to the picket lines behind the hogans.

These were not the logs-stacked-up houses he was so used to. They were the more primitive type of dwellings. They were the forked-together-house whose form and structure had been handed down by the Talking God. The Indians were shifting restlessly around the fires. None of them seated themselves until Banner returned and lowered himself, cross-legged, on a sheepskin by Cristina. She was handed a dish of Pueblo pottery. He was handed a dish. From a communal pot, stew was ladled out. One by one the men began to seat themselves. Watching with those smoldering eyes. They ate silently, watching.

"I told you it would be bad," Cristina said in a low voice. "This is a wild clan. This last year has made it worse. They cannot understand why the government gave some of their land to the railroad that way. I see many of the Talk-In-Blanket clan. I heard they came north by wagon after being forced off their land in the Corn River bottoms."

"That wasn't the government's fault," he said. "Hackett brought pressure to bear in the Bureau."

"It does not matter. All these people can see is that their treaty has been violated."

She began eating once more. Sitting cross-legged beside him, eating the stew with her hands, licking the grease off her fingers. She seemed to take on the primitive savagery of these people. When she was finally finished, she put the plate down. She looked at the chief, around the circle of gleaming bronze faces. Then she made a ceremonial gesture with one arm.

"*Di banaxosinini. Toaxei* Mexican Hat, *Hosteen* Jahzini *la yah abi dolte* . . ." Of this you have been told. At the place called Mexican Hat, Old Man Black Ears has been put in jail . . .

Banner followed it that far, but she was speaking so swiftly that he soon began to lose it. After she finished, the chief spoke to her, and then turned and spoke to some of the others. It went along too fast for Banner to get more than a vague idea of what they were talking about. Some of the others began answering sullenly, warily. Then Cristina asked the chief something. He answered. Cristina looked quickly at Adakhai, and asked something. It stopped there.

"They have seen no strangers," Cristina said. "I asked if any of them had been as far south as Yellow Gap. The chief said Adakhai had hunted down that way."

"And Adakhai wouldn't answer?"

"I asked him if he had been through Yellow Gap. He was silent."

"Did you explain we were looking for an eyewitness to Wright's killing? That it would save your father's life?"

"I explained that. They are not convinced that you have truth in the heart. They say how can I trust you when you work for Henry Dodge, who will prosecute the case? These are the wild ones, Lee. They do not understand. I think we can find no more this way. I will be sleeping with the women in the hogans tonight. Perhaps I can learn more from them."

The crowd began to disperse. The women washed the dishes, the kettle, the few utensils in sand. Half a dozen of the men began playing conquian with Mexican cards. A few rolled out their sheepskin pallets by the fires and lay down. Cristina was taken to a hogan by a pair of old women. Banner was left alone, with Adakhai sitting across the fire, staring at him from those smoldering eyes.

He built a cigarette, offered it to the Indian. Adakhai rose and walked away. Banner lit the cigarette and smoked it himself. Then, despite his tension, the weariness of the long ride began to creep over him. More men were sprawling on their pallets now; the fires were dying. He unrolled his Army blankets, put one under, one on top. He turned on his side and met the un-winking eyes of a Navajo lying on a sheepskin five feet from him. He turned the other way. The Navajo on that side was sitting up, watching. He turned on his back, staring at the sky. Even the stars seemed to be watching.

He smoked the cigarette down, put it out. The breathing

around him gathered volume, grew stertorous. The card game broke up and the men rolled in. Still he could not sleep. Ada-khai's bay horse was on his mind again.

The Indian had been south, hunting. Had just returned. That could mean he had been there during the week of the murder. When they asked him about Yellow Gap, he had refused to answer. It all fitted in. But the bay horse on the rim of Yellow Gap had been shod. If Adakhai's horse was shod . . .

The impulse ran through Banner so strongly that he almost rolled over. He knew the chance he would be taking. If they caught him, and misinterpreted it, there was no telling what they would do. Yet he had to take it. Adakhai was already suspicious. If he was really the one, and did not want it known, he might get rid of the horse during the night.

One by one Banner slipped his boots off. Then he listened again. He rolled to one side and stared around the circle of men, dark mounds in the moonlight. All of them seemed asleep.

He slid from his blankets, rolled to hands and knees. A man flopped over. Banner froze. The man settled back, snoring.

Banner crawled away from the blanketed bodies into the night, behind the forked-together houses. The horses were picketed here. They shied nervously, began shifting around, snorting as he came to his feet among them. In the moonlight, he moved through the animals, seeking the bay. At last, near the end of the lines, he found it.

The horse tried to sidle away from him but he followed it to the end of its rope and caught it there, murmuring to it, sooth-ing it, till he had the animal quiet. He put his weight against the horse, shifting it off balance, and then bent to lift its right front leg.

There was no shoe. The hoof looked strange. Its heel was pinched; the frog squeezed in. But there was no shoe.

He dropped the hoof and straightened with the sense of fluttering motion from the hogans. The horses began snorting and running on their picket ropes. Then he wheeled, with the shocking surprise of the shape hurtling out of darkness upon him, and the guttural shout: *"Tchindi!"*

The body came so heavily into him that he stumbled backward, falling. He had the instantaneous impression of moonlight making a glittering sliver of something above his head and all he could do was throw his arm up to block it as it came down.

He hit on his back, a stunning blow, with the man straddled above him. Breath knocked out of him, he felt the shift of the body, heard the grunt as the man struck again. He jerked aside. The knife ripped his collar, dug hilt deep into the earth by his ear.

The man's face was a foot above Banner's. It was Adakhai. Banner hit him with an upflung elbow. Adakhai's head jerked back. Banner caught his wrist in both hands and used it as a lever to heave the Indian over.

He rolled on top, still holding the knife wrist in both hands. He twisted it, heard the Indian shout in pain. But before he could get enough leverage to make Adakhai drop the knife, the man lunged up beneath him.

The tigerish fury in the narrow body shocked him. He couldn't retain his wristlock and stay on top. Too late he let go. He was already pitching over.

Adakhai came on top of him, smashing him fully in the face with his free fist. The stunning pain of it incapacitated Banner. Dimly he saw Adakhai raise the knife to drive it down. Tried to jerk over. Couldn't.

Then the Indian gave a great shout. His weight was torn from Banner. A shrill voice was screaming something. Banner rolled over, dazedly, onto his hands and knees. He saw a slim figure writhing with Adakhai on the ground, shouting.

"I-chai . . . tchindi . . . juthla hago ni . . . !"

Cristina.

Adakhai rolled her over, tore free, tried to come to his feet and lunge at Banner again. The girl caught at him. Banner saw her hand flash before Adakhai's face. Saw the four parallel stripes leap into Adakhai's face, from brow to jaw.

The Indian shouted in pain, eyes squinted shut, and reeled back. By then Banner had gained his feet, shaking his head to clear it. Running figures were pouring in between the hogans now. A pair of them blocked Adakhai off as he tried to lunge at Banner again.

The chief ran between Adakhai and Banner, a squat, frog-like shape in the moonlight. The others gathered around. Adakhai stopped fighting, held by the two men. He was trembling with rage.

"What was it?" Cristina panted. "What were you doing?"

"The bay," Banner told her. "I had to see its hoofs."

"Lee!" Her eyes were wide and dark with anger. "Why could you not wait? Why must you always do things without thinking . . . ?"

"I couldn't wait," he said. "Adakhai was suspicious. If he's the one, he might have gotten the horse away tonight."

She shook her head, mouth twisted. "But this was the worst way you could have done it. He was probably watching you. He must think you were trying to steal the horse."

Defeat left a sick taste in his mouth. "Try to make him understand, Cristina. I was only doing it to help your father."

She shook her head, eyes squinted almost shut. "It will not help. I doubt if you will ever learn anything from them now. You have violated . . ."

The chief cut her off with an angry gesture, turning to speak to Banner.

"He says he is very angry with you," Cristina told Banner.

"They all hate you. He says you must go."

Banner's shoulders sagged. "What about you?"

"They will not let me go off with you at night, a white man. They will take me back to my home tomorrow."

"You'll be all right?"

"These are my people, Lee."

As he turned to go, he saw Adakhai's eyes. They glittered like a naked blade in the moonlight.

VII

Banner did not go far that night. He was too played out. He found a *tchindi* hogan about four miles from the Indian camp and slept there, knowing he would be safe, for no Navajo would approach a building in which someone had died.

It took him all of the next day to get back to Mexican Hat. He reached the house sodden with fatigue and turned his horse into one of the stalls in back, forking out hay and dropping his saddle beneath the ramada where all the rigging was kept.

There was a light in the parlor and he heard Dodge's soft laugh. Going down the hall, he felt a rush of warmth. How many times had he come in like this to hear the old reprobate chuckling over some ironic twist of a case in Chitty or Coke?

"Henry?"

There was the creak of a hide-seated chair, the sound of boots on hard-packed adobe. "Lee. Where in the devil have you been?"

"Up to Chin Lee, Henry. Trying to turn up the eyewitness to the killing . . ."

"The eyewitness?"

"We found his tracks out at Yellow Gap that time. A man on a bay horse who saw the murder."

"Now, son, this isn't the time to talk about . . ."

"It can't wait," Banner said. "I think I've found the witness. An Indian boy named Adakhai. He was down there hunting during the week of the murder. He has a bay horse. When . . ."

He broke off, as the other figure was silhouetted in the doorway. Dodge made an apologetic gesture.

"I told you it wasn't the time to talk about it, Lee."

"Go ahead," Julia Wright said. Her voice had a strained sound. "Did this Adakhai say he'd seen Jahzini murder my father?"

"You know I'm not trying to convict Jahzini," Banner said. "I think he's innocent, and I'll prove it."

"By stealing my father's trunk and going through his papers?" Her voice was bitter.

"Julia, I had to do that. I'm sorry, but I had to. Did Henry tell you about the letter I found?"

"That's exactly what I came here for tonight. You got those papers under false pretenses. Claude Miller says the only one with authority to impound them is the sheriff. This whole thing is so stupid. The case against that old Indian is open and shut, and here a man right in the prosecutor's office is trying to mess the whole thing up. Lee . . . I . . ."

She broke off with a sound of utter exasperation. Then she turned, tight-lipped, and walked across the living room, snatching her cloak from a chair. She had opened the front door and stepped outside before Banner caught up with her. He grasped her arm, pulling her back around.

"Julia, this isn't like you at all. Would it help your father, now, to kill an innocent man for his murder?"

"But he isn't innocent. All the evidence against him . . ."

"Is as circumstantial as the evidence I've found defending him," he said.

She started to fight—then the tension went out of her suddenly and she sagged against him.

"Oh, don't go over it again, Lee. I'm so tired, so confused. You're the only one who could really give me any help and here you are fighting me . . ."

She broke off, leaning heavily against him, and turned her face up. He felt all the anger drain from him. He dipped his head to hers and held her against him and kissed her.

For a moment she met it with the old passion, her body straining against his. Then he sensed the subtle change. Her lips altered their shape, grew stiff and unyielding, slipped off his mouth. It brought her cheek against his chest, with her face hidden from him.

"You're not still angry with me, Julia?"

"No."

"Then what is it between us, Julia?"

"Nothing, Lee. Nothing."

"There is something." He caught her chin in a cupped hand, forcing her eyes up to his. "I always thought it was something in your past. You came from Denver three years ago. Every man in Mexican Hat started buzzing around. You wouldn't have anything to do with them for months. Then, suddenly, the barriers came down. For a while I didn't know whether it would be Hackett or Elder or me."

She fingered his lapel, pouting. "You knew there was never any question."

"But even then you wouldn't talk about Denver," he said. "It always chilled things to bring it up. Was it a man, back in Denver?"

She tried to pull away. "Lee, please . . ."

"It's got to be something like that, Julia. I keep feeling it, between us."

"Lee, will you stop it, will you stop it! I can't talk about anything like that now. There's nothing. It's all in your mind. Please don't, please . . ."

103

He held her tightly, eyes turned bleakly to the darkness beyond. "I'm sorry. Maybe I'm wrong."

Her breathing seemed to abate; she was quiescent in his arms a moment, her full body softly molded to him. She spoke so low he could hardly hear.

"You'll come to see me tomorrow evening, then?"

"If I can. We'll probably be in court during the day. That Morgan litigation."

"And you won't go riding all over the country like that?" She tilted her head up when he did not speak. "There must be a hundred men with a bay horse around here, Lee. A dozen of them could have passed through Yellow Gap during that time." The expression on his face stopped her. She grasped his hands tightly. "Lee . . . you won't . . . ?"

"How can I promise that?" he said stiffly.

A dull red flush crept up her neck, into her face. She stepped back, out of his arms. "Maybe you hadn't better come to see me tomorrow night, Lee."

Dodge was sitting in his big leather chair by the fireplace when Banner came back in.

"Clear things up?" he asked.

"No," Banner said emptily. He shook his head. "Her hatred of Jahzini seems so blind, Henry."

"She's had a shock, Lee. Give her time to get over it."

Banner lowered himself into a chair, staring moodily at the floor. "I suppose you're right."

"Yes." Dodge heaved himself up and went to the ivory-topped table. He pulled open the drawer and shoved aside the ancient Dragoon Colt he kept in there, to get at his box of cigars. He bit off the end of a long black smoke and padded over to the fireplace to spit it out. He lit up, rolling it between thumb and forefinger till it was drawing well. Then he cleared his throat.

"Just how much did you get out of this Indian . . . this Ada-khai?"

"I told you the important part."

"Don't you see what flimsy evidence the whole thing would be, son?"

Banner stood up. "We went through that before, Henry. Why do you keep insisting on the technicalities of the case? I've turned up more than enough to cast doubt on Jahzini's guilt."

"All right. I'll admit what you've turned up changes the aspect of the case. But that's as far as I can go, Lee. Even if I accept the cigarette butt and the tracks you found as valid evidence, they aren't conclusive proof to me that Hackett had Wright killed. Hackett just doesn't operate that way."

Banner stared at him a long time. "You've changed in the last years, Henry. I guess I've been working too close with you. I wasn't aware of it. Suddenly you look older."

"We all get older, Lee."

"And as we get older, Henry, do we get more afraid? Does our job, our position, get to mean so much to us that we can't face anything that might endanger them?"

"Son . . ." Dodge said it sharply, rocking his weight forward. Then he stopped, staring wide-eyed at Banner, the blood darkening his face. At last he settled back, the choleric anger mingling with a look of helplessness.

Banner forced himself to go on. "Jahzini doesn't have money for a lawyer. 1 understand the court's assigned Farris, from Flagstaff."

Dodge seemed to dredge it up with great effort. "Yes."

"I know how Farris feels about Indians. I certainly wouldn't feel safe having it in his hands." Banner frowned intensely at the floor. "Farris wouldn't be needed, if Jahzini already had a lawyer, would he?"

Dodge held out his hand. "Lee . . . son . . ."

"It's got to be that way," Banner said in a strained voice. "I've got to take the case, Henry. I've even got to leave this house . . ."

Dodge grasped his arm. "You'll ruin your whole career this way. You don't have enough evidence to win the case, son. Lose it and you'll never get a private practice in this town. The feeling's too intense."

"That's why I've got to move out of your house, Henry. The Indians know you're prosecuting the case. I'll never get anything out of them as long as they think I'm still with you."

A stricken look filled Dodge's eyes. When he finally spoke, his voice was rusty and trembling with suppressed rage. "I guess you're right. You'd better go."

VIII

Aztec Street ran six blocks southward from Courthouse Square, then dipped into Gayoso Wash, becoming no more than a wagon road, and ran three blocks more to the railroad. In these three blocks was the Mexican section of town. At the street called Calle de los Léperos, Banner turned off Aztec, riding between sagging spindle fences that surrounded dark dooryards.

Banner's portmanteau was on the rump of his horse and he was still sick from leaving Dodge under these circumstances. He realized his own anger had led him to hurt the old man, to express suspicions he wouldn't have put into words if he had stopped to think.

He drew his horse up sharply as a screaming voice burst from one of the adobes farther down the alley. A woman's voice, shrill, vitriolic, cursing in Spanish.

"*¡Tu bribón, se las tendrá que haber con el papá de ella, lo agarró con las manos en la masa . . . !*"

There was the crash of crockery, a man's voice shouting wildly: "*Madre de Dios,* what are you make . . . ?"

106

Light blossomed from a door flung open. The man's figure was silhouetted in the yellow rectangle, squat, bowlegged, primitive. A dish hit him and broke all over his skull. He howled and ducked low, wrapping his arms around his head. A clay jug spun over him and struck the street and shattered.

"*¡Vayase con la música a otra parte!*" screamed the woman.

The man was running toward Banner; the woman was silhouetted in the door, heaving another plate. It spun by and smashed against a wall. Other doors were opening, people were shouting ribald advice, laughing. The man wheeled into a cross alley. Banner reined the horse in after him. At the other end of the alley, the man came to a halt, puffing.

"So she caught you red-handed," Banner said.

The man brushed pottery from his hair, muttering angrily: "I was just show Camilla how they do it in Durango. She tell me her mother won't be home till midnight. What a little liar."

"So you'll have her father to answer to."

"Is that what the old witch she was shouting? What an old *bruja* . . ." Tilfego broke off, turning. "*Amigo,* I thought it was the voice of my conscious."

"Conscience."

"*Sí.* Conscious."

"How about bunking with you?"

"Is pleasure." Tilfego rubbed at the back of his neck, staring up at Banner. "So you're going to defend Jahzini. And Henry Dodge he has kick you out."

"Is it that clear?"

"Your bag you got. I see it coming a long time. You cannot have the blame for Henry. Even I can see that you do not have enough evidence for the court."

The Mexican's two-room adobe was farther up the Street of the Beggars. They turned Banner's horse into the spindle corral out back and went into the house. While Tilfego lit a candle,

Banner slumped wearily on the bed, head in his hands, and told Tilfego about Chin Lee, about finding the pinched heel and squeezed frog on Adakhai's bay. Tilfego agreed that it might mean the horse had been recently shod, for that condition usually developed from poor shoeing. The Mexican had seen no sign of the bad frog in the tracks at Yellow Gap. However, it was possible that the condition had developed after the Indian had been to Yellow Gap, and he had subsequently removed the shoes to let the hoof get better. It gave Banner a little hope.

He slept like a dead man that night, not waking till 10:00 the next morning. Tilfego was out back, currying Banner's chestnut. They went into town for breakfast. There was not much movement on Reservation at this hour. Banner was about to cross the street with Tilfego when he saw the wagon coming in from the east.

It was like the shock of a blow at the pit of his stomach. Jeremiah Mills was driving the wagon, and one of the horses in his team was a bay.

Tilfego put a hand on Banner's arm. "You jump too quick again, Lee. I thought that was too easy, ride out over the weekend and find everything."

"But it all pointed to that Indian . . ."

"You did not really think you would be that lucky?"

Banner's shoulders sagged. "I guess not. Mills is north of the tracks, isn't he?"

" 'Way north."

"And he'd have to come through Yellow Gap to get to town. Is that a cinch sore on the bay?"

"Looks like it. She has been under saddle, and not too long ago."

Mills pulled into the rack before Price's Mercantile, climbing slowly out of the wagon. He was tall, gaunt, with the chronic stoop of the dry land farmer in his heavy shoulders. He shambled into the store.

Banner and Tilfego walked the half block to the Mercantile, and Tilfego squatted down to study the hoofs of the horse, lifting one at a time.

"Same size as that one at Yellow Gap."

"Could this be the one?" Banner asked eagerly.

"Hard to say. The one at Yellow Gap have little dent on rear hind shoe. This one she is smooth."

"Riding over a lot of talus could have ground it down."

"Maybe." Tilfego rose.

Mills came through the door with a fifty-pound sack of flour on one shoulder. The man glanced dourly at Banner and lowered the sack into the bed of the wagon.

"That's a pretty bay," Banner said.

Mills leaned against the wagon. "She ain't good for nothin'," he said. "So lame I can't ride her."

"You ain't had her long?" Tilfego asked.

"Not long. Victor Kitteridge owed me some money for alfalfa. He couldn't pay it. I needed a wagon horse so I took the bay instead."

Banner stepped close to him. "You know Wallace Wright was murdered in Yellow Gap last Thursday, Mills. That same day a man on a bay horse rode through the gap. We have every reason to believe he saw the killing."

The first shock left Mills's face blank. Then his eyes narrowed. "I didn't have this horse then."

"I can check with Kitteridge easily enough."

"Go ahead, damn you." The man turned to climb into the wagon.

"Are you that afraid of Hackett?"

It stopped Mills, with his hand on the wagon. He turned to look at Banner again, surprise in his eyes. Then something else filled them, almost a look of pain, and they swung away, and he lifted his foot to climb in. Banner stepped up beside him and put a hand on the side of the wagon. It blocked Mills from stepping up. The man stared down at Banner's arm.

"Take it away, Lee. I'll bust you open like a sack."

"Will you, Mills?" Banner asked softly.

The man continued to look at the arm for a long time. Without looking up, he spoke, his voice strained and husky. "What do you want?"

"I always thought hard work put that stoop in your shoulders, Mills," Banner said. "But that isn't it. You're afraid. You've been afraid so long you've forgotten what it's like to give a man a good punch in the nose. Five years ago it was another big man you were afraid of, back in Missouri or Arkansas or wherever it was. Now it's Clay Hackett."

The man settled slowly, heavily against the wagon, letting a husky breath flow out of him, staring at Banner's arm without seeing it. Finally the words began to creep out, not directed at Banner, or at anybody in particular, just words. "We were a long time getting this place. I owned two farms back in Missouri. I was flooded out. Owned one in Ohio. Crop failure lost me the mortgage. Homesteaded in Wyoming. The Johnson County War finished that. I guess I've squatted in a dozen places between here and there. Sometimes the cattlemen squeezed me out, sometime the land failed me. It digs into a man to lose that many times, Banner. It digs into a man."

"And if it wasn't for Hackett, now, you couldn't even stay where you are."

Mills's head lowered. "He could kick me out if he wanted to. I had squatter's rights on that land. Even the government recognized them till the railroad come through and they gave it alternate sections along the right of way. My land fell in one of those sections. The railroad leased it to Hackett. I know cattlemen, Banner. Ninety-nine out of a hundred would have kicked me off. He's let me stay."

"Your land runs right across the northern end of the railroad section, doesn't it? Ever had trouble with the Indians?"

"A dozen times. You know that."

"Don't you see what a buffer you make for Hackett, Mills? He's using graze he'd have to fight the Indians for if you weren't there. All the reports that come in have you in trouble with the Indians in that section, not Hackett."

Mills stared intently at him, mouth working faintly. Then he shook his head.

"Don't try to twist this around, Banner."

Banner felt a frown pull his brows in. "I hadn't realized before how many people in this town were under Hackett's thumb. How can you live on your knees all the time, Mills? I'd vomit."

"You never had a family, did you, Banner?"

Banner looked into Mills's eyes. It was like looking at a hundred years of bitterness, pain, defeat. "All right, Mills," he said.

The man stared at him a moment longer, then started to wheel and a climb into the wagon. He checked himself, looking beyond Banner. His face took on a color of old putty.

"You aren't going to believe everything the counselor says, are you, Mills?" Hackett asked.

Banner turned to see the man standing on the sidewalk, behind the hitch rack. He had his thumbs hooked in his gun belt and his feet planted widely.

Mills licked his lips. "I mind my own business, Hackett. You know that."

"Sure you do," Hackett said.

"I was just leaving," Mills said.

"Sure you were," Hackett said.

The Owensboro creaked as Mills stepped up, settled himself on the seat, shoulders deeply stooped. The little bay snorted, wheeled with the other horse as Mills reined them around.

"This Adakhai," Hackett said. "Do you really think he saw the murder?"

Banner's voice was bitter. "Does Henry run to you with everything?"

"Haven't seen your uncle in several days," Hackett said. "I dropped in on Julia last night, though. Must have been after she'd seen you. She was right upset, had to let it out on somebody. Do you really think that Indian will testify against a man of his own race?"

"If he testifies, it won't be against Jahzini."

"Won't it now?" Hackett lowered his head till his sardonic black eyes were barely visible. "Well," he said absently, "maybe not." He glanced beyond Banner, at something down the street. "Maybe not." He turned and walked toward Blackstrap Kelly's, his spurs setting up a jingling clatter in the quiet street.

"He sure like to drag them cartwheels," Tilfego observed.

Banner turned to see what Hackett had looked at. Arles was sitting his horse near the corner of Aztec and Reservation. He met Banner's gaze for a moment, then reined the horse around and rode toward the desert.

They ate breakfast at one of the Mexican *cantinas,* and then Banner went back to Tilfego's house to get some paper and pencils from his bag. He went to the extreme west end of town first, meaning to work eastward. The station was the last building on Reservation. From his cubbyhole of a ticket booth, Si Warner saw Banner coming, and turned back into the waiting room. Banner and Tilfego followed him in. The man had his back turned and was assiduously sweeping out beneath the seats.

"When I was a kid," Banner said, "you used to tell me stories about the time you were an engineer."

"Don't make it hard on me, Lee. Blackstrap Kelly's my friend, too. I got to eat my meals there every day. I got to drink his liquor if I want to see my other friends."

"I knew the feeling was bad in town, Si. I didn't know that it extended to you."

"Damn it, Lee." The man shook his head exasperatedly. "Everybody in town knows you're goin' to defend Jahzini. Dodge's cook heard you and you know what a gossip she is. Feeling's high on Reservation Street and you're goin' to run smack into it. Like this rumor that some Injuns are goin' to try and bust Jahzini out of jail. A lot of men are sayin' we should hang Jahzini before they can try anything. Caleb Elder said anybody that defended Jahzini ought to be hung, too."

"Let me hear him say it," Tilfego growled. "I'll string him up by his thumbs."

"Elder's got a right," Si said. "Some Injuns burnt out his Cherry Creek line camp last night."

"I've still got to ask you some questions, Si. Did you see Jeremiah Mills in town on June the Twelfth?"

"Can't recall."

"If I have to bring you into court, Si, and you lie, they can jail you for perjury."

"Dammit, Lee, I still didn't see him."

"Victor Kitteridge, then."

"Seems so," Warner said reluctantly.

"Riding a bay?"

"Seems it was that hammerheaded roan of his."

"What time, Si?"

"How the hell can I remember all that? Morning, I think. I don't know."

After Si, it was Sam Price. And then Blackstrap Kelly. And all along the way, he met the same resentment, the same withdrawal, the same anger. But he persisted, and by the end of the day he had gotten down to Fifth Street. He had filled five sheets of paper on both sides. He had the names of seven different people who had been in town from the north country during the day of the murder. Five of them were Indians known to the townsfolk, but none of these had ridden a bay. The other two were whites, Caleb Elder and Victor Kitteridge. Of the eight people who remembered Kitteridge being in town that day, three thought he had been riding a buckskin, two remembered a hammerheaded roan, one thought it might have been a bay, if it wasn't a chestnut.

IX

Banner ate at Tilfego's that night, and went to bed right after the meal, dead tired. It seemed only a second before he was awakened. He lay in the bunk, staring around him, with the sense of having been shaken. He was surprised to see dawn filling the room with a milky light.

"Somebody belch big?" Tilfego asked.

"It wake you up, too?" Banner said. He heard somebody calling from next door, something about an explosion. He sat up sharply, throwing the covers off.

"What you make?"

"I'm going to see about it." Something was working in Banner, an apprehension, a premonition. He dressed, slipped into his coat, even buckled on his Colt. Then he went outside. A few people stood in the squalid lane.

"*¿Qué pasa?*" Banner asked.

"*No se,*" a man said. "*Un explosión, al norte . . .*"

To the north? Banner went to the corral and saddled up his chestnut, the premonition still tugging at him. He could hear Tilfego snoring again, from inside. He turned down the street to Aztec, then up toward Reservation. Little knots of people were gathering on the corners.

114

A thin trickle of them was moving up the street. A buggy passed Banner, going hard. He was almost to Reservation, now, could see the crowd around the courthouse. Sam Price came running from the alley between Reservation and First, a six-shooter in one hand.

"He's not down there!" he shouted. "Carey's starting a search of the houses now!"

"Somebody said he got a horse down on Second!" another man called. "He'll head north for sure. What the hell is that sheriff doing?"

Banner pulled up on the fringe of the crowd around the jail, saw Blackstrap Kelly. "What happened, Kelly?"

"Somebody blew up the jail safe. Jahzini got out the hole."

Banner swung down and shouldered his way through the men. The splintery cedar door was wide open; there were more men inside, examining the blackened hole in the back wall of the office. The safe had been knocked over on its side by the explosion, the heavy door bent open like a piece of tin. Charlie Drake was down on his hunkers, pawing through what was left of the papers. He gave a tremendous wheeze, coming to his feet. He had a few burned pieces of paper in his hand, and Wright's saddlebags.

"That's all I can find," he said. "The rest must have been burned up. I had a lot of exhibits on that Johnson case, too."

"You're wasting a helluva lot of valuable time," somebody said hoarsely. "Let's get after him."

"We'll get after him," Drake said. "Somebody can go get them Papago trackers for me right now. I can use a dozen men in the posse. I'll deputize the first twelve of you that come back with a horse and two spares, two five-gallon canteens, and food for three days."

There was an eddying shift around Banner as the men started going out. He stepped past Judge Prentice, speaking to Drake.

"That cigarette butt is gone?"

"Hello, Lee. What cigarette butt?"

"The exhibit Dodge gave you Saturday."

"Oh." Drake wiped the wrinkled back of his hand across a ruddy nose. "I guess it is. This is all I found."

"And Wright's letter?"

"I told you." Drake held up the saddlebags. "This is about all anybody could recognize."

Judge Prentice irritably pulled his coat shut over his nightshirt. "I don't see how they got in to do it in the first place, Drake. It looks like willful negligence to me."

"I don't think you can blame Drake, Judge," Kelly said. "Somebody started a fight in the alley back of my place. Drake was the only one on duty over here. He come running with his shotgun."

"Who was it?"

"I didn't catch 'em," Drake said. "The explosion came when I was out back of Kelly's. Time I got back onto Reservation, whoever'd done it was gone, Jahzini was gone, too." The sheriff waved the saddlebags at the breach behind the safe. "Jahzini's cell was on the other side of that wall. When they blew the safe, it made a big enough hole for him to crawl out."

Banner began backing out of the room, into the crowd, getting his horse. At the corner of Aztec, just about to mount, Banner saw three men swing onto Reservation at the next corner. Each one had a saddle roll, a pair of canteens, and two spare horses. And one of them was Big Red.

Banner stepped aboard and kicked the horse into a run, heading eastward out of town. Beyond the last house he pulled the animal down to a walk-canter trot that kept the miles unraveling behind him without draining the beast completely. His mind was on Big Red, and the implications of that, but he was also calculating how much of a head start he'd have. It would take them twenty minutes to get the Papago trackers, in their camp west of the railroad station. Maybe another ten to deputize the men, to get the group organized. Half an hour. It wasn't much.

The sun was up now and the heat waves were beginning to dance along the buttes. He turned off on the Yellow Gap cut-off, went through the gap itself, rose to the higher land northward. Two hours later he was riding through the mesquite forest south of Jahzini's. Then he rode into the rocky bench-lands. An hour of this brought him out of the rough country into the wash where the hogan stood.

Cristina must have heard his oncoming horse, for the wicker-work door was pushed aside, and she stooped through and straightened, a slim figure in her blue velvet tunic and voluminous skirt. He checked the horse before her.

"Your dad's escaped, Cristina. A posse's after him. We haven't got a minute to waste. Is he here?"

"He isn't here, Lee. How . . . how . . . ?"

"Somebody got into the sheriff's office this morning and blew up the safe. It knocked a hole in the wall. Your father got out that way. The only evidence destroyed was the stuff I'd gotten that might have proved your father's innocence."

He could see the fear begin to shine in her eyes. "What are you thinking, Lee? Don't try to spare me."

"Big Red was there," he said. "One of the first to join the posse. Why would he be in town at this time? Hackett needs every man on roundup."

Her eyes grew darker. "My father is liable to get drunk. He always got drunk when he was mixed up about the white men. He has friends all the way up to Corn River. If he gets hold of liquor . . ."

"That's what I figured, too. He'll put up a fight if they catch him."

"And they will shoot him." There was a dead sound to her

voice. "That is what you mean, isn't it? Hackett did this on purpose. He wanted my father to escape, so they could kill him."

"It would clear things up for Hackett," Banner said. "Maybe he was beginning to feel the pressure. To be afraid of what I was turning up. This way, the case would be closed quick. No court battle. No evidence turning up in favor of your dad. Just a posse, a fight, a coroner's inquest."

She frowned. "When Jahzini was in trouble before, he always hid with a friend north of the Corn River. Few know where the place is. It is two days from Mexican Hat, pushing hard. I had better go with you. You could never find it alone."

The old woman had come from the hogan. She seemed to shrink a little when Cristina told her what had happened.

"We will stop by some of my cousins," Cristina told Banner. "They will come back to take care of her."

He helped her saddle up. Then they rode. Westward the benchlands began lifting upward till they reached a rim that ran northwest for miles and then petered off in ridges shaggy with another mesquite forest.

The sun rolled toward its zenith, turning the sky's turquoise bowl to an arch of blinding brass. Banner was sodden with sweat and giddy with the heat. They found a trickle of water in a narrow gorge and let their horses drink and drank themselves, and then hitched the animals in the shade of scrub oak. Banner settled onto the baked earth, beside the girl.

"Did you find out anything more at Chin Lee?"

She gazed somberly at the stream. "The women knew little. They said Adakhai was one of the really wild boys. His father was killed in one of the fights over grazing trouble. They said Adakhai had been south, and might have been through Yellow Gap on the day of the murder. I tried to speak with him the next day, but he had gone hunting again." She looked up at him, a wondering expression parting her lips. "When everything was happy, when the world was peaceful, I saw very little of you. How strange that it should take death and pain to bring us together." Then: "Will you come to me . . . as you go to Julia Wright?"

He almost smiled. Something in her eyes kept him from it.

"Are you jealous of Julia Wright?" he asked.

A fathomless blankness dulled her eyes.

"Why do you look at me like that?" he asked. "Did I say something wrong?"

"Would you say a foot separates us, Lee?"

He smiled wryly. "No more than a foot, certainly."

"A thousand years separate us."

"Cristina . . ."

"I saw your face up at Chin Lee when you stepped down among those people. They smell like wild animals, don't they? You were stepping down into the past. A man cut off from all he knew, surrounded by people he could never understand."

"That has nothing to do with you."

"They are my people, Lee."

"They may be of your blood. But you've lived among us. You speak our tongue. Your mind works like ours."

"How do you know how my mind works? Does your mind work like an Indian because you lived with us for a year? You proved it did not at Chin Lee. They hated you, yet they gave you hospitality. You violated that. You did not even understand what it would do to Adakhai if he found you with that horse. You will never get his trust now."

"Cristina, please . . ."

She shook her head, eyes dropping. "It is no use, Lee. You showed me up there how impossible it is that our two races will ever understand each other. That thousand years will always stand between us."

"No!" He caught her arms savagely. "Only a foot separates us. We can cross that right now."

He pulled her toward him, bent his head to hers. There was a silken warmth to her lips. It was a transitory thing, a hint of satiny passion. Then it was gone; she tipped her head back, pushed him away.

He stared down into her face, trying to understand what had happened to him. Looking down at her, still trying to define what was happening within him, he could not help smiling, his rueful quirk of a smile. She reached up to touch his mouth with her fingers.

"When I think of you . . . I think of that," she said.

She took her hand away suddenly, swiftly as if from a burn. She stood up and turned around and walked to her horse. He got up and followed her and took her shoulders in his hands and turned her around. Her eyes were squinted shut and tears were running down her cheeks.

"Cristina . . . I didn't mean . . ."

"What didn't you mean?"

He gazed down at the piquant oval of her face, helpless before the turmoil of his own feelings. "I don't know," he said in a low voice. What should a man mean, or not mean, when he suddenly realized that a girl had become a woman? He shook his head wonderingly, still holding her arms.

"At least that thousand years is gone from between us now."

Her head came up. "You still don't see it?"

"Cristina, don't talk that way again."

"You're right. I shouldn't talk. If you don't see it, talk won't explain."

She twisted away, toed her stirrup. Her skirts flared as she swung up. She wheeled the pinto on down the cañon. He went to his own horse and pulled the latigo tight and stepped aboard and turned to follow her.

X

In the afternoon they reached Cristina's cousins at Ta Lagai. They came out of the highlands again into the greasewood flats and logs-stacked-up house. As soon as Banner and the girl appeared, there was a call from somewhere, and people began to pop up like ants swarming from the earth. Banner was surrounded by a cacophony of Navajo and English. When an ancient headman had finally quieted them, Cristina looked at Banner.

"Did you understand? Jahzini passed here on his way north. He sneaked in without any of them seeing him and got hold of some liquor and a gun. All the young men have gone south to sell the wool. They couldn't keep Jahzini here and had nobody to send after him when he left by horse."

"Did I catch Drake's name?"

"Sheriff Drake and his posse got here by horseback an hour after Jahzini left. The Papago trackers didn't have any trouble following him on north."

"Then we're too late."

She shook her head. "If Jahzini is going north of Corn River, I know a short cut between here and Turquoise Buttes that might get us ahead of Drake."

She turned to tell the palsied old headman of her mother. He said he would send one of his wives to take care of her. They watered their mounts, then pushed on.

The heat became more intense, sucking moisture from Banner till he was drenched in sweat, yet felt dry as a husk. His eyes ached; his face felt flayed raw; he began to have the sensation of riding in a feverish stupor. The girl accepted it all with expressionless calm.

They topped Turquoise Mesa and rode westward for three miles along its rim, and then saw the stain of dust against the steely northern sky.

"That is probably Drake," she said. "It looks like they are heading west. That means they have struck the river and are following it. If we cut straight through these benchlands ahead of us, we might reach Mogul Ford before they do."

It was a cruel stretch, studded with lava that would have cut a horse to ribbons if a man didn't know the trail. They finally reached the ford. The water was sullen and brassy under an afternoon sun. The strain of dust against the sky was to their right, now, coming toward them, and they knew they had beaten Drake. Cristina took one glance at what looked like the fresh tracks of a shod horse, lining through the sand toward the river. Then she led Banner into the water, slopping across three hundred yards of brazen shallows to the narrow strip of beach on the other side. A great sandstone escarpment rose beyond the beach, ruptured by a single cañon directly ahead of them. Cristina rode unhesitatingly into this.

It was a narrow gorge, a place of shadows, of silence. Sometimes it was so narrow it scraped Banner's legs. It twisted and turned, back-tracked and looped. Sunset was turning the sky to a bloody stripe between the rocky walls far above them when they began to smell the stench.

A few yards on they found the dead horse. Cristina stared down at it, compassion darkening her eyes.

"Jahzini must have run it all the way through this heat. He would never do a thing like that if he was sober."

They rode another half mile through the narrow chasm, crossing shale where the clatter of their hoofs ran before them. Then Cristina pulled to a halt, staring at the rim above.

"There is a foot trail up here to the mesas. It will take him a mile across them to the northern rim and then down again. It is the shortest way. I think he would use it. If we both go up here, he might get away at the other end."

"Could we split up?"

122

"That's the only way. A half mile on, this cañon opens onto the desert. You turn west along the mesa rim for a mile to where that foot trail comes down again."

"Do you want me to go that way?"

"I had better. You couldn't find where the trail comes down. You'll have to leave your horse here when you go up."

Cristina turned her horse and rode on into the cañon, into the shadows, out of his sight.

He hitched his horse to some mesquite and started climbing. It was talus slope at first, treacherous going in his high-heeled boots. He squirmed over the lip at the top, débris rolling down to make a small roar in the gorge.

He rose to his feet on a narrow ledge that shelved upward, switching back on itself, becoming a defile between outcropping rocks. It was a steep, laborious going. He had to stop for a breath more than once.

In one of those pauses he felt his head jerk up in reaction. Had there been motion above him? He could see nothing.

He began moving upward, for the first time realizing the full implications of what he might meet up there. Jahzini might start shooting without taking time to recognize him.

Banner's eyes began to ache with the strain of trying to find something on the twilit rim of rocks. There was no movement above him. No sound. Nothing.

The ledge widened, fanned out through a studding of rocks that hung on the lip of the plateau. His breathing was loud and gusty. He neared the top of the cliff, his eyes lifted above the tops of the last rocks. He stopped.

"Belinkana?"

A sly, nasal, questioning tone to it. American? A cunning tone, matching the cunning light in Jahzini's eyes, in his blandly smiling face. He sat there like a paunchy, leering Buddha, in the rocks, with the *tusjeh* beside him, uncorked. The Remington six-shooter in his lap was pointed at Banner.

"Jahzini . . ."

The gun snapped up, stopping Banner short. Jahzini held it in both hands. Banner could see no recognition in the drink-glazed eyes.

"Belinkana!"

High and nasal. American! Rolling it around the tongue. Savoring it. Banner sought swiftly for the right words to say now, trying to avoid the verb forms that could put so many different, wrong meanings onto it.

"Jahzini . . . Hackett did this on purpose . . . Big Red is in the posse . . . they know you will fight. They want you dead, don't you understand? They want you dead . . ."

"Dead!"

The gun jerked as Jahzini said it. His whole body seemed to lift up, a wild light in his eyes. Then, the small click.

Jahzini was staring at Banner over a cocked gun. Banner felt the sweat break out on his palms. He knew he had to speak again. There was so little time left. He sought desperately for the right thing to say. "Jahzini, you remember me. You remember Tsi Tsosi."

"Tsi Tsosi?"

"Yes. Yellow Hair. And Keet Seel. Remember the lion at Keet Seel? Who was it saved your life? You cut our palms. We mingled blood. We were brothers. Look at your hand."

Suspiciously the Indian let that pass through his mind. It seemed to take forever. Then he let go of the gun with his right hand, stared bleary-eyed at the palm. The old scar was faint and white against the dirty brown skin. Slowly the Navajo's eyes raised. Just as slowly Banner held his hand out, palm up. It bore a faint white scar, too. Jahzini squinted. The effort of remembering etched the million wrinkles deeper into Jahzini's nut-brown face. The drunken cunning faded from his eyes.

"Tsi Tsosi?" he said wonderingly. Then he grinned tentatively, and his voice was touched by all the chuckling warmth with which he had imbued the name when he had first called Banner Yellow Hair. "Tsi Tsosi."

Banner knew a glowing triumph, and started to move toward the old man. Then he stopped. Jahzini's head had lifted sharply. The wild look was back in his eyes. They were staring beyond Banner.

And the young man could hear it now, too. Down in the cañon. A hollow rustling. A far-off clatter of hoofs across shale in the cañon bottom. Then there was a shout from below.

"Jahzini, is that you?"

It was Drake's voice, coming from the depths of the gorge, echoing and reëchoing till a hundred men seemed to be shouting. It filled Banner with the impulse to turn. But the expression on Jahzini's face checked him. The Indian's features looked shrunken with rage. The gun was pointed now at Banner's chest, and the wrinkled thumb was clamped hard over the cocked hammer.

"Jahzini," Banner said, "I didn't bring them here. You've got to believe me. I didn't betray you."

"All right, you old fool!" Drake called out loudly. "We're coming up. Cut loose just once and we'll shoot you off that cliff."

The creak of leather, from below. The first rustle of climbing men, from below. The irony of it filled the young lawyer bitterly. He was skylighted on the rim, and the men down there thought he was Jahzini.

The gun was trembling in the old Indian's hand. Banner stared across its black bore into those yellow-tinged eyes.

Then somebody started the first landslide. He must have kicked a sizeable rock loose, for it made a startling crash of sound in the cañon.

"Belinkana." Jahzini jumped to his feet, shouting it, and fired down into the cañon.

In sheer reflex, Banner threw himself at the man, knocking him backward. A dozen guns must have gone off below in the following instant. A hail of bullets took vicious bites out of the rocks where Banner had stood the moment before. If Jahzini had been on his feet, he would have been cut to pieces.

Jahzini struggled to free himself from beneath Banner. But the young lawyer caught at the gun, twisted it from his grasp. The old man clawed him like a cat. Banner hit him across the side of the head with the barrel of the gun. Jahzini went slack beneath him.

The guns were still racketing from below, filling the gorge with a gigantic roar. A ricochet screamed like a woman in pain. Deafened by the din, Banner crouched low over Jahzini.

Without raising up, he tried to drag the old man farther back from the edge. There was furtive movement from among the rocks. Banner jerked the gun up. Cristina crawled into view. Banner let his pent breath out.

"I had to hit him," he said.

"I know." She came closer, shouting in the din. "We cannot go back to my horse! Those Papago trackers must have known about this foot trail. They led Arles and another man around to that end of it. I saw them reach my horse as I got to the top of the mesa. They will be coming up after me."

"Is there another way down from here?"

"A mile to the west. It is dangerous, but we might make it."

"And from there, how far to the nearest place we could get horses?"

"Ten or twelve miles to Kitteridge's place. We could lose our tracks in the Corn River."

They pulled Jahzini back into the brush. He crouched on his hands and knees, shaking his head. Finally he looked up at Banner. The blow seemed to have sobered him somewhat.

"*Bahagi*," he groaned. "I have committed a great offense."

"You did nothing of the sort," Banner told him. "You fired past me, down into the cañon. I should have known you couldn't ever get drunk enough to shoot me."

"I thought you were an evil *belinkana*. I thought you were Nayenezrani himself come to strike me down with all four of his lightnings."

"We've got to make a run for it, Old Black Ears. Can you stand?"

"Stand? I can fly. The wind cannot keep up with me." He tried to rise, swayed, would have fallen if they hadn't caught him. He shook them off. "Let us go," he said. "Cry out when you grow tired and I will carry you on my back."

XI

Somehow they made it down the treacherous, forgotten trail on the west end of the mesa. They knew it would be hard for the Papagos to track them at night, and in that lay their hope. They left a false trail leading north, and then gained the Corn River and turned south in its shallows. For the first few miles the old man showed a surprising stamina, slopping through the muddy water. As Banner moved beside him, Jahzini chuckled roguishly and gave him a poke in the ribs.

"I should escape jail more often, if that is what it takes to see my white son again. I have missed those nights in the hogan. With Cristina gone away to school, there was no one I could tell the myths to."

"Those nights will come again. You must help them come. You must tell us what happened."

The old man nodded. "I was all mixed up. They showed me Wright's saddlebags and said they had found them in my hogan and said I killed him. I was drunk when they found me and I couldn't remember anything anyway and I thought maybe I did kill him and couldn't remember it."

"But you didn't."

"No. Now I do not think I did. I was taking wool to town by wagon that day when I heard the shot in Yellow Gap. When I came upon Wright, he was dead. It gave me great fear. I had fought with Wright over the land. His death would make great trouble for my people. I went to the hogan of my cousin."

"And got drunk."

"Sometimes just running is not enough."

"Never mind, Old Black Ears. You are with your people now."

"That is good. It gives me strength. If you grow tired, we can sing *hozhoni* songs. They will make us holy and give us wings to our feet."

So they sang *hozhoni* songs as they ran, because they knew it would help the old man. They sang the "Lightning Song" and "Pounding Boy's Song" and the "War God's Song" and all the old songs that Jahzini's people had been singing for hundreds of years when they set out upon a journey or started off to war.

But finally the old man began stumbling and they had to slow down to a walk and even the songs were too much effort. Banner did not know what time of night it was that they reached the fork in the river and left the shallows and made their way into the broken country west of Chimney Buttes. Then the old man stumbled and fell to his hands and knees in the sand, his breathing shallow with exhaustion. When they helped him up, he shook his head.

"It is a bad thing to have a father who will lie to you. I really could not carry you on my back if you got tired."

Banner slapped him affectionately on the back. "You can't fool me. I am on to your jokes. You pretended to be tired that time when we were racing for the blankets and I slowed down because I thought I had beaten you and you passed me up before I knew what had happened."

A feeble roguishness lit the oblique glance Jahzini sent him. *"Ai,"* he said, giving Banner a sly poke in the ribs. "I did beat you that time, didn't I? You make me young again, bringing back the old days. Very well, let us run some more."

"And sing some more," Cristina said. "Sing us the 'Clown Song', like you used to."

"I cannot thump my belly to make a drum any more. It seems to hurt me or something."

"I will thump my belly," Banner said. "You sing."

So they sang another song, moving across the broken land in that unremitting Indian dog-trot, with Banner thumping his belly and the old man chanting the "Clown Song" in a husky, wavering voice. It helped for a while. Then the old man began faltering, and they had to slow down to a walk, and finally he fell again, and they had to stop and rest. Banner lost count of the times they ran, the times they rested. He thought the night would never end.

But the dawn came at last, revealing Chimney Buttes on the horizon. And when the sun rose, they were in sight of Kitteridge's house, backed up against the wall of a mesa.

Banner and Cristina were half carrying Jahzini now, each holding him up by an arm. He was stupefied with exhaustion.

"Just cry out if you cannot go on," he mumbled. "I will carry you on my back."

Banner saw the hammerheaded roan and half a dozen other horses in the corral. Kitteridge opened the door before they reached it.

His gaunt frame seemed to stiffen as he saw them. His eyes widened with his first surprise, then squinted almost shut, and he watched their approach with a suspicious withdrawal on his face.

"Let us get Jahzini inside," Banner panted. "I think he's

passed out."

"I ain't harboring no murderer."

"He's not a murderer, damn you. Let us in. You'd help a dog if he was in this shape."

Reluctantly Kitteridge moved out of the way, and they staggered into the room, carrying Jahzini to a chair. When they got him into it, Cristina had to hold the old man to keep him from falling. Kitteridge still stood at the door. Banner pulled the table across in front of Jahzini so he could lean forward without falling. When Cristina let him go, he dropped his head into his arms. She took the other chair, leaning heavily against the table, her eyes blank with exhaustion. Banner let a long gust of air run out of him, his eyes glazed with weariness.

"Now," he said, "we'll need three horses."

"The hell you will. I told you . . ."

"I'm trying to get Jahzini back to Mexican Hat," Banner said. "They set this up so Jahzini could escape. They wanted to kill him before this case came to trial."

"Is that so?" Kitteridge said cynically. "Who set it up?"

"I haven't got time to explain that, Kitteridge. But Jahzini's innocent. You've got to help me save his life. There's a posse on our trail now and they'll kill him if they get him."

"I ain't helping no murderer."

"He isn't a murderer, damn you . . ." Banner broke off, staring in frustrated anger at the cynicism in the man's long face. Kitteridge slouched across the room to the spindled Mexican cupboard. From this he took a coffee pot, shook coffee into it from a sack.

"Shouldn't've let you spoil my breakfast," he said. "If you want to get away from that posse bad enough to walk all this distance for my horses, you sure as hell won't let them catch you here, whether you get the horses or not. *Ipso facto*, Counselor?"

Banner's voice was pinched with restraint. "You won't give us the horses?"

Kitteridge set the pot on the stove. "I told you."

The restraint left Banner; his words exploded in a gust of anger as he wheeled toward the back door. "Then we're taking them!"

Kitteridge did not seem to move fast. He straightened and stepped toward the front. Cristina jumped from her chair, trying to block him. But somehow he was at the door before she reached him.

"No, you ain't," he said.

At the rear door Banner half turned, to see the man standing by a heap of rigging. He had pulled a Winchester from its boot. It was crooked in one elbow, pointed toward the lawyer.

"There ain't so much as a rope out in them corrals," Kitteridge said. "You'd have to come back here anyway. The halters are in this pile."

Cristina had stopped, halfway to the man. Now the look of her face altered subtly. She began to walk toward Kitteridge. He did not even shift the gun.

"I never shot a lady," he said. "But I'll sure as hell swipe the barrel of this gun across your head if you come any nearer."

"Don't do it, Cristina." Banner's voice was sharp. "He means what he says."

Cristina stopped. A long breath left her. It made a hissing sound in the room. Banner stared at Kitteridge.

"I always thought they misjudged you in town, Kitteridge. I'm beginning to believe they didn't."

"I mind my business. I expect other people to do the same."

"Why?" Banner asked thinly. "Are you running from something, too? You've been here three years and haven't made a friend. There's a lot of people who think you're on the dodge. What are you, Kitteridge? A thief? A murderer?"

A whipped look crossed Kitteridge's face, and he started to lean forward. Then he checked himself. "You're not in the courtroom now, Counselor," he said.

Banner hardly heard him. He was looking at the gear beside Kitteridge. The yellow color on the saddle had been visible all the time, but his anger had blinded him to its significance. It came through at last. A yellow stain on the bottom of a stirrup. Clay. The bright yellow clay a man would pick up at Yellow Gap.

"That's a little saddle," Banner said. "Was it the bay's?"

Kitteridge revealed his surprise. "What bay's?"

"The bay you gave to Jeremiah Mills."

Kitteridge's grin held no humor. "You think of the funniest things, Counselor."

Banner felt his hands closing into fists. "That tree looks too small to fit any of the horses you've got here."

"The bay was a little horse. I'll get me another little horse."

"Then you haven't used that saddle since you rode the bay?"

"What's that got to do with anything?"

"A lot. Did you go through Yellow Gap the last time you rode the bay?"

The coffee started to boil. Its hissing was the only sound in the room. Kitteridge was studying Banner.

"Why should I want to kill Wallace Wright?"

"I'm not implying you killed Wright," Banner said hotly. "There was an eyewitness to the killing. We have every reason to believe he saw it from the rim of the gap. He came from up here and he rode a bay horse."

Cristina was watching the man intently. The hiss of boiling water became a gurgle. At last he spoke. "All of Mills's saddles were too small for that bay. He used this one for quite a while after I gave him the horse."

"Mills said you gave him the horse after the killing."

"He's a liar."

"You're saying you didn't see the killing?"

"A man that minds his own chores don't go around poking his nose into things like that."

"Damn you, Kitteridge, it isn't a matter of poking your nose into other people's business. You'd be saving a man's life. If you didn't talk, it would be the same as murdering Jahzini."

"Save your howling for the jury, Counselor," Kitteridge said. "I didn't see any killing. I didn't see nothing."

Banner felt his whole body grow rigid in frustrated anger. He began to pace across the room.

"Isn't there anything that can touch you? They're set to kill this old man, shooting, or hanging, or however else they can do it. The man who saw that murder is the only one who can save him."

"Looks like you're getting impatient," Kitteridge said. "It's true you ain't got much time left. That posse's had a lot of daylight to track you now. They might be riding up outside right now."

Banner checked his angry pacing.

He knew the man was right. The trick of hiding their tracks in the river wouldn't fool the Papagos for long.

The lid of the coffee pot began to clatter and dance, and Kitteridge glanced at Cristina. "Move it off, honey. It's fixing to boil over."

The girl rose, going toward the oven. She picked up a dirty rag to use as a potholder and bent over the coffee. It was then that she glanced at Banner. He looked at Kitteridge. Then he took a lunging step toward the man.

"Damn you, Kitter—"

"Stay there," the man snapped, jerking his rifle up.

For that moment it took his attention completely away from Cristina. She picked up the coffee pot and threw it.

133

The man reacted instantly, turning toward her motion. But he was too late. The top fell off as the pot struck him. The boiling water cascaded over his head.

His shout of pain filled the room. He dropped the rifle and staggered backward, hands clapped to his scalded face. Banner jumped to the Winchester, scooping it up. Kitteridge stood rigidly against the wall, hands spread tightly over his face. His breathing was a sobbing sound in the room. Banner gave the rifle to Cristina and turned to get the can of beef tallow on a shelf.

"Stay away from me," Kitteridge said.

"Don't be a fool," Banner told him. "You'll be scarred for good unless you get some of this on your face."

He had to pull the man's hands down. Kitteridge's eyes were squinted shut, his face intensely contorted. Banner put the grease on his cheeks in great gobs and rubbed it in gently.

Cristina held the Winchester on the man, mouth pinched and tight.

"I am sorry," she said. "You forced us . . ."

"If you was a man, I'd kill you," Kitteridge said. "I'd kill you right now."

"It was my father. You made me do it. I could not let them kill him. You must understand."

Kitteridge leaned back against the wall, drawing a thin, whistling breath between his teeth. "All right. So you couldn't let them kill him."

"You do understand, you don't hate me?"

"Hate you?" The man opened his eyes to look at her. They were watering and twitching with the pain of the burn. "No, honey," he said finally. "I guess I don't hate you."

Banner looked at him in surprise. He turned to put the can of grease on the table and took the rifle from the girl.

"I'd better hold him here while you saddle up, Cristina."

"That ain't necessary," Kitteridge said. "If you want the horses that bad, you got 'em."

"You disappoint me," Banner said. "I thought you were all vinegar."

Kitteridge took a weary breath. "Nobody's all anything, Counselor. Just get out of here before that posse shows."

"You'd better get a doctor as soon as you can."

"I don't need a doctor." The man turned to pace across the room. He stopped by the fireplace, staring blankly at the wall. His voice lowered. "I don't need nobody."

Banner stared at his back with a new insight into the man. "I think that's where you're wrong, Kitteridge," he said. "I think you've needed somebody for a long time."

XII

Evening had come before they got back to Mexican Hat. They came in from the south, across the railroad tracks, through the Mexican district. Tilfego was not home but they left their jaded horses in his corral. They went up the alley between Aztec and Central to Judge Prentice's house. But the place was unlit. The only other chance they had was that the judge was working late in his chambers at the courthouse.

It was a tense journey to the square, and into the gaunt old building, but they were not stopped. Light showed under the judge's door. Banner knocked softly. Prentice's voice sounded muffled, asking them to enter. His swivel chair shrieked as he leaned back in utter surprise at Jahzini's appearance. Banner towered behind Jahzini in the doorway, his eyes red-rimmed and feverish, deep lines of weariness about his mouth.

"He came back of his own accord, Judge. You've got to believe that. I brought him to you because you're the only one I can trust now."

The chair groaned more softly as Prentice leaned forward

again, putting his hands on the desk, littered with the manila-backed briefs of his cases. Then he rose abruptly, coming around the desk.

"Sit down," he said. "You look all beaten out." He went to the scarred highboy by the window and got a bottle of brandy and three glasses from one of the cupboards. While he poured the drinks and handed them around, Banner helped Jahzini into a chair. The old man was stupid with exhaustion and sat huddled over, gazing blankly at the floor. Banner spoke swiftly.

"The posse can't be far behind us. I want your word on something before they come. If you won't give it, I'm taking Jahzini right back out, Judge."

Prentice smiled ruefully. "Don't put me on the spot, Lee."

"I only want your word you'll put Jahzini on the first train out of Mexican Hat. Send him to the Territorial Penitentiary at Yuma till the date of his trial."

Prentice moved to the window and stared out, his hands locked behind him.

"I know there's a lot of feeling against him. There's even been talk of lynching. But I doubt if it will come to that . . ."

"You know what I'm talking about."

The judge was silent for a long moment. Then he took a reluctant breath. "All right. Talk has also been going around that you think Hackett had Wright killed. I asked your uncle about it. He said that was your theory."

"It's more than a theory," Banner said. "I turned two items of evidence over to the court that might have proven Jahzini's innocence. Doesn't it strike you strange that they were destroyed in that explosion, while all the evidence against him was saved?"

"I've been thinking of that . . ."

"Thinking of it!"

Prentice turned toward him. "Take it easy, Lee. I know you're perfectly sincere in what you're doing. But have you stopped to think what this has done to Henry? Not only his personal feelings for you, but his position . . ."

"Have you stopped to think what it's done to Jahzini?"

Prentice flushed, started to speak, checked himself with effort. Then the thud of hoof beats came from the street, the faraway shout of a man.

"They're here," Prentice said.

"Judge, please . . ."

The man frowned at him. The heavy echo of boots ran down the outer hallway. Cristina came up out of her chair, hands clenched at her side. There was the rumble of voices outside, the door shook to a knock. Prentice glanced apprehensively at Jahzini, then said: "Come in."

Sheriff Drake was the first to enter, with Clay Hackett and Big Red and Blackstrap Kelly pushing in behind. Drake halted his gross bulk a couple of paces inside the room, staring at Jahzini.

"How do you like that?" he said with weary disgust. "Chase all around the country and find them right back where we started." He seemed to settle against the floor, emitting a long, wheezing breath. "We tracked you to Kitteridge's. He said you was coming back here. I wouldn't believe him."

Anger made Hackett's prominent cheek bones stand out whitely. "That was you up on the cliff?" he asked Banner.

The lawyer ignored him, speaking to Drake. "Jahzini came back of his own accord."

"After trying to ambush us," Hackett said.

"He was drunk. He didn't know what he was doing."

"Well, we know what we're doing," Hackett said. "Charlie, slap those cuffs on him. He won't get away again."

Drake started to move. Banner took one long step that put himself between Jahzini and the sheriff.

"Don't get in the way again, Lee," Hackett said.

Banner spoke to Prentice without moving his eyes from Drake. "Judge?"

Prentice had been watching Hackett closely. "How do you happen to be in the posse?" he asked.

"I wasn't," Hackett said. "There was a card game at Blackstrap's."

"I understand you were represented, anyway. Good of you to spare Big Red, right at roundup time."

"And Arles," Banner said.

Hackett turned sharply toward Banner, a biting anger filling his eyes. But he did not speak. As if feeling Prentice's gaze on him, Hackett closed his mouth and wheeled slowly back till he was looking at Prentice again, his gaunt features wooden and enigmatic. "So it's bad to join a posse now," he said. His voice was silk-soft. "Maybe you'd rather chase your murderers next time without one."

Drake shifted uncomfortably. "Now, Clay . . ."

"We didn't mean to criticize your public spirit, Mister Hackett," Prentice said. He studied Hackett quizzically for another moment. "The feeling's bad enough in this town. After this little escapade it might get dangerous. I think we'd better send Jahzini to Yuma for safekeeping till the trial."

"And give him another chance to escape?" Blackstrap Kelly said.

"Not many men have escaped Yuma," Prentice answered dryly. "I'll sign the order. You can wire Yuma for confirmation tonight, Charlie. I think there's a train at ten thirty-eight tomorrow morning. You can send a couple of your deputies to guard him."

As the pen began to scratch, Hackett turned to look at Banner. For a moment, he let the anger show in his eyes again, naked and ugly. Then, without a word, he wheeled to the door. Big Red followed Hackett out. Prentice raised a brief glance to

Banner. Then he lowered his head and began to write again.

Cristina was bent over her father, explaining to him in Navajo what had happened. He began to nod, frowning. When she was finished, he held up an arm, and Cristina caught it, helping him to stand. Then he shuffled over to Banner, putting his sinewy old hands on his shoulders. He was smiling and his eyes were suspiciously wet.

"*Shiye,*" he said, patting Banner gently with both hands. "My son."

XIII

Next morning, Banner boarded the train with Jahzini and two of Drake's deputies. Hackett had little power outside Navajo County, and Banner felt sure the man could not touch Jahzini beyond Flagstaff. So he rode that far, checking each passenger who got on, making sure that none of the cars held anyone remotely connected with Hackett. Banner said good bye to the Indian at Flagstaff, returning to Mexican Hat on the next train.

And again he set out on the process of elimination. It took him two days to finish questioning the people of Mexican Hat. No new suspects arose. Mills and Kitteridge were the only white men from the north country that had been seen in Mexican Hat during the day of the murder.

After finishing in town, Banner rode out to the trading post. Besides meaning to question Calico Adams, he had half hoped to see Julia. But it was after 3:00 P.M. and school had already closed, and Calico said Julia had already gone on her usual afternoon ride. The trader told the lawyer there had been no stranger on the reservation who might have come south through Yellow Gap during June. And although Adakhai had not been at the trading post since April, several Indians had seen him hunting in the country west of Yellow Gap on the week before the murder.

After leaving Calico, Banner rode north to begin his routine check of the remaining whites between the railroad tracks and the reservation. He reached Caleb Elder's about 5:00.

The man was a big, taciturn cattle operator who had been Banner's rival for Julia two years ago. That old antagonism, and the trouble Elder had been having with the Indians filled him with a hostility he did not try to veil.

But Banner told him that the trial would probably be in September, and that unless he cleared himself of any suspected connection with the murder, he could be subpoenaed to testify, and would undoubtedly lose a lot of time from fall roundup. This made him admit that he had been driving cattle across the reservation to St. Michaels during the week of the murder. He gave as witnesses Joe Garry and Breed, who he had met holding some Hackett cattle on the Río Puerco. Banner would not accept them, and Elder included the priest at St. Michaels, to whom he had delivered the cattle on the day of the murder. It completely obviated any chance of Elder's being at Yellow Gap, seventy miles away, on the same day.

However, the fact that the two Hackett riders were holding Broken Bit cattle deep in reservation land was direct evidence that Hackett was violating the treaty, and Banner knew it would be a strong item of subsidiary evidence for the defense. So he prepared a statement, including the names of Joe Garry and Breed as witnesses to Elder's claim, which Elder signed.

The trail back to the Ganado Road cut across a vast, broken country, and Banner free-bitted his horse through the soft dusk. He wound into a cut, red with crumbled sandstone, puckered with the mounds made by kangaroo rats. He emerged from the mouth of the cut and crossed a sandy flat to Parker's Sink, the only water hole between Elder's and the railroad.

Two riders were already watering their animals at the sink. One of them was Julia Wright, a handsome figure in her riding habit of dark green suede, a pork-pie hat tilted saucily on high-piled hair. The other one, sitting slackly on a hammerheaded roan, was Victor Kitteridge.

There was a long space of awkward silence. Then Kitteridge's saddle creaked as he shifted his weight. "Seems like everybody's out riding tonight."

"Seems like," Banner said, nodding a sober greeting to Julia. "Did you get your three horses back, Kitteridge?"

"Your Indian boy brought 'em back all right."

"How's the face?"

"No uglier'n usual."

"It didn't seem to leave any scars."

"Take more'n that."

"You don't seem mad."

"Bygones."

"Then maybe you'll tell me about the bay, now."

"No."

"When they hang Jahzini, will you come to see it?"

Julia stiffened in the saddle, her face going white. Kitteridge showed no reaction.

"I'll be dragging," he said.

He gathered up his reins, nodded to Julia, heeled his horse around, rode out through the trees. Banner was watching the small changes of expression pass through Julia's face.

"Did you know him, back in Denver?"

She flushed. "I told you I didn't. I stopped here to water my horse. He was coming back from Ganado."

"A man saw your father murdered, Julia. I've narrowed it down to three possibilities. Kitteridge is one. If you know him, I need your help the worst way."

"Oh, stop it," she said bitterly. "Do you have to go on hurting

141

everybody?"

"You know I don't mean to hurt you."

"Then why don't you stop? It's not only me. Can't you see what you're doing to Henry? It used to be I couldn't go into town without seeing your uncle out there on the corner, talking with some friends. Now he's never there. Do you know why? He's up in his office. He's hiding, Lee."

"Julia . . ."

"He's the laughingstock of the town. You've made a circus of this thing. Can anybody take Henry seriously with his own son turning on him like that? Everybody's come to look on you as practically his son."

"I can't help it. Do you think I'd turn on Henry if there was any other way? Don't you think it's tearing my insides out to see him cross the street to avoid me?"

She turned her head sharply aside, squeezing her eyes shut. "Oh, Lee, why does it have to be this way? I'm so mixed up. I still want to believe Jahzini killed Dad. I want to hate him for it."

"But you can't," he said. "Admit it."

"All right"—she shook her head savagely—"I admit it. I admit it."

She put her hands over her face; her shoulders began to tremble with her sobs. He stepped over to her horse.

"Julia," he said softly, persuasively. "Julia."

She looked down at him, her throat working.

"You would have come down to me before, if you'd really relented," he said.

"I've admitted I couldn't just let Jahzini hang, if there was any chance of his innocence. What more can you ask?"

"Things have changed," he said.

Her throat stopped working. "I suppose they have."

"Hackett?"

"Don't be a fool."

"You've seen a lot of him lately."

"It isn't Hackett. Can't you leave it at that?"

He stared up at her, searching her face. "Then you'll help me with Jahzini," he said. "You'll tell me about Kitteridge."

"Lee, I don't see what possible connection . . ."

He reached up to catch her hand. "I've checked at the post office. Ed tells me that in the three years Kitteridge has been here he's gotten one letter, from Denver. If you knew Kitteridge up there, you've got to tell me, Julia. I can't seem to reach him. He knows that if he saw the murder, he could save Jahzini's life by testifying. But he won't admit anything."

"Maybe he actually didn't see the killing."

"I can't cross him off till I'm absolutely sure. If he did see it, Julia, what's keeping him from admitting it? He must have some powerful reason. Is it something in his past?"

She gave that savage shake of her head again. "If it was, could you ask me to betray him?"

He tightened his grip on her hand. "If you don't tell me, I'll have to wire the district attorney in Denver. I'll have to give him a description of Kitteridge, the date of Kitteridge's arrival here. I'll ask him if anyone is wanted in Colorado who would fit the description."

Her voice was barely a whisper. "You wouldn't."

"I'm trying to save a man's life, Julia."

She looked away, biting her lip. She took a deep breath, and finally spoke. "I did know Kitteridge up in Denver." Her words were flat and toneless. "He was Victor Morrow then. You probably remember the case."

"The Morrow-Ware Land and Cattle Company." Banner's eyes were wide with surprise. "About five years ago, wasn't it? One of the biggest swindles in the Southwest. As I remember, the chief bookkeeper was the only one they caught. Sheffield, or something."

"Shefford," she said. "His testimony led to Victor Morrow's indictment. Victor escaped before they could jail him, came down here, changed his name to Kitteridge. But he didn't have anything to do with the swindle. It was Ware who engineered the whole thing, with the bookkeeper's help."

"But the grand jury didn't even indict Ware. He got off with a clean slate."

"Of course he did. He framed Victor. As general field manager for the company, Victor only got into the office twice a month. He had no idea how Ware was pyramiding the stocks or appropriating the company funds. They made him the goat. Shefford falsified the books to make Victor seem responsible. But something must have slipped, and Shefford was caught."

"Then why didn't Shefford expose Ware and get a chunk of his term knocked off for turning state's evidence?"

She shook her head. "Shefford was playing for bigger stakes. Victor did have access to the books, but they probably let him see only innocent figures. As he remembers it, though, even those figures didn't turn up at the trial. The only thing we could figure out was that Shefford had kept two sets of books. The falsified ones, which made Victor seem guilty, and which turned up at the trial, and the real ones, which nobody ever saw."

"Why would Shefford do that?"

"Because the real ones would prove Ware's guilt," she said. "Shefford was keeping them as sort of insurance against Ware. Ware must have made a couple of hundred thousand on that swindle. He'd certainly pay to keep Shefford from turning the real books in."

"It sounds logical," Banner muttered. "But if those real books would prove Ware's guilt, they might prove Morrow's . . . Kitteridge's innocence."

"Don't you think I've told Victor that a million times?" she said bitterly. "I spent weeks talking with Shefford, trying to get him to admit the truth, to tell us where the real books were. It was no use. But I'm convinced I'm right."

"And you really think there's a chance Kitteridge could prove his innocence?"

"I know he could, Lee. It would just take someone who knew how to work, someone with more connections than I had. Ware disappeared shortly after the trial. A couple of years later we got word that he was separated from his wife. She was living somewhere in Kansas. I even tried to follow that down. I ran out of money . . ."

She trailed off, close to tears again. She was stooped in the saddle, her head hanging, all the spirit drained from her.

"I always wondered what lay between us," he said.

She looked down at him, frowning intensely. Then she shook her head. "No, Lee. You're wrong. I knew Victor had come down here and changed his name to Kitteridge. When Dad got a chance to transfer to the Navajo Agency, I asked him to do it. Maybe I still hoped to help Kitteridge clear himself. Maybe I had some fool notion that we could go on. I was wrong both ways. He's so changed, Lee, so bitter, not the man I knew in Denver at all. It took me a year down here to finally admit it to myself."

"And that was where I came in?"

She nodded slowly. "About that time." She glanced at him quickly, apprehensively. "Don't think I was using you merely to forget Kitteridge. What you and I had would have happened whether I'd known Victor or not. It was good, Lee. Maybe I still wasn't completely over Kitteridge. Maybe that's what you felt between us. But it isn't between us now, Lee. Whatever I had with Kitteridge up in Denver is over."

He studied her face somberly, and his voice was dark and wondering. "Is it, Julia?" he asked.

XIV

All the way back to Mexican Hat a dozen different thoughts gnawed at him, a dozen different emotions. He didn't know yet, whether he believed Julia when she said she and Kitteridge were through. He didn't think she knew herself. He didn't even know what he felt for Julia now.

In this frustrated confusion he reached Mexican Hat. The bright hardness of burning sun was gone from the streets. The buildings etched a broken silhouette of roof tops and false fronts against a moonlit sky. Kerosene torches flared from a score of wooden overhangs, dappling the rutted street with miniature lakes of yellow light.

He saw Tilfego's buckskin yawning at the hitch rack before Kelly's, and swung his own animal into a slot between two horses.

He got off and stepped up to the sidewalk. Over the tops of the batwing doors he could see a thin evening crowd lined up at the Brunswicke bar, a few scattered diners at the tables. Tilfego sat near the wall, a plate of tortillas before him. As Celestina maneuvered her jiggling hulk past him with a tray, he reached out to pinch her on the hip.

Banner saw his uncle, then, sitting at a corner table. He started to push through the doors, but something about the man's posture checked him. The white-haired lawyer sat stiffly in his chair, facing the wall. His meal was only half finished, but he was not eating. One of his hands was gripping the edge of the table so tightly that the tendons stood out in bluish ridges. It struck Banner how many of the men at the bar were looking at Dodge. There was derision in their drink-flushed faces, and a couple of them were grinning broadly.

The two Hackett riders Elder had seen on the reservation stood at the far end of the bar. Joe Garry was a short, broad-girthed man. Breed was taller, with a slouching, stoop-shouldered way of standing.

"Hey, Henry!" Joe Garry called. His voice was slurred with drink. "Give me the latest. They tell me you don't have enough evidence to convict Jahzini. You just sent Banner out to raise all this ruckus so you wouldn't have to prosecute."

A general laugh went up from the men at the bar. Banner saw the artery in Dodge's temple throbbing, saw the deep red flush of his face. But his back was to Garry, and he did not turn to answer the Hackett rider.

"Leave the old man alone," Tilfego said. "His supper you are spoiling."

"We're just asking him the latest." Garry laughed.

"Yeah," Breed said. "I hear the Indians are going to run one of their men for district attorney. If they can murder the agent and get away with it, they figure they can do anything."

Banner saw Dodge's body begin to tremble faintly. Hot with anger, the young man pushed through the batwings, but the scrape of Dodge's chair checked him once more. The old man had pushed it back and was rising. He started to walk stiffly toward the door. Then he saw Banner.

He stopped, eyes wide with surprise. A corner of his mouth twitched. Banner moved swiftly between a pair of empty tables.

"I've got to see you, Henry."

The flush of anger remained in Dodge's face, but a strange, pleading look filled his eyes, like that of a man clutching at his last straw. "You mean you're ready to admit you're wrong about Jahzini?"

"No, but we can't go on like th—"

"Then we have nothing to talk about."

Dodge's face was so set it looked frozen, and he started to go around Banner. The young man tried to grab his arm.

"Henry."

Dodge jerked free. It unbalanced him and he stumbled into a

chair, almost upsetting it. Half a dozen of the men at the bar began to laugh, and Joe Garry shouted again. "Why not take the buggy whip to him, Henry, like you used to?"

One hand on the table, Dodge wheeled toward them. He made a strangled sound of rage. Sending a last, torn look at Banner, he wheeled and stamped out.

"Looked like the old mossyhorn was goin' to bust a gut." Garry laughed. "You oughta have more respect for your uncle, Lee. You're both shysters under the skin."

It brought laughter from the whole line at the bar. Banner spun toward Garry, but he felt a hand on his arm, and Tilfego's bland voice came through his anger.

"Toss the slack out, Lee. Let them ride you and every man in town you have to fight."

Banner stood rigidly, staring at the crowd, trying to gain control of himself. He shook his head helplessly, allowing Tilfego to guide him to an empty space near the front end of the bar. Joe Garry put down a silver dollar for his drinks and turned toward the front door, followed by Breed.

Blackstrap Kelly stumped along on the other side of the bar till he was in front of them. He put his hairy hands flat on the mahogany, staring unwinkingly into Banner's face.

"What you like?" Tilfego asked.

"How about some of that Old Kentucky?" Banner said.

"All out of it," Kelly told them.

"Make it beer then."

"All out of that, too."

Banner took his foot off the worn rail, straightening up. "What have you got?"

"Nothin'."

"You make it pretty clear, Blackstrap."

"It hurts my business to have you in here. But I wouldn't serve no Injun lover anyhow. It's you oughta be strung up, after letting him escape like that."

"He didn't escape. They took him to Yuma."

"I'll believe that when Charlie Drake's deputies get back."

Joe Garry stopped before passing Banner. "What's this about the deputies? I hear Jahzini tried to escape at Flagstaff and they had to shoot him down."

Banner wheeled to him. "Don't be a fool. I rode as far as Flagstaff with . . ."

"Don't take it so hard, Lee." Garry's greasy jowls were flushed with drink. "You're the one to crow now. You're collecting so much evidence there won't be any left for old Henry."

Tilfego grabbed Banner's rigid arm. "Cut it out, Garry," he said.

"What the hell." Garry chuckled. "Lee knows all the latest news. Don't he, Breed?"

"Tha's what they tell me," Breed said.

"Give me the latest, Lee. They say you was building up such a case for Jahzini that Henry knew he couldn't win if it reached court. He blew that safe open hisself so the old Indian could escape."

Banner hit Garry. It smashed the man backward into Breed and then he twisted off and fell to the floor. Breed had been thrown back into the bar. He recovered with a violent lunge, slapping for his gun.

"Stop it," Blackstrap said.

Breed's whole violent movement halted with his hand on his gun. Slowly he turned to Blackstrap Kelly. The saloonkeeper had a sawed-off shotgun resting on the bar.

"I don't want no killing in my place," he said. "Get out of here. All of you."

Garry got to his feet. He stood before Banner, swaying faintly, his eyes muddy with a seething anger. Then he turned around and pushed his way through the batwings. Breed followed, his hand still on his gun. Banner waited till he saw them both cross the sidewalk and drop off to their horses. Then he went out through the doors with Tilfego.

The kerosene torches on the edge of the overhang splashed their smoky yellow light across Garry, standing between two animals at the rack. He seemed to be tightening the cinch on his paint. But the light caught the whites of his eyes, turned obliquely toward the sidewalk.

"Can you see me as well as I can see you?" Tilfego asked softly.

Garry went on tugging at his latigo without answering. But he was plainly visible, in the torchlight, while Banner and Tilfego stood in the black shadows beneath the overhang. Garry must have realized the advantage that gave them, because he finally tossed his reins over the paint's head and swung aboard. He held the fiddling horse, waiting for Breed to mount.

"You made a mistake, Banner. Twenty men ride for Hackett. Every one will just be waiting for you after they hear about this."

He wheeled his horse out and spurred it into a dead run down the street, followed by Breed. Banner moved to the edge of the sidewalk.

"I didn't know what I was doing," he said. "It happened so fast I didn't know what I was doing."

"Because you still love the old man and you been work so hard you are jumpy as the jack rabbit," Tilfego said. "And I am glad you hit Garry. The hell with him."

"It's true, then. Julia told me. I guess I hadn't realized it. I've made Henry a laughingstock. Did you see his eyes, that last time he looked at me? Like I'd stabbed him or something."

"Is something you cannot help," Tilfego said softly.

Banner shook his head, broad shoulders stooped. "Maybe I'm wrong, Tilfego. Maybe there isn't really an eyewitness.

Maybe I'm doing all this for nothing."

"You cannot give up now."

"I can't go on hurting Henry this way. He was right. I'm too impulsive. Get an idea and I jump. Don't care who I hurt or why. All I can think of is myself."

"You are not think of yourself. Everything you do is for Jahzini."

"I'm beginning to doubt myself. I can't go on hurting him this way. If something doesn't break soon . . ."

He broke off, realizing Tilfego was not looking at him. He raised his head, following the man's gaze, out into the street. At first he thought it was Joe Garry returning. Then the rider pulled into the flickering light.

"Cristina."

She pulled her mare to a halt. Before he could step out to aid her, she swung down.

"I thought you'd want to know about Adakhai," she said. "Two of his people passed our hogan this afternoon with the news. They told me Adakhai had disappeared. Over a week ago he left by horseback for a hunting trip up near Navajo Mountain. He was going to stop at Tonalea and get his cousin. But he never got there. Some of the young men from Chin Lee tried to trail him. They lost his trail."

He stepped into the street, staring down at the troubled darkness of her eyes. "Eight or ten days isn't so long for a hunting trip that far north."

"But he did not appear at Tonalea. His cousin is still waiting there."

Tilfego was beside them now, his eyes squinted thoughtfully. "Hackett know you thought Adakhai was the eyewitness?"

Banner turned to him. "Yes," he said, "Hackett knew."

They were all silent. The horse snorted. The kerosene torch spat softly. Tilfego moistened his lips before he spoke. "I was

151

pass by the roundup camp of Hackett on my return from Army job. Arles and Big Red they was not there. A Mexican hand he say they been gone many days."

Slowly, heavily Banner asked: "Would they know that country up there?"

"Arles would," Tilfego answered. "Remember when he was a kid. He kill a man in Tucson. He out around Navajo Mountain for two years. Then he hook up with Hackett and Hackett have the influence to get a self-defense ruling on it."

Banner's voice was dull with defeat. "I don't want to believe it."

"You put Jahzini out of Hackett's reach," Tilfego said. "This is all Hackett has got left. Without an eyewitness, you do not have a case."

Banner was staring beyond Cristina. "How could we ever do it?"

"A man he leave sign," Tilfego said.

"But the trail's over a week old. And even the Indians lost it."

Tilfego looked hurt. "You are give me the insult."

Banner shook his head. "I couldn't ask you to do it. If it's true, if Arles and Big Red are really up there . . ."

"Leave me out of good fight and I never call you *amigo* again." Tilfego chuckled. "You do not have to ask me. I volunteer."

The girl's skirts rustled softly. "I will go, also."

Banner shook his head. "We can't take you. No telling how long it's going to be. Just tell us where the Indians lost the trail and anything else you can think of."

She hesitated. "They followed it as far as Dot Klish. You know how to find that. In the land beyond is where Adakhai's people lost his trail. It is sand country, and the wind had covered his tracks."

He nodded. "We'll start right away."

"Thank you, Lee. I must get back to my mother now." Her

eyes clung to his a moment longer. Then she turned to Tilfego, putting her hand on his arm. Banner saw Tilfego's eyes widen. They held an indefinable, luminous expression. "You are very good," Cristina said. "It is my wish that more people realized how good."

She smiled up at him, a fleeting little smile, and then started to turn away. Banner held out his hand.

"Cristina."

She faced back quickly. "Yes?"

He stared down at the soft oval of her face, turned to burnished copper in the flickering lights. "Nothing," he said awkwardly. "We'll let you know as soon as we get back."

She seemed to understand. The smile came again briefly, shyly. "Thank you, Lee."

Her skirts whirled and rustled as she swung up on the horse. She heeled it around, sent them a last look, and rode down the street. Banner finally turned to see that Tilfego was still staring after the girl with that shining look yet in his eyes. Banner grinned.

"You didn't ask her to marry you," he said. Tilfego did not seem to hear him. Banner put a hand on the man's beefy shoulder. "Tilfego?" he said.

The Mexican turned. "*¿Sí?*" he asked blankly.

Banner frowned wonderingly at him. "Don't tell me."

Tilfego's primitive face colored with embarrassment. He looked at Banner, trying to grin. "*Qué barbaridad,*" he said.

"Yes," Banner said, "what a barbarity."

XV

They left before dawn the next morning. They rode north in a hot wind that seemed to be sweeping the world clean. The sand blew into their faces all day and all night and they had to stop every half hour to clean out the clogged nostrils of their horses.

North of the Corn River, north of the Hopi villages, farther north than Banner had ever been before, they began to ascend the Shonto Plateau.

Near the end of the second day they reached the tributary gorge called Dot Klish by the Navajos for the blue clay in its walls. Erosion had eaten out all the sand around the clay, leaving a labyrinth of weird blue shapes that covered the walls like twisted gargoyles waiting to pounce. The wind was still blowing. It had sifted three feet of sand into the bottom of Dot Klish. Banner pulled his animal to a halt.

"No wonder they lost him here. He might as well have walked in water."

Tilfego's eyes were squinted almost shut against the stinging sand. "If they trail him this far, it means he come into this cañon. He come from Chin Lee? That means he travel west. He was go to Tonalea? She is north. So he leave this cañon by either the west or the north."

They knew the cañon only ran a few miles, east and west. But that was a lot of ground to cover when you were looking for sign. They made camp at its east end, leaving the horses there, so they would not obliterate any of the marks left on the land. Then, on foot, they began their search. Slowly, painfully they studied all the ground adjoining each exit through the north wall of the cañon. When daylight failed, they returned to their camp and ate and slept. They were up before dawn.

They worked through the forenoon, sweating under a brazen sun, faces whipped raw by the wind-blown sand. By late afternoon, they were only a mile up the cañon, working on the fourth exit. It was a rocky gully, and one of the boulders rose like a jagged tooth from the sand covering the bottom. Tilfego squatted over the rock for ten minutes, giving its glittering surface a minute inspection.

"Lee," he said. Banner waded through the sand to him, staring down at the rock. He could see nothing. "The little hole," Tilfego said. "Something chip it out."

At last Banner made out the tiny pockmark in the rock, hardly bigger than a pinhead. He was filled with a great sense of helplessness. It was so tiny, so insignificant. Yet he had seen Tilfego's uncanny faculties at work before.

The tributary gully cut through the wall in a northwest direction, and the Mexican started working his way down its sandy bottom. Banner followed. Inch by inch. Foot by foot. Yard by yard. With the sun dying and the light failing and night coming again. But just before dark Tilfego found it. He stooped over a bench of sandstone, wet his finger, rubbed it across the surface. Then he looked at Banner and Banner went to him. It was a chip of granite, no larger than the head of a pin, glittering like a miniature jewel.

"A horseshoe could have chip it out back there," Tilfego said. "It could have caught in the nail, be carried this far, be knock out again. Will do?"

"Will do."

Night again. Dinner again. Sleep again. Up with dawn and eating a cold breakfast and into the tributary gully with the first light of the sun. Working along the twisted walls and in the bottom where the sand was piled high as a man's knees. For half a day they worked, without finding another sign. Then the gully petered out and opened up and they were faced with a vast plain, cloaked densely with creosote.

"If a man he went through here he had to brush against that creosote somewhere," Tilfego said. "You start one side, I start the other. Cover all the ground in between."

It was a heartbreaking job. Again sand had drifted across the ground beneath the bushes, covering any tracks that might have been made. The bushes were knee-high, for the most part, and Banner had to squat all the time. His clothes were sodden with sweat; his back ached; he was dizzy with the intense heat. They met in the middle without having found anything.

"Dammit, Tilfego, maybe that was some animal we're tracking. Why don't we go on to Tonalea and ask if they saw him?"

The Mexican chuckled. "His own people do that. You are tracking now, *amigo*. Is not sit down and turn to page ten and find the rule. I have spent a week looking for one sign."

"But we haven't got the time. If Big Red and Arles are on his tail, we haven't got time."

"You tell me a better way, *amigo*?"

Banner drew a weary breath. "All right. What now?"

"Same thing."

Same thing. Bending their aching backs to the task again, studying the creosote and the greasewood and the cactus till their eyes burned and began to lose focus. No telling how much later it was that Banner found the cholla, stout-trunked, short-branched, covered thick with glistening spines that could stab like a dirk. Banner called Tilfego. The Mexican came.

"Does it look like that joint's been torn off recently?"

The Mexican stared at the healing end of the branch, chuckled, clapped Banner on the back. "A tracker you are. The spine she catch in something and pull the whole joint off." He glanced behind them. "Is almost due north from gully. We go in same direction. Somewhere that spine she drop off."

Half a mile on they found the cholla spine, broken, lying in an open patch of ground. A triumphant grin tilted Tilfego's eyes into that Oriental mask.

"Finally we know this he is man. There is nothing around here the spine could have brush off on. The man broke it when he pull it from his horse, or his saddle leather. Will do?"

Banner could not help his husky laugh. "Sure as hell, will do."

They had their direction now, and they clung to it. They got their horses and moved northward. They found more sign on the brush, but soon it got patchy, and finally ceased growing altogether, and they found themselves on the edge of a sand flat that stretched beyond sight. They camped there that night and started hunting the next morning, and after half a day Tilfego admitted there were times when the land hid all from a man. So they had to gamble. They moved on north across the sandy wasteland. They had used up all the water in their canteens by now, and came across no new water holes. By noon Banner's throat was burning; the horses were spooky and wild with thirst.

In the late afternoon a great escarpment rose before them. And in the towering rock wall was the knife-blade crack of a cañon. They turned off their course toward it. Distance was deceptive, and it took them till sunset to reach the escarpment.

There was soft earth about the entrance of the gorge. It had recorded the imprints faithfully. They had been made by an unshod horse. Its right front hoof left the mark of a squeezed frog.

The two men stared down at it for a long time. Then their eyes lifted, met. Banner shook his head.

"I knew you were the best tracker in the world, but this is one I didn't think you could pull out of the hat."

They gigged their jaded horses into the rock-walled chasm. The sky was a tortured thread of turquoise above them, striped with crimsoned cloud banners. Against this, the circling birds were silhouetted darkly. Banner looked at Tilfego, felt something tighten in his chest. Without a word they heeled their fretting animals into a sluggish trot. A few hundred yards on the cañon formed an elbow turn.

Rounding it, they startled the feeding buzzards. The birds rose into the air with a funeral whir, a ghastly squawking. The smell of putrefying meat almost gagged Banner. But there was enough hide left on the carcass to tell its original color. It was the bay.

Reluctantly Tilfego stepped off his horse and walked toward the carcass. Grimacing with the stench, he forced himself to stand over the dead animal, studying the signs.

"She fell hard." He pointed to the earth at one side. "There Adakhai he hit and roll and get to his feet."

He began to follow the tracks. They led up a talus slope to a ridge of cap rock. Here he stopped, beckoning Banner to bring the horses. Banner gigged the animals up to him.

"What do you think?" Banner asked.

"I think somebody they shoot. Hit horse instead of Indian. He run up here. I could try to follow his sign. But an Indian on foot is the hardest thing in the world to track."

"What else can we do?"

"Look at our horse. Crazy for water. Smell it somewhere near."

"I guess you're right," Banner said. "We'll find his sign at the sink."

"Not find his sign, even if he go there. But if they are follow him, their sign we will see."

They let the horses have their heads. The beasts led them unerringly down the twisting gorge. Soon they reached the western mouth of the cañon, cut into another skyscraping wall of rock, and rode out into rough benchlands of rusty sandstone. The mesa was not far behind them when Tilfego reined his horse in. His head was lifted and his splayed nostrils were fluttering.

"Now, listen," Banner said. "Not out here."

Tilfego asked angrily: "Do not these horse know when there is water near?" He thumped his chest. "Then Tilfego he know when there is chile peppers near."

"All right. So you know. We haven't got time to look for them."

"Tilfego he always has time. I look around, I sniff the air, I turn the corner. *¡Hola!* Chile peppers."

"Tilfego, this may mean a man's life."

The Mexican settled sullenly in the saddle. Pouting like a child, he grunted. "Very well. No chile peppers today."

They wound on through the broken benches, with the horses fighting to break into a run. Finally they reached the lip of a drop-off and looked down into the shallow valley ahead, where the lake lay. Banner had never been here before, but he recognized it as Red Lake, named for the ruddy sandstone surrounding it. As the horses broke into an eager scramble toward the water, Banner saw the sagging Studebaker wagon at the edge of the water. An old Navajo, wrapped to his chin in a blanket, sat on the seat. The horses had been unhitched and led to the lake. Standing beside them was the figure of a girl.

"What I tell you?" Tilfego thumped his chest.

"All right, you old horse thief," Banner said.

They could not hold their horses so they let them run right into the water and drink their fill, before trying to talk with the Indians. When Banner's animal had finished, he rode over to the wagon, stepped off, loosened the cinch. The girl had brought her team back to put them in harness again, and, after the formal greeting was over, Banner asked them where they were from. She said they were from Tonalea. Her grandfather had dreamed of bear during the summer, and was very sick. He could be cured by the ceremony of the Mountain Chant, and that was why they were traveling south. A Mountain Chant was to be held near Yellow Gap.

Banner asked her if she had seen any men during the journey, an Indian, or two white men. She said her grandfather had seen something last night. Banner spoke to the old man. The Indian started a quavering oration. The girl went around to hitch up the traces on the other side. It took Banner a long time to pin the old Indian down to the fact that the only people he had seen were the ones in his dreams.

Disgustedly Banner turned around. The girl was not in sight, and Tilfego's horse stood ground-hitched and empty-saddled a few feet off. Banner heard a giggle from behind the covered wagon. He walked around the tailgate. The Mexican was rubbing noses with the girl.

"Tilfego."

The man looked up in surprise, then grinned at Banner. "That is the way the Digger Indians do it, amigo."

"These people don't know anything. We've got to go on."

"A Zuñi tell me. He say he learn it from a Digger Indian."

"Tilfego."

Pouting, the Mexican walked back to his horse with Banner. They led the animals to the lake again, and, while Banner filled the canteens, Tilfego began hunting for sign, following the shore eastward. He finally stopped, hunkering down.

"Adakhai?" Banner asked.

Tilfego pointed to the prints. "These are two shod horses. See the left hind shoe on this one. Sharp edges. Nails nice and clear. Want to bet?"

"On what?"

"That she is a new shoe. That a week ago she was change for a shoe with three nails gone."

"You mean Arles?"

"I mean Arles."

They followed the tracks of the shod hoofs northward, through a broken country, a country of giant mesas, of tortured cañons. When it grew too dark to see, they ate supper. When the moon came up, they started again.

Nowhere could they find Adakhai's trail. But Arles and Big Red would not have gone farther north unless they were following the Indian. And if Tilfego could not find Adakhai's trail, the other two men certainly couldn't. There was but one logical answer. Arles and Big Red were following the boy himself, rather than his tracks. Adakhai was on foot, and they were ahorse, and though he had been able to keep out of their reach, he had not been able to get out of their sight.

This knowledge filled Banner with a sick foreboding. It could not last long, that way. It drove the two of them, when the moon rose, to follow the tracks of Arles and Big Red through the night, until the moon died and there was no more light. At dawn they were on the trail again, with Navajo Mountain in sight far ahead, lonely and serene in the desert solitude.

The sun rose. Weariness bore them down in the saddle. Still they pushed ahead.

Here Arles and Red had stopped, had held their horses in the cover of twisted juniper. Adakhai must have holed up across the cañon, in the rocks there, and kept the white men off with his gun, for here in the sand were two spent bullets. And then the Indian must have started running once more, for the two horses had bolted suddenly from their cover. And the white men had shot at Adakhai, for here were more spent slugs, of different caliber than the first.

And then Tilfego found the dark spots. He pulled his horse up, staring down, and finally got off. Banner could see the stains against the bone-white sand, like faded rust. Tilfego squatted there a long time, running his finger over it.

"Blood," he said. "Days old. He was hit bad to lose this much. He cannot go much farther. I think we hitch our animals here. Whatever we find, it will be close ahead."

XVI

Saving their animals, they took their Winchesters and worked their way slowly through the brush-choked cañon, finding more spots of blood in the sand. Then the cañon broadened, its walls receding into great broken benches. And high on those benches, on the west side, were the buildings. They were of adobe and rocks, ancient, crumbling, so close to the earth in hue and texture that they seemed to have grown from the land. In countless places their walls had fallen in, and the rubble supported the smashed ends of fallen beams, immense and smoke-blackened.

They were the same kind of aboriginal cliff houses Banner had seen at Chaco Cañon and Cañon de Chelly, deserted by their makers centuries before the white man had come to this country. The stains of dried blood led up through tile benches and into the buildings, while the prints of the two shod horses continued on down the cañon, disappearing around a turn. The picture was plain to Banner.

Adakhai had taken refuge in the cliff houses like a wounded animal, unable to run any longer, finding a hole to crawl into where they couldn't get at him. And they were down in the cañon somewhere, keeping the boy up in the ruins till he died of his wounds, or starved to death.

"Those *chingados*." Tilfego's voice had an ugly sound.

Then they did not speak for a space, gripped in the musty silence of the ancient place, a silence so intense it almost hurt. Banner studied the cañon with slitted eyes, trying to decide where Arles and Big Red were. There was not much cover on the sloping, broken side of the cañon opposite the cliff houses. They had probably taken up their watch in the ruins along the bottom. Above these ruins were two more levels of buildings, and high above the top level, beneath a deeply overhanging cliff, was one lone, circular structure.

"Looks like one of those kivas these people used to worship in," Banner said. "It's the most logical place for Adakhai to be. They couldn't reach him from above. That cliff hangs clear over it. And he's got command of the whole cañon below him."

Tilfego nodded. "The bloodstain they lead up that way."

Banner pointed to a series of steps built into one of the walls. "That stairway leads to the second level. If I can get up there, I'll be above Big Red and Arles."

"You forget the Indian. He is liable to shoot you just as quick as them. He can see you even on that second level."

"Not right back against the wall."

"You are guessing."

"All right, so I'm guessing. I'll take the chance. It's almost dark already."

Tilfego shook his head. "Henry is right. Always jumping in without a look . . ."

"So I'm always jumping in. If you don't want to . . ."

Tilfego slapped him on the back, grinning broadly. "Slack up, *hombre*. Who would like you any other way? Is what make you Lee Banner. Go ahead and jump. I am right on your back."

Banner could not help grinning, sheepishly. He studied the buildings a moment longer. He looked at Tilfego. The Mexican nodded. Banner lunged out into the open.

There was thirty feet of bone-white sand between the brush and the walls. He was halfway across when the shot crashed. It came from the kiva, high above. He saw sand spew up five feet to his right.

Before it had settled, another shot smashed. This came from the ruins at the bottom of the cañon, but it went even wider. Then the steady crash of Tilfego's Winchester blotted out all the other firing, and Banner had reached the wall.

Crouched there, he was cut off from Adakhai above, and from Arles and Big Red in the cañon. Ahead of him a flanking wall was molded into steps that led to the roof of a building. And from the roof was another stairway that led to the bench above. He would not be exposed to Adakhai till he reached that roof. But as soon as he left this wall, Arles and Big Red would have a shot at him. The knowledge brought clammy sweat to his palms.

And what if he did gain the bench? Maybe he was mistaken. Maybe there was no cover from Adakhai up there. Maybe . . . What the hell!

He sucked in air and jumped out and ran for the steps. There was one shot, from the direction of Arles and Red. It ate a piece of adobe from the wall behind Banner.

Then Tilfego's gun was going again, filling the cañon with an awesome din. Banner reached the stairway, was scrambling up the narrow steps and jumping onto the roof.

It was one of the few roofs left intact but it almost gave way beneath him and the instant he reached it Adakhai's gun smashed from the kiva above and kicked earth out of the roof a foot from Banner.

He ran on across the trembling roof and started up the second tier of stairs. He was out of sight of the white men now. Tilfego had shifted his fire to the kiva, and was keeping Adakhai down.

Then the top step crumbled beneath Banner.

He felt himself falling and threw himself in a wild dive for the lip of the bench just above. He reached it, sliding across it on his belly. At the same time, Tilfego must have run out of bullets. The echoes of the shots rolled down the cañon. The silence came while Banner was still sprawled on his belly on the edge of the bench. And then, like a thunderclap, Adakai's first shot.

He felt the smash of a blow against his foot and didn't even know what it meant because he was rolling, flopping over and over, with the gun crashing again and again from above, until he came up against the wall of the buildings on that second level. He lay there, cut off from Adakhai again, gasping.

He felt no pain in his foot and saw that the bullet had only knocked off the heel of his boot. He got to his hands and knees, and then stood up against the wall, chest swelling in its need for air.

The Indian had quit firing once more. He began to work his way swiftly down the front walls of these buildings toward the north end of the cañon. He passed doorways so low he would have had to stoop double to get through. His feet crunched through shards of pottery that had been broken hundreds of years before. Finally the long adobe wall angled out toward the edge of the bench and brought him abruptly into sight of the man below.

It was Big Red, crouched on a roof top, behind the parapet formed by an extension of the wall. He was not looking for Banner. He was watching Tilfego.

The Mexican must have figured Banner was in a position to cover him by now. He had run across that stretch of sand and was beginning to work his way through the lower level of the city.

Banner saw him duck across a courtyard, run into a long passage, pass through its end. It opened into a roofless room. Tilfego hesitated at the end of the passage, then darted into the open.

"Tilfego!"

Banner's warning shout was cut off by the blast of Big Red's gun. Banner saw Tilfego halt in surprise, look vainly for a man he couldn't see, then wheel and run for the doorway from which he had come. Banner saw Big Red pump his lever, and he swung his own gun around till the blot of Red's body covered his sights, and fired.

The man shouted in pain and flopped over. The weight of his great body hitting the flimsy roof made it collapse and he fell through with it. Tilfego gained the safety of the doorway and checked himself, wheeling back.

"Arles!" Red shouted. His voice sounded muffled. "They

broke my arm. Come and get me, damn you. They broke my arm."

There was scurrying movement below Banner that he could not see. He heard husky cursing. Tilfego took a chance, knowing Banner was covering him now, and scuttled once more from the doorway, crossing the courtyard. Banner moved on down the bench, keeping in the shelter of walls that would protect him from the Indian above. Finally the buildings ended, the bench ran around a point where the cañon turned, cutting Banner off from Adakhai's sight. Then the bench became a shelving trail that led down into the cañon.

Banner could hear them running down below, the rattle of rubble underfoot, the crunch of that broken pottery. There was a wild whinny from a horse, somewhere within the ruins. He stopped, trying to place it. The frantic beat of hoofs filled the cañon. He heard Tilfego calling him, and answered. The man appeared in a few moments, coming from a black doorway.

"You save my neck on that one." The Mexican grinned. "Must have hit one of them good. He left his rifle."

"They're through, then," Banner said. "They must know they can't do anything with one of them wounded." He moved close to the point, staring up at the corner of the high kiva.

"You cannot go up there," Tilfego said. "He shoot you as quick as them."

Banner moved closer to the point. "If he's still losing blood, another night might kill him," Banner said. "We've got to get him now, Tilfego." He raised his voice. "Adakhai? Tsi Tsosi. *Dance-has, shichi handsi.*"

There was a protracted silence, then the answer came, a feeble cry in the thin air. *"Chindash."*

"What you say?" Tilfego asked.

"I told him I was Yellow Hair, asked him how bad he was hurt."

"What he say?"

"Go to hell."

Neither of them spoke after that. The silence of the gorge was tomb-like. Night was settling velvety darkness into the cañon. Banner was trying to think of the right words.

Finally he began to talk, telling Adakhai that they only wanted to help him, that they had chased away the men who had done this to him, that he would probably die if he stayed up there much longer. Then he stopped and waited for the answer. For a long time he waited, in the velvet darkness, in the musty silence. There was no answer. Finally Tilfego snorted disgustedly.

"Is how much good the talking does with them."

"Then we'll have to go up there," Banner said. "The only way is right through the buildings."

"Do not be loco. They would have get him if it was possible."

"They didn't have to take a chance," Banner said. "All they wanted him to do was die, and they could wait for that. I want him to live. And I can't wait. We haven't got much time before moonrise. You cover me from below. Don't shoot to hit him. Just try to keep him down while I'm in the open spots."

He handed Tilfego his rifle. He turned to go back up the trail, around the point, against the front walls of the buildings on the second bench, which hid him from the kiva above. It was so dark he could see but a few feet in front of him.

He could not find any more outside stairways to the next level. But he found a notched beam in a room, and knew it was one of their ladders. He finally made out the hole in the ceiling, a vague square, only faintly lighter than the blackness of the roof. The beam was almost too heavy to lift. He finally got it up, leaning slantwise against one corner of the hole.

It was a precarious climb. The beam threatened to roll beneath him any moment. He finally reached the hole, lifted himself through onto the roof. His foot hit the tip of the notched beam. He heard a crunching sound; the corner of the hole gave way; the beam fell with an echoing crash.

Before the sound was dead, there was a wild yell above him. A gun made its smashing detonation. He heard the bullet strike the roof somewhere to his left. He was completely exposed here, with the wall of the kiva ten feet away, and no cover between. He had that moment of choice, with the impulse running savagely through him to drop back down through the hole.

Then Tilfego's gun began to clatter from down below. Banner heard bullets chopping into the wall of the kiva.

He lunged to his feet and headed in a wild run for the round building. Adakhai fired again, but Tilfego's gun was still going, and would give the Indian no time to aim. It was so dark that Banner only made a shadowy impression of a target anyway. And he reached the wall, throwing himself up against it, panting heavily.

Tilfego's firing ceased abruptly. The echoes rolled down the cañon, dying.

The Indian was right above him now, on the roof of the kiva, behind the parapet formed by the top of the wall. In order to shoot Banner, he would have to poke the rifle over the side. And Banner would see it against the sky.

It was the only way Banner could get him. The wall was about seven feet high, and he could reach the edge with his hands. But it would be suicide to try and get up onto it. He had to bring the boy down.

Deliberately he sucked in a deep breath, and exhaled in a noisy gust. He heard a faint scraping from above. His body stiffened.

Then he saw it, skylighted above him. Like a thin strip of darkness, barely darker than the heavens. He lunged up, knocking the rifle aside as it went off, grabbing it in both hands and throwing all his weight against it. He heard the wild shout.

Adakhai must have held on too long. He plummeted down on Banner. The lawyer had that last instant to throw himself from beneath the Indian. But the thought of those wounds flashed through his mind. He let Adakhai strike him, cushioning the fall.

It drove him to the ground, knocked the wind from him. He caught at the Indian's flailing arms. Adakhai rolled over and began fighting immediately. It caused them to flop over and over down the slope leading to the top of the buildings below. Banner saw one of the Indian's hands slap at his belt, saw the flash of a knife.

As they rolled out onto the roof, he was beneath. But he lunged up with both hands and caught the man's arm as the Indian raised it to strike. They were still rolling and Banner came on top, throwing all his weight against the arm.

It twisted Adakhai's wrist back on itself. He shouted in pain. The knife slipped from his hand. Banner tried to keep the Indian beneath him, but he held onto the arm too long. With a tigerish lunge, Adakhai flopped them over again, and Banner could not release his hold soon enough to stop himself from going under. Then Adakhai tore his wrist free and his hands found the white man's throat.

Banner's eyes swelled in their sockets with the pressure. His head was smashed against the roof. With the Indian straddling him, he fought to tear the sinewy hands free, battered wildly at the catgut muscle of the arms. But he came against the same savage strength he had met at Chin Lee. His head seemed to be bursting with the pressure. The night spun about him. In a last desperate effort, he twisted against the throttling hands and drove a blow for Adakhai's belly. He heard the explosive gasp torn from the Indian.

It jerked the hands off Banner's neck, unbalanced Adakhai in that moment. Banner heaved him over and sprawled on top. He let his whole weight sag down onto the Indian and lay there, gasping, drained. For a moment Adakhai was too spent to struggle.

Then, in a new burst of savagery, he tried to fight free. Banner caught his arm, twisted it around into a hammerlock.

"Do not struggle, you fool," he said in Navajo. "We come to help you. We made your pursuers leave by horseback. Can't you understand that?"

"Thish bizedeigi," Adakhai gasped, still fighting. "You are the spit of a snake. I swear it."

The Indian's struggles grew gradually weaker, however, and finally he stopped, lying slackly beneath Banner. His wounds had started to bleed again and Banner was soaked with blood.

"Tilfego!" Banner called. "I've got him. Bring a rope."

Tilfego had to get the rope off the horses, and he led them back to the ruins on the lower level. Then he brought a coiled dally up and they tied Adakhai hand and foot.

"Is helluva thing to do with wounded man," Tilfego said.

"It's the only way we can keep him quiet," Banner said.

Adakhai lay on his back, staring at them balefully. In the moonlight, he looked like a wild animal. His hair was matted and dirty; the bones stood out so whitely in his gaunt face that it looked like a skull. There were two wounds. The one in the shoulder was clean. But when Banner unwound the dirty strip of buckskin from the boy's thigh, he saw that the leg was badly swollen.

"He'll die if that blood poisoning isn't stopped," Banner said.

"You mean dig the bullet out?" Tilfego shook his head. "If you do that and he die, you have every Navajo on reservation after your scalp."

"He'll die if I don't do it. Maybe you'd rather not be involved."

"Don't be a *burro,*" Tilfego said. He pulled his Bowie. "You can use my knife."

They built a fire and heated the blade till it was red. The boy made no sound. His body lunged up just once when the blade entered. From then on he lay rigidly, his eyes open, staring at the sky. Banner finally got the bullet out, and sank back, as sodden with sweat as the Indian. Tilfego brought him the water he had boiled, and, while Banner cleaned the wound, he sent the man after as much prickly pear as he could find.

Tilfego came back with a hatful of prickly-pear paddles. Banner pounded it to a pulp between two rocks and mixed it with water till it was paste and put this poultice on the boy's wounds, binding them with his neckerchief and strips of blanket.

"Jahzini taught me that," he said. "The prickly pear will draw the pus out like nothing you ever saw." When he was finished, he went over and sank down on the parapet of the wall, utterly played out. "I feel like I've run a hundred miles."

"What you need is a quart of coffee," Tilfego said. "Let's get the boy down into one of these houses, and then I'll fix something to eat."

They carried the boy as gently as possible down one of the wall stairways and into a room that was still intact. Then Tilfego built a fire and fixed coffee and heated tortillas and made a stew from some of their smoked meat. The Indian would not eat, and Banner did not want to force anything on him in his weakened condition. They spent the night sleeping and watching in shifts. The Indian would still not eat, at breakfast.

"We've got to get him to a doctor," Banner told Tilfego. "You can get a wagon at Tonalea. Bring a couple of men with you and a stretcher, and we can carry him out to the wagon. It should take you three or four days."

"Anything you want me to leave?"

"All the coffee. That bottle of whiskey. Food for at least four days. And that pack of cards you always carry."

Tilfego frowned. "They will do you no good."

"We'll see," Banner said. "They don't call him The Gambler for nothing."

XVII

A little while after Tilfego was gone, the boy began to get delirious. He thrashed around and fought the ropes and Banner could not keep the blanket on him. Then he stopped sweating and began to shudder with chills, whimpering like a lost puppy. Banner threw all the blankets on him and finally he started sweating again. It lasted all day and by the time the boy finally dropped into a deep sleep, Banner was trembling with tension and fatigue.

He went to sleep himself and did not wake up till the middle of the night. The boy was still sleeping and Banner walked out onto the bench that overlooked the ruins below. It was a weird ghost city in the moonlight. He sat down against the wall.

He fell asleep sitting there and was awakened by the first daylight. It showed him nothing but empty ruins below, and he went back inside. The boy was conscious, lucid again, watching him from eyes black with hate.

Banner made some ash cakes from meal and water and fried them in the pan with bacon. Then he put the coffee on and let it boil till its fragrance mingled with the rich odor of crackling bacon. He saw Adakhai lick his lips.

He put the frying pan beside the Indian, poured a cup of coffee. *"Ko adi yih,"* he said. "You may eat."

The Navajo closed his eyes; his lips became a thin line of defiance. Banner sat, cross-legged, beside him and took one of the cakes out of the pan, putting a strip of bacon across it, eating. He finished and went out on the bench again, spending fifteen minutes in a search of the cañon.

When he went back in, the cakes and bacon still lay uneaten

in the pan beside the boy, cold and congealed in their own grease. Banner wrapped them in a piece of buckskin, scoured the pan with sand. Then he sat down against the wall and got out Tilfego's cards and began idly shuffling them. He saw the boy's glance run involuntarily to the pasteboards.

"I'm pretty good at coon-can," Banner said. "Never been beat in Mexican Hat." No answer. He began to play solitaire. "Maybe poker's your game. I bet I could beat you. In the past I played with Jahzini. You would like him. It is a wonderful thing when a Navajo will take in a *belinkana* and treat him as his own son."

"You lie!" It was torn from the boy. His face was contorted. "No Navajo would take in a white man!"

"Would I know the story of the Emergence, if I had not lived with your people?" Banner asked. "I remember it well. Jahzini was a wonderful storyteller. It is told that there were four worlds, one above the other. There was a great flood in the underworld. People were driven up by the waters. First Man and First Woman brought with them earth from the mountains of the world below. With this they made the sacred mountains of Navajo land. To the east they placed the sacred mountain Sisnajinni. They adorned it with white shell and fastened it to the earth with an arrow from the War God's bow . . ."

"They fastened it with a bolt of lightning . . ." Adakhai broke off suddenly, staring angrily at Banner.

Banner looked down at the cards so the boy could not see his eyes. He had not forgotten about the bolt of lightning.

"Jahzini told me a long time ago. The details are not all clear. So they attached Sisnajinni with a bolt of lightning. And to the west they placed the sacred mountain Doki-oslid. They adorned it with haliotis shell and fastened it to the earth with a moonbeam . . ."

"A sunbeam."

"Yes. A sunbeam. I remember now. And when they had finished putting down all the sacred mountains, the holy songs were sung. Jahzini used to sing the 'Mountain Song' to us. He was a wonderful singer of songs." Banner leaned back and closed his eyes and began to chant.

> Piki yo-ye, Daichl nantai,
> Piki yo-ye, Sa-a naral . . .
> Singing of the Mountain, Chief of All Mountains,
>   thither I go
> Singing of the Mountain, Living forever blessings
>   bestowing . . .

Singing all the verses, almost forgetting Adakhai, forgetting where he was, because it was bringing back those half-forgotten nights when he had sat with Jahzini in his hogan, when he had sat with the old man, listening to him sing these ancient chants, transported in space and time by the old Navajo's mystic incantations, as only a child could be transported, until he was one with the gods, coming up through the hollow reed from the underworld, seeing Haliotis Maiden and Twilight Youth, riding with the Sun God on his turquoise horse, or his silver horse.

When Banner was finally finished, there was no sound in the room. He did not open his eyes for a while. When he did, he found the Indian watching him with a strange expression.

"How you sing." It was barely a whisper from Adakhai. "I could almost believe you had our blood."

"I have." Banner held out his hand so the Navajo could see the scar on his palm. "Jahzini and I became brothers. It was after I saved him from a mountain lion. He cut my palm and his palm and we clasped hands."

The boy did not answer but continued to watch Banner. The balefulness did not return to his eyes. Banner went over and heated the coffee and cakes and bacon again and set them before the boy once more.

"Perhaps you would like to eat now. If you are too weak, I will help you."

"I am not weak."

"You will be if you don't eat."

Adakhai looked at the coffee. At last he rolled on his side and picked up the cup. He spilled some, lifting it to his lips. But Banner knew the boy's pride, and made no move to help.

The effort of eating left the boy weak and listless. Banner changed the poultices and found that some of the infection had been drawn out.

In the afternoon, the boy went to sleep. Banner went out onto the bench to watch. With dusk falling, he went back inside. The boy was awake.

"You think those others are still about?" he asked.

"No."

"Why did they want to kill me?"

"One of them is the man who murdered Wallace Wright. He thinks you saw him kill Wright. If you told, he would hang for it."

"And you saved my life."

"I want you to tell if you saw the murder. It will save Jahzini's life."

"You are helping Jahzini because you are his friend. But you are not my friend."

"Only in your own heart am I not your friend," Banner said. "My heart has no hatred."

The boy turned restlessly to one side. "White men killed my father. I vowed I would not forget that."

"If an Indian killed your father, would you hate all Indians?"

Something that was almost surprise shone in Adakhai's eyes. Then he veiled it. Banner built a fire for supper, letting the Indian think it over. When they were eating, he asked Adakhai how Big Red and Arles had known where to find him.

"Some Navajos from Chin Lee went down to the trading post on horses," Adakhai said. "They must have passed through Hackett's cattle camp and made mention that I had just left by horseback for Navajo Mountain."

Banner poured the coffee. "I guess Arles knew the country well enough to figure you'd come up here by way of Dot Klish."

Adakhai nodded. "They waited for me at Dot Klish. They shot at me there and missed me. From Dot Klish there is no trail on north. A man may go any way he wishes."

"That is why your own people did not know where to look for you."

"I suppose so. I ran for Zuñi Cañon. But the two *belinkanas* got on the rim above me there and shot again. They hit my horse. I tried to lose them by hiding my tracks after that. But they kept me always in sight. With my gun I prevented them from getting too close. Then one of them hit me in the cañon back there. I had been up here many days when you came. I would have been dead by now."

Banner scoured the pan after they had eaten, and then sat down to begin idly shuffling the cards again. He nodded at the knife they had taken from the boy. "That is a beautiful weapon."

"Those are cannel coal beads in the hilt," Adakhai said. "I won it from a chief."

"I have five dollars," Banner said, taking the silver from his pocket. He saw the Indian's eyes begin to glow. It was much more than the worth of the knife. Then the Indian lay back, shaking his head. Banner smiled thinly. "When I go to Mexican Hat, I will say that The Gambler has been misnamed," he said. "From now on they will know him as Old Squaw."

"*Tchindi!*" With an explosive oath, the Indian lurched up on an elbow, staring hotly at Banner.

"I have two Mexican dollars, also," Banner said, adding them to the others.

The Indian stared at the little stack, winking in the gloom. Banner picked up the knife and tossed it to him. The Indian stared down at it, the temptation working through his face.

"Coon-can?" Banner asked.

The Indian dropped off his elbow, but remained on his side, breathing shallowly. Finally he said: "Poker."

Banner shuffled again, let the Indian cut, then dealt. Adakhai studied his cards, then pushed the knife out between them. Banner had a pair of tens. He put $2 beside the knife.

"Will that call you?"

"Yes. I'll have two cards."

Banner dealt the Indian a pair, drew three himself. He didn't get another ten. Adakhai took off his bow guard and added it to the pot. Banner put another dollar in.

"Call you."

Adakhai showed two pairs, kings high. Banner put down his two tens. Without changing expression, the Indian pulled the knife, the bow guard, the $3 back to him. Banner passed the deck over. As the Indian dealt, Banner found his eyes going to the man's *bizha,* which hung from his belt by a thong. It was the personal fetish every Navajo carried. For a gambler it was a piece of turquoise, because Noholike, the gambling god, had always been made successful with it.

Turquoise alone was of great value to the Navajos for its deep religious significance. Banner had known men to trade a horse for a single turquoise. The fact that it represented a man's personal fetish made it doubly valuable. Banner felt sure that if he could win it, the boy would gladly pay any price for its return. Even to telling if he had seen Arles kill Wright.

"You opening?"

Banner glanced up to see the Indian watching him narrowly over the tops of his cards. Banner picked up his hand, saw a pair of queens, opened with a dollar. The game went on, lasting long into the night. When they finally quit, the Indian had won Banner's money, his $10 Stetson, and the silver buckle off his belt.

Adakhai was more cheerful the next morning. After breakfast his eyes kept going to the cards, and, when Banner suggested playing another game, the Indian accepted eagerly.

It went back and forth, as it had the night before. Banner won his money and his hat back, lost the money again.

They ate lunch. After lunch they played again, and Banner lost his Winchester. The Indian's gambling fever was running high. He was dealing, when Banner got the hand.

It was three kings, an eight, and a four. The right draw would give him a full house. He found his eyes lifting to the Indian's *bizha* once more. He realized this might be the time.

"How much is my shirt worth to you?" he asked.

The Indian glanced at the stack of seven dollars. "A dollar."

"I'll open with it."

"Raise you a dollar."

"How much for my boots?"

"Four dollars."

"Then they'll raise you a dollar."

"I'll raise another dollar."

"How much are my pants worth?"

"A dollar."

"I'll call you with them," Banner said. "And I'll take one card."

He discarded a four. The Indian dealt to him, then dealt himself two cards. Banner picked up his card. It was an eight.

Sitting there, looking at his full house, he could feel the blood pounding at his temples. It was hard to keep his face expressionless. But he could not help thinking of the *bizha* again. He knew it was within his reach now.

"I'll open with my hat," he said.

"I have bet all the money. Will the rifle and my bow guard raise you?"

Banner nodded, studying the Indian's face. He could not believe the man would have gone along this far on a bluff. Adakhai had not been playing that way. Then the Indian held a good hand. Was it good enough to carry him all the way to the *bizha*?

"My clothes are all in the pot," Banner said. "Will my revolver raise you?"

"I'll take it. Will the silver buckle off your belt and my bracelet raise you?"

Banner's mouth felt dry. He knew this was the moment. He might well be gambling for Jahzini's life.

"All I have left is my horse and saddle," he said. "I'll raise you with both of them."

He saw the light go out of Adakhai's eyes. "I thought you were bluffing, and would not risk them," he said in a low voice. "I have nothing with which to call your bet."

"You have your *bizha*."

Banner saw surprise widen Adakhai's eyes. Then the Navajo masked it, the sullen woodenness returning to his face. "I would not bet my *bizha* against the wealth of three men. I dreamed that Noholike came to me and said that if I would go to Bead Spring, I would find the *bizha* for which I would be named. I found this turquoise. From that day on my name was changed from Slim Man to The Gambler, and I have been invincible."

"You mean you are going to let me take this whole pot without a fight?" Banner asked.

The Indian shook his head without answering.

Banner said disgustedly: "What power can your *bizha* have if you fear to wager it? If you let me have the pot now, how will you ever be invincible again? How can they call you The

Gambler when you are afraid to gamble?"

The Indian came up onto his elbow, eyes smoldering. The lawyer waved his hand at the pot.

"With the horse and saddle, it must be worth three hundred dollars. What will your people think when they hear you did not have the courage to gamble for such wealth? They will laugh behind your back. They will change your name to Man Without Heart."

Banner could see the combination of pride and gambling fever gnawing at the Indian. His mouth began to work. His face was flushed. At last it was too much for him. He unfastened the turquoise. Holding it in his palm, he looked down at it.

For that instant, the anger, the bitterness, the pride were washed from his face. His eyes grew dark with all the primitive beliefs and superstitions and fears bound up in the *bizha*. It did something to Banner. He had realized objectively how much the fetish meant to Adakhai. Now he felt it emotionally.

It was as if the fetish was his own. It was as if the warp and woof of his life had been bound up with that bit of turquoise for as long as he could remember. The relationship had no comparison in the white man's world, except, perhaps, his belief in God. The immense value of the *bizha*, the crushing possibility of its loss, was borne against Banner with all its overwhelming ramifications.

He felt like a fool. Dodge was right. Always going off half-cocked. He had made the same mistake at Chin Lee. Knowing enough about the Indian's reactions to use them against him, but not taking the time, not going deeply enough into them to see what the end result would mean to the Indian. Could he really use the *bizha* to force the truth about Yellow Gap from Adakhai? Or would he gain nothing but the Indian's undying enmity by winning it? He searched Adakhai's face for the answer. And as the Navajo put the turquoise down, and raised his eyes, with the intense bitterness returning to his face, Banner had his answer.

He knew he had only one chance left. The Indian had called his bet. It was Banner's obligation to show the first cards. His only hope was that the immense strain of the moment would blind Adakhai to custom.

"What have you got?" Banner asked.

The Indian hesitated. Then he turned his hand over. All he had was two pairs.

Banner put his full house on the floor, face down. "You win," he said. "Your *bizha* is truly invincible."

The Indian stared blankly at Banner for an instant. Then, with a whoop, he flopped over, clawing for the turquoise. Holding it tightly in his fist, he gazed at the heap of loot. Then he laughed. Like a child he laughed, all the dour impassivity gone from his face. Too elated to question Banner's hand, he lay back, weakened by his effort, still laughing.

"You are lucky you did not wager that beautiful yellow hair. I would have had to scalp you."

Banner smiled, picking up his cards and shuffling them into the deck. "It is as I told Tilfego. They do not call you The Gambler for nothing."

XVIII

Tilfego came back with the wagon the third day. Banner saw them moving down among the ruins and waited for them on the bench. Tilfego and a pair of Indians climbed up the precarious tier of steps molded into the wall and gained the bench. The Mexican introduced the Navajos as Hosteen Red Shirt, a half-breed trader from Tonalea, and Running Man, Adakhai's cousin. They all stooped through the low door and crowded into the room. Tilfego stared blankly at the heap of loot beside

Adakhai. The Indian grinned broadly, thumping Banner's saddle.

"*Kad xozozo nza yadolel . . .*"

"What he say?" asked Tilfego as the Indian rattled on.

"He says I'll continue to live in peace as long as I gamble like that." Banner grinned. "He says I must come up to his hogan at Chin Lee and we will have another game. He says he won my horse and my saddle and all my clothes. He says you will have to loan me some money when we reach Tuba, unless you want me to walk home naked."

Tilfego threw his head back and let it shake the rafters. The Indians were laughing, too. Adakhai lay back on his pallet and laughed till he was too weak to go on.

"I never think I see this," Tilfego said. "Like you been pardners all your life. How did you make it, Lee?"

"There's some willow saplings for stretcher poles down the cañon," Banner said. "I'll tell you while we chop them down."

As they stooped out through the door, Tilfego turned to Banner. "If he feel like this toward you, now . . ."

Banner shook his head darkly. "I haven't gotten him to tell me whether he was at Yellow Gap yet."

Tilfego clapped Banner on the back. "Never mind. You cannot expect the miracle overnight."

Tilfego and Banner rode as far as Tuba with the wagon, where there was a doctor. Tilfego had to loan Banner all his Army money to get a ratty Navajo pony and some old clothes and boots. They impressed upon the Indians the necessity of keeping Adakhai hidden from Hackett till he was well. The Indians assured them Adakhai would be kept safe, and they took their leave.

It was two days back to Mexican Hat. They arrived late in the evening. Tilfego wanted to see Celestina, so Banner left him at

Blackstrap Kelly's and went on down to the two-room adobe on the Street of the Beggars. He was thinking about bed when the knock came at the door.

It was Ramirez, the husband of Dodge's cook, a furtive little man with an immense black mustache. He told Banner he had seen Tilfego at the saloon and had known they were back. He said he had word that Dodge wanted to see Banner as soon as Banner returned.

Banner thanked the man, and stood motionless in the doorway after he had left, a warmth flooding him. He knew Dodge's pride. The old man wouldn't send for him unless he was willing to admit he had been wrong. Suddenly Banner shut the door behind him, walking swiftly down to Aztec.

A deep nostalgia filled him with his first sight of the house in which he had spent so many years. The windows made yellow slots against the dark adobe; the recess of the front door lay in black shadow. There was no answer to his knock.

He tried the door. It was not locked, and he opened it, pushing it ajar, stepping into the penetrating reek of Dodge's cigars. But the room seemed empty. He let his hand slide off the doorknob and took another step inside, calling: "Henry . . . ?"

There was a faint sound from behind him. He started to wheel. The man came from behind the door and struck him on the back of his head before he was all the way around.

It drove him to his hands and knees. For a moment he swam in the shock of it, barely able to support himself. His arms were grabbed. He was dragged heavily over to the high-backed chair by the fireplace and lifted into it and his arms were twisted around his back and tied. Vision was returning. Arles stood by the front door. He had shut it again. The six-shooter was still in his hand.

Hackett towered before Banner, black-haired, black-eyed. Joe Garry stood by the ivory table, his hands tucked like horny claws into his sagging shell belt.

Banner leaned his head sickly against the high back of the chair. "Where's Henry? What've you done with Henry?"

"Don't worry about the old man," Hackett told him. "He's probably on the train by now. Some will to make out in Flagstaff. Ramirez didn't know about it. When I told him Dodge wanted to see you, Ramirez thought it was straight from the horse's mouth."

Banner squinted his eyes against the throbbing pain of his head, glance shuttling to Arles and Garry. "Not using Big Red any more?" he asked thinly.

"Never mind."

"Maybe he got hurt or something."

"I said never mind!" It came sharply from Hackett. "So you think Adakhai saw the murder."

"Do *you*?"

A little flutter of muscle ran across the gaunt angle of Hackett's jaw. "Where is he?"

"I don't know."

Arles moved from the door, still holding his gun. "I could make him talk," he said.

"Now, listen, Lee," Hackett said. "We understand each other. You know why I want Adakhai."

"To kill him?"

"We'll just get him out of the country till the trial's over."

"Then they'll hang Jahzini. One of them dies either way."

"I'll see that Jahzini isn't hanged."

"Maybe you'll let him escape again so you can put Big Red and Arles in the posse to kill him."

"Damn you, Lee"—Hackett's voice had risen close to a shout—"I didn't have anything to do with that."

"I thought we understood each other."

Hackett was bent toward Banner. His right hand was fisted.

184

Arles was watching with an avid light in his eyes. Finally Hackett slapped his hand savagely against his leg.

"All right. We do understand each other. I'm in this too deep to back out now, Lee. I won't stop at anything to make you talk."

"I think you would have tried to get me killed a long time before this, if you thought you could get away with it," Banner said. "But you'd lose the whole game then, Clay. I've raised too touch stink. It would point the finger right at you to get rid of me that way."

"Nobody talked about killing, Lee," Hackett said.

He walked to the ivory-topped table. He opened the cigar box and took out one of the long black smokes. He bit off its end. Joe Garry lit it for him. Then Hackett came back to Banner, rolling the cigar to make it draw.

"Lee, you've pushed me against the wall and you'll wish to hell you'd kept yourself out of it before I'm through."

"I think Wallace Wright had you against the wall a long time before this."

"You know he did. If they move me south of the railroad again, I'm through."

"He was only trying to protect the Indians," Banner said. "If you'd let them alone, you would have been all right."

"You know that damn' railroad land isn't anything. There isn't enough water on it to keep half my stock alive. The sheep have cut all the grass off." Hackett gestured savagely with the cigar. "It was just a damn' sop they threw us hoping we'd knuckle under. But the association had a bill up to open that southern reservation for homesteading. In six months they would have given our land back to us."

"*Your* land back to you?"

Hackett wheeled on him. "Damn' right! Who opened this territory? You wouldn't have a railroad if it wasn't for cattle. You wouldn't even have any town. We build a country for you and you try to take it away from beneath us . . ."

"Are you trying to convince me, or yourself?"

Hackett stared dourly at Banner. "All right. You just poked a sore and the pus had to come out. I shouldn't have wasted the time on you." He began to draw on the cigar till its end glowed cherry-red. "You know you can't take this, Lee. I guess you've got as much guts as the next man, but you can't stand up under something like this. You'd better tell me now while you've still got your face."

Banner stared at the glowing tip of the cigar. A fear welled up in him—he could not deny it—a fear of pain that came from the animal depths of him. He felt his fingers curling up behind the chair.

"I don't know where Adakhai is," he said.

Hackett drew a breath, a thin little breath. Garry wiped one hand across the dirty belly of his shirt. Arles's boots made a restless scrape against the floor.

"In his eye," he said. "Put it in his eye."

Hackett was looking into Banner's eyes. His glance slowly dropped to Banner's cheek. "Hold his head."

Garry stepped to one side of Banner. The lawyer tried to jerk aside, tried to overturn the chair. Arles jumped forward and stopped that. Garry caught Banner's long yellow hair, jerking his head against the back of the chair. He cupped his other hand under Banner's chin, thumb and forefinger digging deep.

"One more chance, Lee."

"I don't know."

Hackett started to bring the cigar down to Banner's face. Then there was a sound from the rear, the creak of a door, the heavy tattoo of boots on the hard-packed earth of the floor.

"Conchita?" Dodge called. "Why'd you leave all the lights on in front? I thought you were going home early. I got to talking with Prentice and missed that damned train . . ."

Hackett, Arles, Garry, all three of them wheeled toward the back door as Dodge appeared there. The old lawyer halted.

"What the hell?" he said. Then he began to come across the room in a stiff, stamping walk. "Hackett, what in the Johnny hell are you doing?"

Arles raised his gun. Henry Dodge took a last step, staring at it, then stopped. He lifted his gaze from the weapon to Hackett's face. Then he looked at Banner, holding out his hand helplessly.

"Lee . . ."

"Get him out of here," Hackett said. Arles put his gun in his holster to step toward Dodge and grab him, and Garry followed. Dodge swung away from them, fighting wildly. One of his flailing arms caught Arles across the face, knocking him away. Then he wheeled the other way, tearing free of Garry's hands, and lunged at Hackett, his old man's anger flushing his jowls. Hackett tried to jump back. But Dodge caught his arm, clawing at the cigar.

"You can't do this, Clay!" he shouted. "Not in my . . . !"

Hackett's blow cut him off, striking the side of his neck and knocking him heavily to his knees. Again Hackett tried to back off and free himself. But Dodge's face was against his stomach, and his clawing hands caught Hackett's belt. Hackett kicked him in the belly.

Banner shouted and lunged up against his bindings. The kick doubled the old man over with a sick cough, and knocked him violently backward. He crashed into the marble-topped table, upsetting it. The Sandwich lamp smashed against the floor, and the smell of raw camphene flooded the room.

In the sudden darkness, Banner writhed savagely to free his hands. He could hear Dodge making sick, retching sounds.

"There's another lamp somewhere by the oven," Hackett

187

said. "Light it up."

There was the stumbling sound of boots, a curse. Finally light blossomed at the other end of the room, revealing Joe Garry bent over the lamp on the *banco*. Banner could feel his wrists bleeding, but he was not free. The overturned table had kept Dodge from being thrown completely flat, and he sat in the wreckage, leaning heavily against it.

"You damn' old fool," Hackett said. "If you'd gone to Flagstaff, this wouldn't've happened."

"Hackett"—Dodge almost gagged on the words—"what is it, what is it?"

"I guess you'll find out now," Hackett said. "I'm through wasting time."

He put the cigar in his mouth, drawing on it till the tip began to glow again. Dodge cried out and tried to rise. But the effort cost the old man too much. With a low moan of pain he fell back against the table and slid down till he lay flat, one arm thrown across the broken drawer that had fallen out. Hackett took out his cigar and held it in front of Banner's face.

"Tell me where he is, Lee."

Banner stared fixedly at the glowing point of light. The sweat slid down his face. Arles and Garry watched tensely.

"All right, Lee," Hackett said.

"If you do that to my boy, Hackett, I'll shoot your belly out."

It came from Henry Dodge. It checked Hackett. Slowly he turned to look at Dodge. The old man still lay on his side. But in his hand was the old Dragoon Colt he had always kept in the drawer.

"Back away," he said. "Drop that cigar and back away."

Hackett's face was dead white. His black eyes were pinpoints of rage. As he started to take a step backward, Aries made a vicious motion to Dodge's right. Dodge turned and fired.

The shot was deafening. The bullet plucked Arles's tall hat

off and carried it halfway to the wall before it dropped. Arles stood transfixed, his hand gripped around an undrawn gun.

"Next time it'll be your head," Dodge said.

Arles removed his hand from his gun. Hackett dropped the cigar. Dodge grasped the edge of the overturned table and pulled himself to a sitting position. Banner saw that the heavy gun trembled faintly in his hand.

He picked up a shard of glass from the broken lamp and crawled over behind Banner, still aiming the gun at the men, and began to saw at the ropes. When they dropped off, Banner stood up, rubbing at his wrists. He took the Colt from Dodge's hand. The old lawyer got to his feet with difficulty, worked his way around the chair, and lowered himself into it.

"Shall we put them away?" he said. "We've got a dozen counts. Trespassing. Assault and battery."

"Is that what we want them for?" Banner asked.

Dodge looked up at him. "No. I guess it isn't."

"You'd better go, then," Banner said.

The intense rage was dying in Hackett's face. Without speaking, he walked to the door. He waited till Arles and Garry went out past him. He was looking at Dodge all the time. There was a thin venom in his voice when he spoke. "They would have called you 'Judge'," he said.

"The hell with that," Dodge said. "All I want is my boy back. Touch him again and I'll kill you myself, Clay."

Hackett stared at them a moment longer, then wheeled and walked out.

Banner went to the door, watching the three men walk up Aztec toward Courthouse Square, where they must have left their horses. Finally he turned to Dodge.

"Want me to get the doctor?"

Dodge shook his head. "Nothing broken. I just can't take it like I used to. Maybe a drink."

Banner stuck the gun in his belt and went over to the spindled Mexican cupboard, pouring two glasses of Dodge's wine. The old man took his glass, raised it, holding Banner's eyes.

"Here's to it, son. It should have been a long time ago." Dodge drank, lowered the glass with a husky exhalation of pleasure. "What did they want, Lee?" he asked.

"They wanted to know where Adakhai was. They think his testimony would convict Arles."

"Then that Indian really did see the murder?"

Banner shook his head, frowning. "I don't know yet. There are still two other possibilities. I don't know whether Hackett is aware of them or not. Kitteridge and Mills are still on my list."

Dodge went over to his leather armchair, dropping into it. Grimacing, he propped one shoe on his knee, began untying it. Banner saw the pain the effort caused him and went over and knelt before the old man, finishing with the laces, pulling the shoe off. Dodge leaned back with a pleased sigh.

"Thanks," he said. "Ain't had anybody to do that in a long while." There was a brooding expression in Dodge's eyes. "You were right, weren't you?" he said. "I'm getting old. And when a man gets old, he gets afraid. He's worked so hard. Wanted something so bad. He sees it just within his grasp. Knows it's his last chance . . ."

"Please, Henry." Banner pulled off the other shoe. "You don't have to. I understand how it was."

"Yes, I have to," the old man said. "I'm glad you wanted to be a lawyer so bad, Lee. You can appreciate how I felt about that judgeship. All my life I'd wanted that spot on the bench. I guess I'd begun compromising for it a long time ago. Letting Hackett become one of my biggest backers was a compromise. He was starting to trade pretty sharp, even then. I told myself it was politics." He shook his leonine head. "But I just couldn't believe he'd kill."

"A man will do a lot of things when he's desperate," Banner said. "Do you think he'll try to get Arles out of the country?"

"Wouldn't do him any good, if you've got an eyewitness." He shook his head. "It's a crazy stalemate when a murderer can walk right in your house and you can't do a thing to him. I guess they're just as blocked, though. Hackett can't move till he's sure if we have the eyewitness. What can I do, Lee?"

Banner was still on his knees, and his face raised to Dodge. Slowly a grin spread his lips, and he clutched the old man's knee. "I know we can lick 'em now," he said. "Wasn't the district attorney at Denver an old schoolmate of yours?"

"D.H. Pine. We almost got expelled for writing a parody on Blackstone."

"You can help then, Henry," Banner said. He went on to tell him how Kitteridge was really Victor Morrow, of the Morrow-Ware swindle. He told how Julia had known Kitteridge up there and was convinced of his innocence. "I guess you'll remember, Shefford was the bookkeeper. He must have planned to get off clean with Ware, but something slipped up. Julia thinks he made two sets of books, though. The real ones, which never appeared, and the falsified ones, which proved Morrow guilty."

"Why would the real ones never turn up?"

"Shefford planned to use them against Ware, in case Ware didn't come through with his share of the money."

The old man nodded. "Been done before. Shefford's term's almost up now. If Julia's right, he'll be waiting to get out and force Ware to come across."

"Do you think there's an angle?"

"If it's set up the way Julia claims, here's what I think. Pine, being a friend, I followed that case closely. Ware got off clean, but the papers had a lot about what a high liver he was, a big spender. It's been close to five years now. I'd bet a box of my best cigars Ware hasn't got any of that money left. If we could prove to Shefford that Ware was broke, Shefford wouldn't have any reason for holding those books out. He'd surely be willing to turn state's evidence to get the rest of his sentence knocked off."

"Julia said Ware and his wife were separated. She was living in Kansas somewhere."

"I did a chore for the Pinkerton division manager in Kansas once. He'd find her for me if she was there."

"And she'd certainly know if Ware had spent that money. Do you think Shefford would believe her?"

"She might even have proof. And if she doesn't, I'll get it."

Banner walked moodily to the fireplace. "We're talking as if we had all the facts. The whole thing's supposition. How do we know Julia's right? Maybe Kitteridge is guilty. Maybe I'm just going off half-cocked like I always did, Henry. I don't want to suck you into something foolish again . . ."

"Don't talk nonsense." Dodge got up out of the chair and padded over behind him, clapping him on the shoulder. "It takes somebody like you to get anything done. If Kitteridge is your witness, we'll find out. We'll damned well find out!"

XIX

Now it was August, with the thunderclouds banked in threatening tiers along the horizon, spilling their rain on the land almost daily, tainting the mornings with the pungent scent of dampened greasewood. Dodge had gotten leave of absence from Prentice to go north, since Jahzini's trial was not set for several weeks yet, and Banner was left to handle the myriad details of the old man's private practice.

There were wills to change, a theft case before a justice of the peace, a brief to draw up on an inheritance contract. Banner kept the office open in the morning to receive those of Dodge's clients who still had enough trust in the old man to come. But through it all, Banner did not forget his primary allegiance to Jahzini. And the second day after Dodge's departure, he rode out to the homestead of Jeremiah Mills.

When he reached the cut-off to Yellow Gap and gained the higher ground, he saw the two riders on the Ganado Road behind him. Wariness squinting his eyes, he rode into the cover of twisted juniper and watched. As they approached the fork in the road, he saw the Broken Bit brand on the near horse. It was Joe Garry in the saddle. The man with him was Breed.

They passed the cut-off and rode on down the Ganado Road in the direction of Hackett's outfit. Only when they were out of sight did Banner turn on north.

Mills's land was on Puffwillow Creek, five miles from the Gap. It was criss-crossed with the crumbled remains of canals built by the ancient peoples who had been here before the Indians, and Mills had dug out sections of these ditches leading from the creek to his alfalfa acreage. Banner followed the winding wagon road past canals filled to the brim with the recent rains till he found the farmer on high ground near the creek, jamming a crude head gate back into place in his brush-and-timber dam. The man straightened with sight of Banner.

" 'Afternoon, Mills," Banner said.

The man looked up at Banner, eyes squinted against the sun. Then he turned to walk heavily down the bank of the canal toward his house. Banner gigged his horse after the man, catching up with him.

"Looks like this rain is going to pull your crop through."

For a space, Banner thought the man would not answer this either. But he was too much a farmer to remain silent on that subject. He spat into the canal.

"Thought I'd make me some money on it this year, but I can't find a cattleman who needs it."

"Not when they can graze on Indian pastures free."

Mills turned to glare at Banner. "If you come up here to make trouble, you might as well ride on."

"I just thought I'd tell you that I saw Kitteridge," Banner said. "He says he gave you that bay before the murder."

This stopped the man. He wheeled to Banner, anger swelling his chest, lifting his whole body for a moment. Then he clamped his lips together, wheeled, and walked on toward his house. Banner saw that his wife had come to the door. Clara Mills was as stooped, as gaunt as her husband.

"Baby's cryin' again, Jeremiah," she said, tugging the cloth wrapper listlessly around her shoulders. "Can't you git the doctor?"

"What with?" Mills said irritably.

"He won't take no more alfalfa for pay?"

"I'll get the doctor," Banner said, "if you'll tell me what you saw at Yellow Gap that day."

At the door, Mills wheeled back again. Before he could speak, Joe Garry stepped around the corner of the house. He had a six-shooter in his hand.

"Just sit still, Banner," he said. "Breed's behind you with a gun."

Banner turned involuntarily to see the half-breed walking from the cover of ragged willows that topped the high creek-bank. He held an old fifteen-shot Henry across one hip.

Garry stopped in front of Mills. "Where's the Indian?" he asked. "We been waiting for this. Where's Adakhai?"

Mills stared blankly at him. "What are you talkin' about?"

"You know. That's what Banner's here for. Get aside and let us through. We'll find him ourselves."

"Don't let 'em in, Jeremiah," Clara said from behind her husband. "They ain't got no right."

Breed walked up by the wall of the house, still holding his rifle pointed at Banner. "Maybe you like some cattle stampeded

194

through the alfalfa," he said.

A squinted look drew Mills's eyes almost closed. "You wouldn't do that. I couldn't stay here without that crop."

"Then let us in, damn you," Garry said.

Mills turned aside slowly, staring at Garry. Breed was next to the door now, with the rifle. Garry passed between him and Mills, to go in. But Clara barred the way, her eyes glowing with anger.

"You can't go in there. My baby's sick . . ."

With a curse, Garry whipped his gun across her face. She reeled back with a sick gasp of pain.

"Garry!"

It came from Mills like the roar of some animal in pain. The man tried to wheel back and meet it, but Mills struck him with an echoing crack of bone on bone. It smashed the short man back into Breed, as Breed tried to swing his rifle around. Before either man could recover, Mills lunged into them, hitting Garry again, an awesome blow that knocked him free of Breed and carried him up against the house so hard the whole building shuddered.

It had given Banner time to pull his gun. As Breed staggered free, swinging his rifle up, Banner called his name. The man checked his whole motion, knowing what it meant, becoming rigid as a statue, with his rifle still pointed at the ground.

Mills had jumped after Garry, catching him against the wall before he could fall, hitting him again. It doubled Garry over. Clara staggered from the door, one hand to her bleeding face, and caught her husband's arm before he could strike again.

"Jeremiah," she begged, putting her whole weight on him, "you'll kill him . . . you'll kill him."

For a space of time Banner couldn't measure, Mills held Joe Garry against the wall, slack as a sack of wheat. The farmer was breathing thickly. At last he released Garry, and stepped back.

The man slid down the wall to a sitting position, chin sunk on his chest, face viscid with blood. Mills stared stupidly at him, then at his wife. She was looking up into his face, with a shining look in her eyes.

The kids had clustered in the doorway now, elfin little figures in their tattered clothes. There was a barefoot girl with tousled hair the color of corn, maybe three years old, and a boy about her same age, round-eyed, open-mouthed. There was an older boy, maybe ten, the first one to gain the courage to move out of the door, his eyes wide and awe-struck.

"Gosh, Pa," he whispered.

Mills looked around at him. The blank rage was gone from the farmer's eyes now. A realization of what he had done deepened the seams around his mouth. His shoulders began to sink.

"Put the rifle down, Breed," Banner said.

The hatchet-faced man dropped the Henry on the ground. Garry lifted his head, groaning with pain. He tried to straighten, wiped feebly at the blood and dirt on his face. Banner jerked his gun at Breed, and the man went over to help Garry get up.

Once on his feet, Garry sagged heavily against the wall. At last, he moved away from the wall, swaying heavily. His voice shook when he spoke to Mills.

"You won't be on this land tomorrow," he said.

Mills held out his hand, started to speak, but Garry turned away. He looked savagely at Banner, then stumbled past him, toward the willows, where they had probably left their horses. Breed glanced at his rifle on the ground.

"Leave it there," Banner said. Venom filled the man's face, but he followed Garry. Mills watched them go, then turned dead eyes to his wife. "You better start packing."

She caught his arm. "No, Jeremiah . . ."

"You know what Hackett will do now. They'll trample the

alfalfa. They'll burn us out. If we're here, they'll just as soon shoot us as not."

All the life seemed drained from his face as he shambled into the house. The kids scurried from his path, round-eyed and frightened. Soundless tears formed silvery tracks in Clara's worn face.

"Did you see him when he hit Garry?" she asked.

"I saw him," Banner said gently.

"That's what he used to be," she said.

"If it isn't completely dead in him, maybe we could give it back to him," Banner said. "Was Jeremiah really here all that day of the murder?"

She locked her hands together and looked down at them.

"It would save Jahzini's life, wouldn't it?"

"Yes."

Her eyes squinted shut; she shook her bowed head. "No. Jeremiah wasn't here all day. He went into town."

"Did he ride the bay he got from Kitteridge?"

"I can't remember that." She looked up, a plea in her face. "I really can't . . ."

"I believe you," he said. He frowned at her a moment. "What if we put Hackett in such a position that he couldn't touch you?" he asked. "Does your husband still have enough guts left to be worth saving?"

She reached up and caught the lapels of his coat, voice fierce. "Of course he has. You saw what he could do . . ."

He gently removed her hands from his lapels, and went around her into the house. Mills had thrown the tattered blankets off a bed and was rolling up the straw tick.

"Mills," Banner said, "in my saddlebags is a statement signed by Caleb Elder. It proves beyond doubt that Hackett is using reservation land for his cattle. If I turn this statement over to the railroad, they'll revoke Hackett's lease. It would finish him north of the tracks."

"Then why don't you do it?"

"Because that still wouldn't pin the murder on Arles. What we can do is hold Elder's statement over Hackett's head. He won't dare touch you."

"Don't try to swindle me into another deal," Mills said bitterly. "I ain't gettin' my kids burned out again." He glanced bitterly at the children. "There used to be five of 'em."

Clara had come in to stand beside the baby's crib. "It was the Johnson County War. The cattlemen were driving out the nesters. Jimmie got caught under a rafter when it burned through and fell. Jeremiah tried to save him. He couldn't."

Banner moistened his lips, then forced himself to go on. "That won't happen again. I know Hackett and know what he wants up here. He couldn't stand to lose those railroad leases. They're his foothold north of the tracks. If you quit now, you'll be running all the rest of your life."

"He's right, Jeremiah." Clara spoke in a pinched voice. "Where will we go? What will we do? We haven't got a cent."

The man shook his bowed head stubbornly. "No . . . no . . ."

"Are you running for their sakes, or yours?" Banner asked. "Why don't you ask your kids what they think? What will they remember? A man who was always running, a man who never had the guts to stay and fight for what he's won. Ask them, Mills. Look at them."

For a long time, Mills refused to turn. But the three children by the door had their eyes fixed solemnly upon him. The baby began to whimper. As if moved by a force outside himself, Mills finally turned. The older boy tried to meet his father's eyes. He lowered his glance. Banner saw it bring the flush of deep shame to Mills's face.

"Is that what you want them to remember?" Banner said.

Mills was breathing shallowly. His fists were clenched and his face was dull red in the gloom.

"What do you want me to do?" he asked.

It was a long ride to Hackett's, down through Yellow Gap, eastward along the Ganado Road, across the brackish waters of the Río Puerco. Finally they reached the sprawling adobe *haci-enda* Hackett had bought from a Mexican in the early years, on the high bluff overlooking the river. Lights winked out of the darkness; the dogs began to bay.

Shadowy figures began moving from the open bunkhouse door. Adakhai had won Banner's own Winchester and six-shooter, and Banner was using the old Dragoon Colt that Dodge had kept in the ivory table, and one of Dodge's Winchesters. He bent to pull the .30-30 from its boot and laid it across his pommel. Mills did the same.

Then the front door was flung open, and Clay Hackett's swaggering, broad-shouldered body was silhouetted in its lighted rectangle. "Who is it, Red?" he asked loudly.

Banner saw the shadowy figure of Big Red halt near the steps, towering above the others, and he rode boldly up to them, rifle pointed at the redhead's chest.

"It's Lee Banner, Hackett," he said. "I've gut my gun on Red. If anybody starts anything, he'll get it first. And Mills can shoot you out of that door just as quick."

There was a general stir among the loosely grouped men. Banner felt his fingers close tightly around the Winchester. But none of them tried to change his position. Banner could see Big Red staring up at him in sullen anger. The man's right arm was in a sling.

"What's on your mind, Lee?" Hackett's voice was sardonic.

"I want to read you a paper." Banner fished Elder's state-ment from his pocket. The light was hardly enough to read by, but he almost knew it by heart now. When he finished, he looked up at Hackett.

"I guess you know what would happen if the railroad got hold of this, Clay. It proves beyond a doubt that you're grazing on reservation land. The last thing in the world the railroad wants is trouble with the Indians. That's why they put that clause in all their leases that any rancher grazing beyond the limits of the checkerboard sections would automatically have his lease revoked. Once the thing got started, it would snowball. A dozen witnesses could be found who have seen your cattle up there. You know what it can do to you?"

Hackett's voice was guttural with restrained anger. "Why show it to me?"

"Because you're going to leave Mills alone. You're not going to touch him, or go near his house again. If you do, if so much as one of your men does, this goes to the railroad."

Garry's voice rose angrily from the group. "Don't let him bluff you, Hackett. I told you Mills is in with Banner. He knows where that Indian is, too. We ought to burn him out tonight."

"It's no bluff, Clay, and you know it," Banner said. "You're going to leave Mills alone. I want an understanding on it before I leave."

Hackett walked across the porch to one of the poles supporting its overhang. Banner could not see his face. It seemed a long time before he spoke.

"All right, damn you," he said at last. "You've got your understanding."

He wheeled around and walked inside, slamming the door after him. Banner jerked his gun at Big Red.

"Walk ahead of us down the road."

Nothing happened on the way out. They could hear the stirring of men, their restless talk, but nothing happened. When they were beyond the fences, Banner released Red. The man stepped to the side of road, letting them pass.

They rode silently back to the Yellow Gap cut-off. Here Mills reined up, sitting heavily in his saddle, shaking his head.

"I never thought you could do it . . . face Hackett on his own ground that way. Do you think he realizes that you know Arles killed Wright?"

"He knows I know," Banner said. "Does that prove the power of Elder's statement?"

"Won't Hackett try to get it?"

"He may. But he's smart enough to realize I won't carry it around on me. And he's got more important things to get."

"You mean Adakhai?"

Banner leaned toward the man. "Mills, it's either that Indian or Kitteridge or you. Now tell me. Did you see that murder?"

Mills shook his head. "No," he said, "I didn't. I swear I didn't."

Banner shook his head disgustedly. "Tonight didn't mean a thing to you. You're still afraid."

"Who wouldn't be, damn you?" It came from the man in a subdued anger. "Whoever saw the killing would have to testify in court, wouldn't he? With Hackett's killers just waiting to cut him down . . ."

"Then you did see the killing?"

"Damn you, I didn't! How many times do I have to say it? Just telling you, that's all. You're asking too much of a man. Any man. Admitting he was the eyewitness would be signing his own death warrant. And letting his family in on it, too, probably."

Banner's eyes grew empty in defeat. "Forget it," he said. "What about now? You're at the crossroads, Mills. Are you going to leave, or stick it out?"

Still stooped in the saddle, Mills gazed down the road. Then his shoulders seemed to lift a little, and he swung in the saddle, looking up toward Yellow Gap.

"I guess I'll be going back to my place," he said.

XX

After that it was the waiting. Through Cristina, Banner heard that Adakhai was healing satisfactorily and would soon return to his people at Chin Lee. The young lawyer had the feeling that he had done all he could with Adakhai, and Kitteridge, and Mills, and that now all he could do was wait.

August passed, and the time set for the trial drew near. There had been no word from Dodge, but that was his way. Banner knew he would write when he had something definite. Over a week after Banner had ridden with Mills to Hackett's, Clara Mills came into town. He was in the office when someone knocked. Clara entered when he opened the door.

After a first shy greeting, she told him eagerly: "First time I been in town since that day. Jeremiah's working in the alfalfa. I got some shopping to do, but I just had to see you before anything, Lee. I just had to thank you for everything you done."

"Hackett hasn't showed up, then?"

"Not a sign. And Jeremiah's got a buyer for the alfalfa. It's all because of you, Lee. We can't thank you enough. You should see how much Jeremiah's changed already. I wouldn't believe it. He's carryin' on like he did ten years ago. More alfalfa in that south forty, a new room on the house."

He smiled. "That stoop gone from his shoulders?"

She caught his hand. "A lot of it has. Every new day takes some more out. Every new day makes him realize a little more that he can stand up to Hackett now, that he hasn't anything to fear, if he'll only stick. Lee, I been tryin' to make him see how he's got to tell if he saw Wright killed. Sooner or later he'll come up to taw. If there's anything to tell, he'll tell." Her voice grew grim. "I'll see to that."

"You give me new hope, Clara," he said.

She pulled her wrapper around bony shoulders. "I got to get on with my shoppin'."

"I'll see you downstairs."

He put his coat on and walked with her to the sidewalk. She took her leave and he stood there on the corner, reluctant to return to the confinement of the office. Sam Price's boy came running down the street. He came up to Banner, holding out an envelope.

"Si said you'd give me a dime for this. Just came in on the telegraph."

Banner found 10¢ for the boy, ripped open the envelope with a sudden excitement.

Denver, Colorado
August 24, 1891
TO LEE BANNER

GOT LINE ON WARE'S EX-WIFE. SHE HAD LETTERS FROM WARE PROVING HE HAD SPENT ALL THE MONEY. SHEFFORD BROKE WHEN HE SAW THEM. TOLD US WHERE TO FIND THE REAL BOOKS AND TURNED STATE'S EVIDENCE AGAINST WARE FOR LENIENCY. BOOKS PROVED MORROW'S INNOCENCE. PINE GET-TING INDICTMENT QUASHED AGAINST MORROW. DON'T NEGLECT YOUR BLACKSTONE.

UNCLE HENRY

Banner realized his hands were trembling. Stuffing the telegram in his pocket, he went to the hitch rack, knocked the reins loose, threw them over his horse's head, and swung aboard. He wheeled the animal around and put it into a gallop down Reservation. Before he reached Yellow Gap, however, he realized he could not go to Kitteridge alone. It was Julia's right to be along when he delivered this. It might help resolve things more quickly.

So he went on to the school. It was past noon when the build-ings rose over the flat horizon. He passed the trading post and saw a dusty horse standing hipshot before the agency living-quarters. It puzzled him but he trotted on to the school build-ing. In the long room, a score of Navajo children were sitting in orderly fashion at the crude desks.

"Where is your teacher?" Banner asked.

One of the older boys stood up, not looking at Banner, recit-ing it like a catechism: "White man he come to house by horseback at a trot. Teacher-woman she go walking fast to see him. Tell us our lessons to do until she come back walking."

Going back to the living quarters, Banner saw that the ratty bay by the door had Kitteridge's Flying Bar brand. He hesitated before knocking, oddly reluctant to see Julia and the man together again. Then he put his knuckles to the door.

Julia answered. Her full lower lip was stiff with tension, and anger made kindling lights in her great dark eyes. Banner saw Kitteridge sitting on the couch within the gloom of the room, smoking a cigarette. With sight of Banner, the man rose slowly.

"Well, Counselor, come after some more horses?"

Banner found all the eagerness swept from him. He glanced at Julia, wordlessly pulled the telegram from his pocket. He saw the flush leave her cheeks as she stared at it. Then she stepped back to let him in. He walked over and handed the telegram to Kitteridge. Kitteridge read it with narrowed eyes, his lips press-ing tighter and tighter. When he had finished, he crumpled the telegram in one fist, viciously, and turned burning eyes to Ban-ner.

"What kind of a fool do you take me for?"

Banner's lips parted in surprise. "You know Dodge wouldn't send anything like that unless it were true."

"The hell I do." Kitteridge flung the crumpled telegram from him. "You damn' shysters! Rigging up something like this. Did you think this would make me tell if I saw anything at Yellow Gap? Do you think I'm a complete fool?"

He wheeled and stalked to the end of the room. He took a

last draw on his cigarette. It made a savage, sucking sound in the room. Then he flung it down.

In the meantime, Julia had picked up the telegram and read it. She went over behind Kitteridge. "This must be true, Vic. I know Mister Dodge went up to Denver. He wouldn't say this unless it was so. You know that. His worst enemies would take his word on anything. You are free, Vic."

It seemed as if he would never turn around to face her. At last, however, he wheeled. There was a hollow-eyed expression on his face. All the sardonic mockery, the impenetrable cynicism was emptied from his eyes. He stared at Julia, and then walked across the room and sat down on the couch again, looking blankly at the wall.

"Free?" he said.

"Free as any man," Banner said. "You can stop hiding up there in the hills. You can make friends. You can come down out of your hole . . ."

"And tell you that I saw who really killed Wright." The thin edge was back in Kitteridge's voice.

"That's what kept you from telling, wasn't it?" Banner asked. "The fear that your true identity would be found out if you got mixed up with the law."

"Yes, Counselor. It was."

"Vic," Julia said sharply, "don't go back to that. Can't you see how much Lee and Mister Dodge have gone through for you? And then you act like this."

"For me?" he asked cynically.

"All right. So they had their reasons. What's the difference? They've given you back something you could never have gotten alone in a million years."

"Slack off, will you?" Kitteridge bent his head, running rope-scarred fingers through his thinning hair. "How can I trust them? I've been framed once, by my best friend. How can I

205

trust anybody after that?"

"Vic," Julia said, "it's not a frame-up. You can take my word on it."

"Your word!" He wheeled on her, bitter-eyed. "Why should I take your word? How did Banner know who I really was in the first place? You're the only one who could have told him. I might as well put you in the same boat as Ware!"

"Vic, don't be like that." She went to him, tried to grab his arm. "Maybe I told, but I knew they only wanted to help you."

"How did you know?" He tore loose, pacing back toward the couch. "I'm not going to be caught short again, Julia! I've put in five years of hell because I trusted someone I'd known since I was a kid. I'm not going to be jammed in a corner again, understand?" He wheeled on them, almost shouting it. "Understand?"

They both stared at him, neither answering.

Banner's face grew dark and somber. "It would take courage to testify against Arles," he said. "Maybe I made a mistake. I thought that indictment was the only thing that kept you from telling what you knew."

For a moment, Kitteridge's eyes were blank with anger. Then he masked it off with his sardonic cynicism.

"Maybe you did," he said. "Maybe you made a mistake about everything. *Ipso facto,* Counselor?"

He picked up his hat off the couch and walked out.

Julia went halfway to the door after him, and then stopped, helplessness in her face. Banner did not move. His first anger was gone, leaving only hollow defeat. Julia turned toward him. She was biting at her underlip; her heavy breathing swelled her breasts. "I thought I knew him. Even the way he'd changed, I thought I knew what he was really like underneath. But . . . now . . ."

He shook his head in deep discouragement. "I've run into

the same thing with Mills, Julia. Maybe we expect them to change too soon. It's been five years for Kitteridge now. A man can't switch back in a minute. You could see the shock it was."

She came to him. She reached up to touch his cheek with the tips of her fingers. Her voice was low, throaty. "I wish . . ."

He waited for her to go on. When she didn't, he asked softly: "You wish what, Julia?"

She stared at him with a luminous darkness in her eyes. Then she wheeled and walked over to the couch, facing away from him.

"Nothing," she said.

He studied the bowed line of her shoulders, sharing her helplessness. "I guess I'll be going," he said.

XXI

Henry Dodge got back on September 8th with a letter to Kitteridge from the Denver district attorney, and one from the foreman of the grand jury, and a half dozen Denver newspapers headlining the story of Morrow's innocence and of Ware's arrest in New Orleans. They had printed a picture of Morrow as he had been five years ago, and Banner could understand how Julia had loved him. The thinning hair Banner knew was a handsome black mane; the cynical sun-faded eyes were bold and laughing.

Dodge and Banner rode up to Kitteridge's together with the newspapers and the letters. But the house was empty, and the horses were all gone. Banner got Tilfego to hunt for him, giving the Mexican the newspapers and letters in case he found Kitteridge. It took Tilfego three days. He returned with the news that he had come across the man with his cattle on the north fork of the Corn. Apparently the man was not running away, but the newspapers, the letters made no appreciable change in him. It left Banner with nothing but a deep discouragement, as the day of the trial arrived.

It was the 12th, and Jahzini was to get in from Yuma that morning. Banner and Dodge had an early breakfast and walked up Aztec to the courthouse. The streets were already teeming with life. A crowd of prospective jurors was talking and smoking restlessly on the courthouse steps; more men were gathered in little groups along the picket fence. Banner could not help looking eastward, toward the desert. Dodge stopped beside him, lighting a cigar.

"Which one are you looking for, son?"

Banner shook his head helplessly. "I don't know. Maybe I've been a fool, Henry. Maybe none of those men saw it."

Dodge cut him off, grasping his arm. "There's still time, Lee. I don't think any one of those three men is the kind to let a man die, with what you've done for them."

Banner hardly heard him. He seemed to be standing in a void, staring down that street. He could feel Dodge's hand tighten on his arm.

"Who is it?" the old man asked. "My eyes ain't as good as they used to be."

"I can't see yet. One rider, leading an empty horse."

Every man in the crowd had seen it now. The silence was an eerie thing, gathering weight, exerting pressure. Then Banner felt the tension washed out of him on a husky breath.

"Who is it, son?" Dodge asked.

Banner's voice had a dead sound. "Cristina."

Talk began to stir again, like the rustling of autumn leaves in a wind. Cristina was a block away now, riding down the center of the street. She had a silver comb in her black hair. She wore her best blue velvet blouse and skirts of black wool.

Then Caleb Elder's voice rose mockingly from the crowd behind Banner. "Hear you've taken the Injun-lover back in your office, Henry. Is this the squaw you're goin' to hitch up with now?"

A jeering laugh rose from other men, and Banner could not help wheeling savagely toward them. Dodge caught his arm.

"Put some slack in it, son. You're going to get a lot of that from here on in."

Banner slowly wheeled back till he was facing Cristina again. She rode up to them and reined in and stepped off. Her eyes were black and depthless with anger.

"Never mind them," Banner told her gently. "They don't count."

"I didn't even hear them," she said stiffly. "I was told my father would be in on the ten-fifteen."

"We were just going to meet him . . ." Banner trailed off, frowning. His attention had been so fixed on her that he had not realized what horse she led. It was his own chestnut, saddled and bridled. She handed him the lead rope.

"Adakhai came past my hogan by wagon last night. He left this gift for you."

Eyes filled with wonder, he stepped over to the chestnut. The horse nickered and tried to nuzzle him. He could not help chuckling.

"It's hard to believe Adakhai would do this. He won it gambling. You know too well how they feel about that."

"It is what gives it so much meaning," she said. "He told me he wanted to see you again. He said his hogan is your hogan whenever you come to Chin Lee. It is something I never would have believed."

Banner held out his hand. "If he'd do this . . ."

His voice died as he saw the darkening of her eyes. "He did not tell me whether he saw the murder at Yellow Gap."

The eagerness fled Banner's face, leaving it somber, older. She came close, caught his arm.

"Perhaps he must think it over longer. If anyone could give him reason to tell, you did. You did more with him than I thought possible for any white man to do. How did you do it, Lee? It couldn't have been merely that you saved his life."

He shook his head. "It was a lot of things, I guess. I think the gambling must have been part of it. Did he tell you about the *bizha*?"

"Yes. He said you knew such great defeat that you put your cards face down on the floor and surrendered completely."

"I'm still wondering if I did right," he murmured. "I know how much that *bizha* meant to him. I thought that if I could win it, he would do almost anything to get it back, even tell me if he was at Yellow Gap . . ."

"No!" she broke in angrily, shaking her head. "Its only value is in the power it gives him in gambling. Of what value would it be if he lost it that way? He could not bargain for it. You would have gained his undying hatred. How could you misjudge him so?"

"That hand I put face down was a full house," Banner said. "He was so excited at winning that he didn't question it. He only had two pairs."

"Lee." Her voice had a breathless sound. "You could have won."

He nodded soberly. "I realized in the last moment what a great mistake it would be."

Her lips were parted and she was staring into his face as if seeing something there for the first time. "I have been wrong," she said. "It is I who have misjudged you. Only a man who understood us could have realized that. No wonder you could change Adakhai so."

"Are you thinking," he asked gently, "that perhaps there isn't a thousand years between us, after all?"

For a moment longer she stared up into his face. Then she

turned away, toward her horse, as she had when he had kissed her out there on the desert. When she finally spoke, her voice was so low he could hardly hear it. "Perhaps I am like Adakhai," she said. "Perhaps I, too, must think it over."

Banner stood looking at her back, wanting to do something, to say something, he didn't know exactly what, yet held from anything by the watching men. Finally Dodge cleared his throat.

"We better get up to the station."

Banner took the reins of his horse and Cristina turned and moved up beside him, and they walked together down the street, running the gamut of veiled comments, of curious stares, of open insults. In front of Price's Mercantile was a growing crowd of Indians, sitting stolidly on the curb or squatting in the shade against the wall. The ruddy mahogany of their faces, the bright silver of their jewelry, the vivid blues and reds of their blankets made a barbaric splash of color against the earth-colored buildings.

"Didn't know Jahzini's clan was so big," Dodge muttered.

"They are not all my people," Cristina said. "A Mountain Chant is being held east of Yellow Gap to cure a man who dreamed of bear. Many of these people came south by wagon to attend the ceremonies. That is why Adakhai came."

"And the only reason," Banner said bitterly.

Cristina's chin lifted. "I have faith that Adakhai will not let my father die. I saw how you changed him, Lee. If he is the one who can save Jahzini, he will come."

The train was half an hour late, and there was little time for greetings when it finally arrived. Sheriff Drake and three deputies hustled the old Indian through the crowds to the courthouse. Banner saw Arles and Big Red lounging beneath the façade of Blackstrap Kelly's, drinking beer. Red's arm was no longer in a sling but a dirty bandage still showed beneath his cuff. As Banner climbed the steps to the courthouse porch, he could not help turning to look over the heads of the crowd, down Reservation, toward the desert. He heard Hackett's brittle voice.

"You really don't expect anybody to come in, do you?"

Banner wheeled sharply to meet the man's black eyes. The biting mockery in them made him lean forward. "Hackett . . ."

"Yes, Lee?" The man's humorless smile grew broader.

Banner settled back, forced himself to turn toward the door. Dodge put a hand on his shoulder.

"Good boy," he muttered. "Just hang on tight."

By the time they reached the rail gate, they saw that Jahzini had been seated at the defendant's table with Cristina. She had brought him some paper bread she'd made the day before, blue as turquoise from the cedar ashes baked into it, and the old man was grinning like a kid at a picnic as he munched at it. Prentice soon came from his chambers, and the bailiff opened court. The first juryman was called.

He was James Wentworth, who ran the feed barn on Aztec, and who did a lot of business with Hackett. It was highly possible that he was under Hackett's thumb, and would constitute a threat to Jahzini, if he got on the jury. Dodge tried to establish this fact, without success, and finally turned the challenging over to Banner. Banner stepped up to the jury box.

"James Wentworth, isn't it true that on June the Twelfth of Eighteen Eighty-Nine you had a quarrel with the defendant?"

"I . . . I don't quite recall."

"He was going home drunk and ran into your barn, knocking off a door. You threatened to take your shotgun to him if he ever came down that street again?"

"That isn't true . . . I . . ."

"You're under oath, Wentworth. I have signed depositions

from two witnesses to the incident. Shall I have them subpoenaed?"

"No, but I . . ."

"I submit that this man be rejected for prejudice he might have against the defendant."

Judge Prentice waited for Wentworth to protest. When the man did not, he nodded frostily. "Sustained."

"Step down," the constable intoned.

The next man was called. He could not be proven prejudiced, and was accepted. The third man was Seth Masters, a small cattleman who had lived off Hackett's bounty for years.

"Seth Masters, isn't it true that your father was scalped by Indians?"

"Damn' right."

"Isn't it true that on a dozen occasions you've been heard to say that the best Indian was a dead Indian?"

"I never said exactly . . ."

"You're under oath, Masters."

"Well . . ."

"I have witnesses to these instances, Your Honor. I submit that Seth Masters be rejected as unfit for prejudice he might have against Jahzini as an Indian."

"I don't think the witnesses are necessary, Mister Banner. You may step down, Mister Masters."

When court was recessed for lunch, only three jurymen had been chosen. Dodge met Banner at the rail gate, grinning broadly.

"I never seen anybody hang it up like this. How'd you ever dig up so much dirt about this town?"

"I've been going through your old briefs for the last three weeks. You've got fifteen years of testimony in there, Henry. It's like the whole history of this town. If Jahzini isn't going to have an eyewitness, he's going to have a fair jury."

As they pushed their way through the sweating, clamoring crowd to the door, Banner saw Julia standing behind the last row of seats. He elbowed his way quickly to her.

"Have you seen him?" he asked. "Has he come?"

She shook her head. "I waited at my place till the last minute. I thought he might . . ." She shook her head. "I haven't seen him since that day. I'm beginning to wonder if you weren't right. Maybe he just doesn't have the courage."

"Now, Julia . . ."

"It's true, Lee. Remember what you said, about Victor still standing between us, about me not even realizing it? I thought that telegram would answer it for me, would bring him back to what he used to be, and I'd know. But now it's even worse. Someone who doesn't even have the backbone to speak up in something like this, who would let an innocent old man die! How could I love a man like that?"

He patted her helplessly on the shoulder, lips compressed, unable to say anything that might help her now. He finally left her and went bleakly out through the crowd. He could not help turning down Reservation, staring out toward the desert again. At last he became aware of Tilfego, pushing his yawning buckskin through the thinning knots of people. The man came up beside him.

"Which one you look for, Lee?"

Banner shook his head helplessly. "I've almost given up, Tilfego. If one of them was going to come, he'd surely do it by now."

"I been wait out in those hills by the Yellow Gap cut-off, like you ask. Nobody he come down from the north. But something is happen I think you should know. Breed and Joe Garry they are waiting there, too."

"That's one of the things I was afraid of," Banner said. "I'm helpless. I should be out there, too, but I've got to see that

Jahzini gets a decent jury." He looked up at Tilfego. "Will you go back? Don't take any chances. If our eyewitness comes, warn him before Breed and Garry can get to him. Will do?"

The man grinned broadly. "Will do."

Banner watched him thread his way back through the crowd, then hunted up Ramirez, the husband of Dodge's cook, and asked him to mingle with the crowd at Kelly's and keep an eye on Arles and Hackett's other men. If any of than left town, he was to tell Banner immediately. Then Banner joined Dodge for lunch.

Though all the windows had been opened, the courtroom was still oppressively hot. Most of the crowd had removed their coats and were shrugging irritably at shirts turned clammy by perspiration. Wiping at his red face, the bailiff reopened court, and the choosing of the jury went on.

By 4:00 Banner's voice was husky from the constant questioning; his back ached; he had a throbbing headache from the heat. He had just finished questioning a juror and had returned to the table when he saw Ramirez beckoning him from the gate. He went to the rail and the man whispered in his ear.

"Joe Garry he come into Kelly's, talk with Arles and Big Red. Then all three they get Hackett and ride out of town."

Banner turned back to the table, sick with the implications of it. Then, swiftly, he slid into the bench beside Cristina, whispering in her ear.

"Tell your father he's got to pass out. Something's come up and I've got to get out of here. Tell him he's got to faint."

She frowned intensely, then whispered to her father. Banner saw the old man's face go blank with surprise. That he grinned mischievously at Banner.

"Shiye," he said in a chiding way. "My son."

For a moment Banner thought he did not understand. Irritably he bent to whisper in Cristina's ear again. Before he could speak, Jahzini's head lulled back and he slid out of the seat to fall limply on the floor. There was an immediate stir in the courtroom. The bailiff ran over to squat beside the old man. Judge Prentice began pounding with his gavel. Banner stood up, shouting to be heard over the babble of voices.

"Your Honor, I request that the court adjourn for the day. The strain has been too much for my client. He could not possibly go on any longer."

"Granted," Prentice said. "Bailiff?"

The bailiff popped up. "Hear ye, hear ye, hear ye, this honorable court is adjourned till nine o'clock tomorrow morning."

XXII

Banner pushed his chestnut unmercifully all the way to Yellow Gap. He had left the court in a rush, without even taking time to explain to Dodge or Cristina. The sense of urgency in him was too great. At the cut-off, he turned north. The sun was dying in the west, turning the shadows crimson in the bottom of the twisting gorges. He saw the pockmarks of fresh hoofprints in the sand. Then, sliding down a steep cut into a broad wash, he sighted the horse.

It was Tilfego's animal, cropping peacefully at a patch of buff sacaton. Banner pulled up beside the buckskin, finding the reins trailing, unhitched. He gathered them up and led the horse on northward, through the gathering twilight. It filled him with a sick sense of guilt that he had sent the man out here. He reached a plateau and heard the cursing from the benches ahead.

"¡Chingados, I hope they get the corajes, como padrotes! I hope they get worse than the corajes, como sinvergüenzas . . . !"

"Tilfego!"

The cursing stopped. The man's immense sombrero and moon face were visible above the edge of the drop-off. His blank surprise turned to a broad grin and he struggled up through the notch till he was on the plateau.

"*Hombre,* what luck, what happiness. I was watch for man from the north like you say. I think I know where Joe Garry and Breed they are. But they get around behind me and start shooting. My horse he spook. I get in arroyo. They kill me I think if other man he do not come."

Banner bent sharply toward him. "What man?"

Tilfego shook his head. "Him I could not see. But they go down in cañon after him. They shoot."

Banner's voice was tight. "Then it must have been our man, Tilfego. How long ago?"

"Hour, maybe two. The shooting sound like they chase him off to the east."

"Then they must have holed him up somewhere," Banner said. "Joe Garry came in to get Hackett and the rest of his crew."

"Maybe we can follow the trail," Tilfego said.

It was not hard for Tilfego to find the tracks. They led away from the Yellow Gap cut-off on one of the dim cattle trails that wound tortuously through the rough and twisted land to the east. But night came, with its blackness, and slowed them down to a snail's pace. At last Banner halted in a narrow wash.

"We'll never catch them going this slow," he said. "We've got to take a chance, Tilfego. Where would a man run to, around here?"

"All flatlands beyond. Not much cover a man could take."

"Then there's only one possibility. The Navajos are holding their Mountain Chant east of Yellow Gap. It can't be too much farther. If that was Adakhai they saw in the cañon, wouldn't it be logical for him to seek refuge with his people?"

Tilfego nodded. "I know where the Indians they build the big corral. Pretty near the trading post. We can reach it in hour."

They forced their horses through the night, keeping to the direction they had already been taking, leaving the benchlands and coming into the vast sage flats. And finally they saw the ruddy glow of the great fire, far ahead, and then the immense corral, built of cedar boughs, piled eight feet high, with only one opening, toward the east.

The Mountain Chant was one of the most important ceremonies of the year and the Navajos had been gathering for days, camping around the chosen spot. Now most of the throng was within the immense corral, but a small crowd still eddied back and forth around the gate, and latecomers were constantly passing through the deserted cook fires and tents and wagons.

The Indians had worn their best clothing and all their jewelry for the annual ceremony, and it gave the scene a barbaric splendor. Banner and Tilfego began passing men laden with silver, great bosses of it as big as saucers studding their belts, silver bow guards and heavy bracelets jangling at their wrists. Women crossed back and forth, draped with necklaces of turquoise and clamshell and cannel coal.

The crowd thickened as the two men neared the gate, and it was slow going. Then Tilfego spurred his horse against Banner and pointed at a copse of cottonwoods near the south end of the great corral. A dozen horses were hitched beneath the trees. Light from a nearby cook fire flickered high enough for Banner to see the black, with the Broken Bit barely discernible on its dusty rump.

"Hackett," Tilfego said. "They must have drive our man over here, all right. He try to escape by going inside corral. They would not leave their horse otherwise."

"Then we've got to get inside, too. We can move faster on foot. How about that hitch rack?"

Another line of horses stood at an improvised hitch rail near the corral. They tied their animals to it, and began to push their way through the Indians. The glow of the big fire inside the corral blossomed against the velvet backdrop of the sky like a rosy nimbus, lighting the coppery faces all about Banner. As they neared the gate, a young man on a pinto shouted angrily at them.

"Haish aniti, ha'at iisha?"

"What he say?" Tilfego asked nervously.

"He asked who we were and what we wanted," Banner told him. "A lot of them don't want white people at these ceremonies." He turned to the Indian, speaking in Navajo. "I am Yellow Hair, the friend of Adakhai. We look for him here."

The young man was unconvinced, and shouted to a pair of friends beyond Banner. They began to force their horses through the crowd, closing in on Banner and the Mexican, their faces ruddy with anger in the smoky firelight. But an old man called to them, telling them to cause no trouble on this holy night. Then an eddy of the crowd carried Banner and Tilfego through the gate.

The roar of the great fire in the center of the corral provided a constant undertone to the cacophony of other sounds. The crowd held back from its intense heat, leaving a large open space all around it, in which the dances were given. When Banner found an empty Studebaker wagon, he climbed up on the seat, looking out across the veritable ocean of sweating faces and barbaric blankets and glimmering silver.

Many of the ceremonies had already been performed, and he saw that the Plumed Arrow Dance had now begun. The patient had been carried out close to the fire, where he sat on the ground, wrapped to the eyes in a buffalo robe. It was the same palsied old man Banner had seen at Red Lake. The two performers were doing a measured dance around him, holding up their plumed arrows, singing the "First Song of the Mountain Sheep."

Yiki Casizini
Kac tsilke cigini
Kac Katso yiscani . . .

Singing of the young man with his sacred implement, the holy young man with his plumed arrow. Giving three coyote yelps and thrusting the long arrows deep down their throats, while the awed crowd watched.

"Can you see anything?" Tilfego asked.

Banner shook his head helplessly. "Not Adakhai."

"Maybe was not him?"

"Who else would have come over here?"

"I would, if they was chase me, and I know this was here."

"Whoever it is, we've got to reach him before Hackett does. You go around toward the north. I'll keep going this way. We'll cover twice as much ground that way and meet on the other side. If you find him first, whether it's Adakhai or not, try to get hold of a chief and make him understand what's happening. If they know Jahzini's life depends on it, the Indians will help you."

Banner dropped off the wagon and shoved into the crowd, away from Tilfego. Through a break in the ranks, he saw that the dancers had pulled their plumed arrows out of their throats, giving three coyote yelps, and the first one had started blessing the patient. He was applying the sacred arrow to the soles of his feet, his knees, his hands, his abdomen, giving three coyote yelps at each spot, until he reached the mouth, and had driven the bear's spirit from the patient.

Then, beyond the patient, beyond the dancers, clear across the compound, in the dense crowd on the other side of the corral, Banner saw Arles. The man was not watching the dancers. He was lighting a cigarette, and watching a point ahead of him in the crowd, and moving inexorably toward that point. In the treacherous firelight, his face looked almost black.

Banner acted without thought, pushed by a breathless sense of urgency. He pushed his way through the packed crowd to the first ranks and broke free and ran into the open, heading straight across the compound toward the other side. The heat of the fire struck at him in a searing wave, but he forced himself on. He was twenty feet out from the crowd when the earth seemed to spin from beneath him. He fell to his knees, blinded, every breath seeming to sear his lungs. A jeering cry rose from the crowd, and one of the young men shouted at him.

"Did you not think it was hot, *belinkana?* Did you not think our dancers were holy?"

Crouched there, shaking his head, Banner knew how foolish he had been. How the dancers ever stood the heat of that fire was one of the things no white man had ever been able to answer. Jahzini had taken Banner to a Mountain Chant when he was a boy, and he had seen a white man try to approach the fire. He had fainted before he had gotten within thirty feet of it.

Banner crawled back to the crowd, reached a wagon, pulled himself to his feet by a wheel. The Indians were still jeering and making jokes at his expense. He looked across the compound again.

He saw that the Plumed Arrow Dance was over; the two young men had retired to the Medicine Hogan. Other dancers were trooping into the compound. On the other side of the corral, in front of the first ranks of watchers, a little girl was swaying back and forth before a blanket on which a feather mysteriously followed every movement of her body. The Mountain Top Shooting Arrows entered from the west with their lightning-sticks that were constructed like folding hat racks that leaped in and out like painted tongues. They sang the ancient song to the Slayer and to the Son of Water, and the drums made the night throb.

The constant whirl of dancers made it hard for Banner to see beyond them into the crowd. But finally he realized that Arles had moved. No matter how Banner searched, he could not see that sardonic face.

He began to stagger through the crowd, moving around the circle toward the other side. That Hackett and his men would think of doing it here was evidence of their desperation. It was their last chance to save themselves. It was Arles's last chance.

Yet, as desperate an attempt as it was, they might make it, with luck. All the Indians were gradually pressing in as close to the fire as possible, to watch the dances. It left open spaces between their rear ranks and the walls of the corral. A man could stand in those black shadows by the cedar bough wall and break through to the outside immediately after shooting. It was possible that he could get away without being identified.

Banner had almost reached the Medicine Hogan in the west end when he saw Big Red. The man stood beside an empty linchpin wagon near the hogan. For that moment the babble of sound seemed to fade. It was only the two of them, staring at each other across the dense mass of the crowd. Then Big Red started toward Banner. Anger ran rawly through Banner, filling him with the impulse to meet the man, to get his hands on something tangible. But he knew he did not have time for that. He turned to shove his way through the crowd in front of the Medicine Hogan, trying to get ahead of the Hackett rider. As he shouldered past a pair of young Navajos, one wheeled in anger, jabbing at him with an elbow.

"*Juthla hago ni . . .*"

Banner blocked the blow, pretending he did not understand the vile curse, and stumbled on. He saw that he had gotten past Red, that the press of the mob was holding the man up. Then, fifty feet beyond, was Joe Garry. Desperately Banner changed directions. But Garry wheeled to cut across and block him again. He tried to turn back, saw that would take him into Red again. He spun around a last time and tried to drive through the Navajos to the front ranks and open ground. It was too late. Joe Garry brutally shoved an old couple aside and stepped in front of Banner, one scarred hand on his gun.

"Don't be a fool," Banner said. "Pull that gun and they'll mob you."

"Nobody needs a gun, Lee," Big Red said.

He was right behind, and Banner started to wheel involuntarily. But Red grabbed his arm, checking his whirling motion, trying to twist his arm into a hammerlock. Banner fought to get free, but Garry lunged in and hit him in the face.

Blinded by the blow, held from behind by Red, Banner lashed out wildly with a boot. He felt it catch Garry in the stomach.

The man reeled back, doubled over, making a retching sound. At the same time, Red twisted Banner's arm up into his back with a violent wrench. Banner shouted with the stabbing pain. It bent him forward helplessly; his wild struggles were useless.

Then he heard Red grunt from behind, and he was released. He fell to his knees, sick with the pain of his twisted arm. It was a great effort to rise, to turn. He saw Adakhai standing above the fallen redhead, a shovel in his hands.

"Ahalani, anaai."

Banner could not help his feeble grin. "Greetings, brother," he answered. "You came out of a cloud."

"I have been trying to catch up with you for some time," Adakhai said. "What are you doing here?"

"I came to help you," Banner said. He gestured at Joe Garry, still sitting on the ground, the pain of the kick turning his face to parchment. "That is one of the men who shot at you on the Yellow Gap cut-off this afternoon."

The Indian looked puzzled. "I was not shot at on the cut-off. I have been here since yesterday."

Banner stared at him blankly. "You mean you were not coming this afternoon to tell that you had seen the murder?"

The Indian placed his hand over his heart. "You saved my life, Yellow Hair. You showed me that a white man could understand our ways and our gods. You are my brother now, and, if I had seen the killing at Yellow Gap, I would tell you. But I cannot say what is not true."

"Then they weren't after you . . ."

Banner broke off, wheeling around, staring into the crowd beyond. Then he began running again, knowing he had lost too much time already. He heard Adakhai call from behind, but did not answer. He passed the Medicine Hogan, plunging into the packed crowd again, pushing his way through. All the dancers had left the compound now. Young horsebackers were dragging in new logs at the ends of their ropes to throw on the center fire. It was shooting up to the heavens once more in a great pyre. The climax of the evening was about to begin—the Fire Dance.

From outside the corral where they had been spraying each other with the sacred medicine, the twelve young dancers began to run in, their naked bodies painted white, their cedar-bark torches blazing, their shrill cries of the sandhill crane filling the air.

"*Prrr! Eh-yah! Prrr! Eh-yah!*"

Banner reached the spot where he had first seen Arles, and began looking frantically for the man, pushed this way and that by angry Indians as he forced his way through their tightly packed ranks. Even here the heat of the fire was so great that the Navajos could not stand still, and shifted constantly back and forth like a restless sea.

Out in the center, the twelve dancers were cavorting about the pyre like fiendish marble statues come to life. Their chant was growing wilder as they circled. They had ignited their torches in the flames and were beating at each other with them, literally bathing themselves in flames.

> *The time when they came out of the earth!*
> *Hostudi's fire is put upon us.*
> *But it does me no harm,*
> *I am holy with the fire . . .*

Then Banner saw Kitteridge. The man was over by a line of wagons, a hundred yards away. The wagons were between him and the wall, but he was moving down toward the end of the line, his back to the wagons, his back to the shadows gathered blackly beneath the wall of cedar boughs. And it was in those shadows Arles would be. Waiting for Kitteridge to move out from behind the last wagon.

"Kitteridge!" Banner shouted at the top of his voice. But the man did not seem to hear him over the chant of the dancers, the frenzied shouting of the mob, the frantic beat of the drums. "Kitteridge, watch out, don't move from behind that wagon!" Banner screamed it. "Kitteridge, for God's sake . . . !"

> *The torch they put on me does not injure me,*
> *The torch they put on me does not injure me.*
> *I am holy with the fire . . .*

Like flaming demons, dancing around the blaze, running into the bed of coals, scattering them and stamping them out, they were whipping each other with their blazing torches. And all the while Lee Banner, fighting to get free of the crowd, saw that there was only a moment left.

Banner did not shout again, knowing the man could not hear. As Kitteridge stepped away from the wagon, exposing his back to the wall, Banner finally broke free of the crowd, clawing at his gun.

In the same instant that he saw the first fluttering motion

from the shadows by the wall. Banner heard the clank of spurs from behind him. His whole body stiffened with the impulse to wheel and meet it. But he knew that if he did, he would never save Kitteridge.

He threw himself full length onto the ground, firing at the movement in the shadows. Hackett's gun roared from behind. But the bullet passed over Banner's head and ate into the earth five feet from him.

Sprawled on his belly, Banner fired again into those shadows, wondering why Hackett's next shot did not hit him, and fired again, and again, till the vague movement became a man, became Arles, staggering out from the wall, doubled over, hugging his bloody belly, dropping his gun, pitching onto his face.

I am holy with it.
I am holy with it.
I am holy with it . . .

XXIII

There was a great silence. The dancers had stopped, the drums had stopped, and the shouting of the crowd had stopped. Banner got to his feet, trembling in reaction now, turning to see why Hackett had not killed him.

The man lay on the ground ten feet behind Banner, ringed by a dense mass of Indians. His great cartwheel spurs held his heels six inches off the ground. He was dead.

Banner stared at him. It was as if his emotions had been numbed. He could feel no shock, no triumph.

He looked finally to see who had shot Hackett. Tilfego stood on top of one of the wagons, far down the line from Kitteridge. His gun was still in his hand. Banner raised his hand in a salute of gratitude, then turned to meet Kitteridge.

"You took a big chance for me," Kitteridge said in a low

226

voice. "I owe you more thanks than I'll ever be able to give."

"Just tell me one thing."

"It's what I was coming down here to tell you. It took me a long time to think it out. A man gets twisted up inside when he's run like that, for five years . . ."

"I think I understand, Kitteridge."

"Hackett's men jumped me in the cut-off this afternoon," Kitteridge said. "They drove me in this direction. When I saw the corral, I thought I could shake them in the crowd . . ." He broke off, moistening his lips. "You were right, Lee. I saw Arles kill Wallace Wright. I was afraid my true identity would be discovered if I got hauled into court to testify. But at the last, I knew that even if you'd rigged that telegram to suck me out, I couldn't let an innocent man die . . ."

Banner gazed at him a long time. Then he became aware of the stirring of the crowd, and turned to see Adakhai, standing on the outer fringe, with Cristina. She was staring wide-eyed at Kitteridge, and Banner knew she had overheard his confession. She seemed to take her eyes off him with great effort, turning to Banner, starting toward him as she spoke.

"Ramirez told me Hackett had left town. I guessed what it meant. I knew that if they were after Adakhai, he might seek refuge here. When I found nothing at Yellow Gap, I came on." She shook her head wonderingly. "But it wasn't Adakhai . . ."

"You and I made the same mistake," Banner said. He turned toward the man, forcing it out. "You'll want to know about Julia. She may have thought I was the one, Kitteridge. But you were always between us. She'll be waiting for you, in town."

Kitteridge met Banner's eyes a long time, as if letting it soak in. Then he grasped Banner's arm, voice husky with emotion. "You're really a man to ride the river with, Counselor."

Cristina was looking up at Banner, searching his face. "It seems to cause you no great pain, to tell him that."

He realized she was right. Somehow it did not hurt him as he had thought it would, to cut the final bonds that held him to Julia. Maybe they had not been the bonds that he had thought they were. There had been passion; there had been intense emotion. But somehow it had not been as fulfilling as merely standing here, looking down into Cristina's face.

"Perhaps, then," she said, "I can answer the question you asked this afternoon. No thousand years stands between us, Lee. I know that now." She lowered her voice, till it was only for him. "Not even a foot, if you want it that way."

He would have taken her in his arms, but the crowd held him from that. He put his hands in hers, and it was enough.

"Yes," he said simply. "I want it that way."

"*Qué barbaridad*," Tilfego said, from behind them. "What are we waiting for? Let us all go in and get married."

ACKNOWLEDGMENTS

"Trouble in Texas" first appeared under the title "Hymn of the Hogleg Hellion" in *Lariat Story Magazine* (7/49). Copyright © 1949 by Real Adventures Publishing Co. Copyright © renewed 1977 by Marian R. Savage. Copyright © 2010 by Golden West Literary Agency for restored material.

"Lawless Land" first appeared under the title "Land of the Lawless" in *Zane Grey's Western Magazine* (7/51). Copyright © 1951 by The Hawley Publications, Inc. Copyright © renewed 1979 by Marian R. Savage. Copyright © 2010 by Golden West Literary Agency for restored material.

ABOUT THE AUTHOR

Les Savage, Jr. was born in Alhambra, California and grew up in Los Angeles. His first published story was "Bullets and Bull-whips" accepted by the prestigious magazine, Street & Smith's *Western Story*. Almost ninety more magazine stories followed, all set on the American frontier, many of them published in Fiction House magazines such as *Frontier Stories* and *Lariat Story Magazine* where Savage became a superstar with his name on many covers. His first novel, *Treasure of the Brasada*, appeared from Simon & Schuster in 1947. Due to his preference for historical accuracy, Savage often ran into problems with book editors in the 1950s who were concerned about marriages between his protagonists and women of different races—a commonplace on the real frontier but not in much Western fiction in that decade. Savage died young, at thirty-five, from complications arising out of hereditary diabetes and elevated cholesterol. However, as a result of the censorship imposed on many of his works, only now are they being fully restored by returning to the author's original manuscripts. Among Savage's finest Western stories are *Fire Dance at Spider Rock* (Five Star Westerns, 1995), *Medicine Wheel* (Five Star Westerns, 1996), *Coffin Gap* (Five Star Westerns, 1997), *Phantoms in the Night* (Five Star Westerns, 1998), *The Bloody Quarter* (Five Star Westerns, 1999), *In The Land of Little Sticks* (Five Star Westerns, 2000), *The Cavan Breed* (Five Star Westerns, 2001), and *Danger Rides the River* (Five Star Westerns, 2002). Much as Stephen

Crane before him, while he wrote, the shadow of his imminent death grew longer and longer across his young life, and he knew that, if he was going to do it at all, he would have to do it quickly. He did it well, and, now that his novels and stories are being restored to what he had intended them to be, his achievement irradiated by his powerful and profoundly sensitive imagination will be with us always, as he had wanted it to be, as he had so rushed against time and mortality that it might be. *Wind River* will be his next Five Star Western.